THE QUIXOTIC FACTION

T. D. KOHLER

The Quixotic Faction

by
Tony D. Kohler

United States of America

Cover Illustration
& Interior Design

All characters, settings, locations, and all other content contained within this book are fictional and are the intellectual property of the author; any likenesses are coincidental and unknown to author and publisher at the time of publication.

ISBN-13: 978-1-949398-19-9
ISBN-10: 1-949398-19-6

Prologue
1948

19 Orogonon Circle Dodge Pond Road, Orogonon, Maine

July 25, 0937 hours

Leaning against a large oak and glass wine cabinet, a well dress man shakes his glass just to hear the ice rattle. “Mr. Washington, how long did you say you have been working with him?”

“Not long, only about eighteen months now.” William feels the new mortar between the grey and black rocks of the walls. “Mr. Sharaf, it is scientist’s dream to be on the forefront of an amazing discovery. Please, if you are doing a biography on Dr. Reich, call me Bill.”

“If you call me Myron.” He smiles, as a bulletin from the Menninger Clinic catches his attention from the table-top. He slides a sheet of paper away to reveal the complete title: “The Strange Case of Wilhelm Reich: The man who blames both neuroses and cancer on unsatisfactory sexual activities.” Myron tries to stifle a laugh.

“Mildred Brady, she was not forthright in telling him she was writing for the FDA, and she took everything about his research completely out of context. Which is why I am relaying my distrust in having someone do a biography on him, nothing personal.”

“I assure you, Bill, no offense taken. I will be forthright in every aspect. Although now I think about it, Orgone, Orogonon, both do seem to be named after the elusive orgasm.”

Guilty laughter fills the room as Myron looks back down at the circled areas on the article.

"Fraud of the first magnitude—the FDA suspected a sexual racket of some kind." Myron raises an eyebrow. "Forefront of an amazing discovery?"

"Yeah, well, I am not going to say there are no perks in his studies; however, I will tell you that he is on the verge of something world changing."

The doorbell rings from the front entrance interrupting the build-up he was shooting for. "Well, Myron, looks like I am saved by the bell."

"Quite literally." Myron nods.

Two well-dressed men in black suits stand in front of an older man with disheveled grey hair and a distinguished, grey moustache. Bill stretches out his hand and tries to ignore the brooding men. "Doctor, we have been expecting you, please come in, my name is William Washington, assistant to Dr. Wilhelm Reich."

The two men escorting the doctor scan the tree line surrounding the house before they allow him to enter. The gentlemen continue to survey the dark, rich wood paneling and the burgundy painted walls. As they make into the grand room, the three come to an abrupt stop.

"Dis is quite remarkable." The older doctor nods as he looks at the bookshelves that surround the room.

Bill gestures to a set of glass doors that lead to the backyard. "Doctor Reich is out back with Mister Neill, a friend of his. He will be honored you have made it to Maine to meet with him."

The aged doctor gives Bill a subtle nod. His escorts block the exit.

The doctor raises a hand. "Gentlemen, vee are guests in a colleague's home. I do not believe, dat dare ist any danger here."

The escorts remain silent, but back away.

* * *

Dr. Wilhelm Reich's hair is blown over his right shoulder despite the lack of breeze. From the edge of the yard, he points to the scenic view of Rangeley Lake. "Orgone energy ist filtered from the lake through nature's curve of the mountains und ist collected in the receptors I placed on the roof."

"Doctor, how do you know this?"

"Mein friend, the evidence ist everywhere. Tell me, when you stand here and look out to the lake, do you not feel alive?"

"I do, the view is truly breathtaking; but, I hardly see that as scientific evidence."

"Ah, but you have witnessed the accumulators fill up with this energy. You cannot simply create something from nothing. zare ist energy all around us."

"That would be accurate to the atomic level."

The gentlemen turn to see the older doctor make his way down the slope of the yard. Dr. Reich claps. "Dr. Einstein! I am honored, that you could make it!"

Dr. Einstein makes his way next to the gentleman and looks out across to the lake.

"The honor ist mein, Dr. Reich. I have to agree the view is truly remarkable."

"Vee are men of science, let's not stand on formalities. Please call me Vilhelm."

Nodding his head, Dr. Einstein reaches his hand out. "Relax, Mister Neill, breathe in this energy." He smiled. "Doctor Reichs, any friend of a colleague is a friend of mine."

"Dr. Einstein, I have read all your work." He quickly looks at Dr. Reichs then back down at his feet, "well most of your work—I read the article in Times magazine."

Dr. Einstein straightens up as he looks back out to the lake. "Zo, you say that it ist this orgone energy, I am feeling right now."

"It ist true, although much like Christopher Columbus, vere he did not discover America but merely discovered the shore line, I've only discovered za shoreline of zee possibilities. If ve can harness, za spectrum of dis energy, dare ist no telling, vut ve can do."

Dr. Einstein rubs his chin. "You say dare is, a spectrum. Dis energy, it is not a constant?"

"Dare ist not a formula for it. It ist, not dissimilar to frequencies of light and za color zat correlates."

"I never could get into Psychology."

"It ist, more den zat. Okay, let's take blue. Za color blue ist supposed to calm you, can even make you sad. However, ven you look at a fresh bloom of Lilacs, do you not feel alive?"

Dr. Reichs studies Dr. Einstein's expressions. "Yet, ven you cut za flowers, color does not change; however, za blooms do not give you za same feelings ven you look at dem.

"As a matter of fact, your mood vill worsen the longer you look at dem. In zat brief moment, you have felt a spectrum of orgone energy."

Noting the stoic expression on Dr. Einstein's face and posture, Dr. Reichs takes a deep breath. "Let's try another approach, vu vill gain more insight. Red, ven you see field of roses, vut do you feel?"

"Love, happiness, even possibly elation."

Trying to contain his excitement, Dr. Reich rubs his hands together. "Precisely, now ist za color zat gave you za varm feelings? If you vere to see a wall of giant splashes paint of the same, identical color. Vould you feel the same? Za answer ist no. You vould experience anger und, even aggression. So, if it ist not za color zat causes zat, ven vut?"

"You say that, zee explanation vould be, this orgone energy."

"If atoms make up everything, za energy zat zey sit in, is orgone energy. Orgone energy is za life energy itself, it even exists vere zare appears to be no life. Ist just waiting to be woke up. I call zat DOR or dead orgone or "stagnant" orgone. It simply needs to awaken. Ist za gateway to life. Yet, I have not discovered za endless capabilities and abilities of za bion particle.

"But vie have I asked you here? Because the bion particle ist radioactive. Und you have, zom experience vit radiation."

"Atomic energy, the discovery of it, vas a mistake. It exists, ve've seen the power it has. Ve cannot put it back in the za box now. If this bion particle can..."

"Vat dis bion particle can do is revolutionize physics. Dis vould be a bombshell zu physics!" Dr. Reichs interrupts trying to contain his excitement. "Ist in fact the very cosmic energy itself. I've even cure cancer."

Dr. Einstein takes in a sharp breath as his thoughts are cut short and raises his eyebrows as he looks at Dr. Reichs. "Are you now suggesting that you have discovered za cure for cancer?"

Waving his hands, Dr. Reichs waves his hands. "No, no, no. Vell, I am not saying zat completely. But the bion particle zat makes up orgone energy has cured some cancer."

"Zare is a man that could help you. But you must understand, zis concept cannot be shown to the public."

Tapping the underside of his chin, Dr. Einstein turns and faces the lake, before clasping his hands behind his back. "Zee information must be kept secret."

"Albert! Za vorld needs to learn about it."

"Vilhelm, you must understand, at least for now. A Mister. Douglas, Lew Douglas, vill be able to explain it better."

Dr. Reichs paced, “I asked you to come here zo I can show you, vut zis discovery can do. And perhaps you vould vant to help me.”

“I vorked with Nikolas Tesla in 1943, a vor effort project. Ve were looking to use his technology to allow American ships to go undetected. That did not go so vell, it had tragic results. My apologies mein freund, but I am not sure I can assist vith anyone yet.”

“Zen, let us go in and have a drink. You must be tired from the walk.”

Dr. Einstein nods and points a finger in the air, “I was, but now that I am here, looking out onto the lake, I feel recovered. Perhaps zare really ist, something with your discovery.

“However, dis energy, like all energy, has the capacity to be very dangerous.”

The Quixotic Faction

2015

Banque Societe Generale de International, Katy, TX

July 17, 1539 hours

Temperature and humidity reached record indexes it the town of Katy, Texas. Heat waves coming off the street and cars make everything look as if it were melting. Outside Banque Societe Generale de International Bank a gentleman wearing a three-piece suit gets out of his brown 1969 Cadillac Deville and assesses the surrounding area.

Scratching his chin, just under his beard, he adjusts his sunglasses and walks into the bank.

The air conditioning washes over him as his skin ripples with goosebumps, giving him the feeling, he is about to walk through a portal into a different world. The bank door closes behind him, shutting out the melting world. Without drawing attention to himself, he takes a deep breath then locks the doors. Turning to count the customers and employees as he sets his briefcase on one of the counters. Sliding a front panel on it, he reveals a series of computerized controls.

Taking a moment, he adjusts the ear pieces to his MP3 player while scanning the customers again. After another deep breath, he reaches to the thumb locks, turning the dials. The briefcase emits silent, but high levels of radio and electromagnetic energy.

Watching a short man with an impressive moustache in front of him fill out a banking slip, he observes his facial expressions. The man starts to furl his brow showing signs of anger.

Making a few more adjustments to the thumb dials, the customer's expression shifts as if he is experiencing pleasure. The stranger whispers to himself, "This is going to be interesting."

Satisfied, he turns away from the briefcase, checks his watch, and walks to take his place in line.

Across the bank, a large man accidentally bumps into a woman with large hips. The woman glances up and their eyes meet, and for an instant, there is an immediate attraction. The couple smile as the middle-aged woman reaches up and caresses the man's cheek. He drops the paperwork he was holding and wraps his arms around her in an intense embrace. The couple kiss as if nobody is around. The stranger notes the passion and a fleeting smile forms and quickly vanishes.

To his right, he notices a motherly woman reaching out to caress the young skin on the woman in front of her. The younger lady looks down and follows the strange hand as it draws her in, she turns and acknowledges the older woman. A faint smile forms as the girl reaches up and gently grazes the nape of the motherly figure. Her hand moves down and cups the larger breasts of the older woman.

Dropping her large purse, the woman takes the younger one's cheeks in her hands and draws them closer as they begin to kiss.

Another fleeting smile forms on the stranger's face again and disappears.

All around him, the bank's customers and employee's attention to each other escalate as the interior scene of the bank takes on a semblance of a Roman bathhouse. Satisfied, he makes his way to the counter stepping over some bodies as he moves to the door to the right of the tellers. Knocking, a pair of semi-dressed employees open the door.

As he enters, the employees continue and no longer acknowledge the stranger. Making his way to a vault room, he searches some of the employees' clothing that was being strewn about, until he finds a key ring of magnetic key cards. Holding them up, he stares at a particular smaller, older safe.

Throwing the key cards aside, he continues to search the piles of clothing.

Inside the lapel of a woman's jacket he unpins a smaller set of two keys. He unlocks part of the safe. Realizing that the safe requires a combination. He looks back at the half-dressed bodies writhing about, tilting his head, he tries to figure out who would have it. Walking over to a woman who has a man pinned to a wall, he taps her shoulder and points to the safe. The woman, without releasing the object of her desire, points to an open door. When he gets to the doorway he sees three men paying particular attention a larger woman.

Knocking on the door, the stranger gets the attention of the large woman. Cupping his fingers, the stranger beckons the woman to come with him. She gets up and gently touches the jaws of each of the men.

When she reaches the door, she looks back at the men to see that have redirected their passion towards each other.

Remaining speechless, she smiles and directs a gleam of bliss at the stranger. He directs her towards the safe. After she works the combination and opens the safe, she hastily makes her way back to the three men in her office.

The stranger pulls out a metal tray holding two, cylinder shaped objects. He picks one up to examine the peculiar bone shape to them. Testing the weight as he lifts them up and down, their light weight surprises him.

Running his other hand over the smooth texture, he notices the strange picture glyphs and other markings that resemble cave writings. He removes his suit jacket, revealing a backpack. He takes a moment to admire the bone-like objects one last time before placing them inside the bag.

* * *

Outside, a police radio blares: "Two-one-one-five silent alarm, robbery in progress." More vehicles pull up as two officers approach the bank doors, trying to see if they can get a visual on the situation. When they reach the door, they see a woman pressed against it, fully nude.

It's apparent to the officers that the woman is being willfully ravaged from behind. They look at each other with disbelief trying not to laugh. They lower their weapons, trying not to laugh, they walk back to their chief.

"Chavez, Green! What the hell is happening?" A seasoned officer with stars on his collar yells out.

Officer Chavez, takes the lead. "Chief, I am not sure how to say this..."

Officer Green, jumps in. "Chief, I, um, we, ummm..."

Chavez puts his hand out, stopping the younger officer. "Chief, there's a full-blown orgy going on in there. I would tell you what we saw, but we are, at least I am, trying to unsee what we saw."

The other officers start to laugh. Chavez turns to his friends. "I admit it's funny; but, you don't have to go and pray to Santa Maria, so you can look at your wife with a straight face."

A Fighting off a "A what? Okay, okay," the chief calls out, trying not to smile.

"I suppose since it would appear that nobody is in danger of getting hurt, we can just wait it out." Picking up a radio handset, "Emily, Daniels, stay alert back there. We are going to wait this out and see who decides to leave the bank."

"Sir, we are not going to breach into the bank?"

"No, Emily, we are not. We are going to be patient on this one. Place all officers on stand-by."

Putting the handset down, the chief turns back to several other uniformed officers on the periphery. "Take a low-profile gentleman; let's get some of these cars out of here."

He points to a young officer. “Jared, we’ll stay here.” Pointing to Officers Green and Chavez he tells them, “As well as you two, since you have already seen what’s happening in there.

The rest of you get out of here before the media arrives and blows this out of proportion.”

The remaining officers moan and groan as they get back in their cars to drive away.

The radio sparks up again, “Emily, Daniels, we are taking a low profile on this; park so not to draw attention to yourselves and wait to see if anyone tries to leave.”

“Copy that, Chief.”

Just then the stranger walks out of the bank carrying the briefcase, the backpack remains hidden under the suit jacket. Realizing the police are there he casually reopens the panel of the briefcase.

Chavez nods towards the bank entrance. “Chief, I believe he is who we are looking for.”

“Shit.” Pushing on Officer Chavez’s shoulder and drawing his own weapon the chief yells out, “You two get over there!” He draws down on the stranger. “Put down the briefcase and put your hands up!”

Chavez and his partner, Green, take to a crouching run to surround the stranger. Officer Jared, standing next to the chief, draws his gun as he takes a few steps away from his supervisor. The stranger sets the briefcase on the hood of his car and adjusts the thumb locks.

Chavez sees this and yells out, “Step away from the briefcase!”

The stranger remains calm and takes a couple steps back, raising his hands in the air. He can see facial twitches on Chavez and Green and he affords himself a subtle smile.

Officer Green begins to walk towards the stranger when his partner grabs him at the top of his Kevlar vest, sending him flying backwards into a nearby car. “What are you doing? Are you trying to get yourself killed?” Chavez screams.

After landing against the car and breaking the driver’s side window, Green recovers and gets up into his partners face.

“He’s unarmed and calm! Wait, you want to take all the glory and be the one to arrest him.”

Chavez pushes his partner away from him. “What the hell are you talking about? I’m trying not to get us killed. That briefcase could be a bomb.”

“Yeah, right.” Getting back up into his partner’s face, he inadvertently points his gun at him. “Now who’s being stupid. If it was a bomb, do you really think he would be just standing there?”

Dodging the gun, Chavez grabs his partner’s vest and throws him to the ground. “Idiot! You don’t wave your gun at me!” Not realizing it, he was doing the same thing.

On the other side Jared steps closer to the stranger as the chief’s attention is towards his officers. “Will you two stay focused and stop trying to kill each other!”

The chief realizes what Jared was attempting to do. "What are you doing? Did I say approach him?"

Dropping his gun and looking frustrated, Jared turns his back to the stranger and walks back towards the Chief, who is stunned, as his two officers fight among themselves instead of apprehending the suspect.

Seeing Jared taking on a defeated posture, he yells, "Jesus Christ, man! What is wrong with you? Why are you dropping your weapon?"

"Stop yelling at me," Jared scoffs in frustration, "and will you make up your mind!"

"I am surrounded by idiots," the chief mumbles out loud as he rubs his temple with his free hand.

Gaining some gumption, Jared stiffens. "Why are we idiots?" He waves his arm in the air and dramatizes. "You are the one that tells us to think for ourselves and then yells at us for not waiting for your instructions!"

With complete disbelief, the chief drops his weapon.

"What? Where is this coming from? Have you all gone mad?"

Jared stares at the chief with complete resolve. Slowly, he raising his gun and points it at him.

The chief readies his gun at the young officer. "Don't do this. You do not want to do this."

Taking slow steps towards his chief, Jared tells him, "There you go. About to lose your life and you are still telling people what they want to do."

The chief recognizes a facial twitch he has seen many times with men are about to fire their weapon. Pulling the trigger of his gun just as the young officer pulls his. Both men fall limp to the ground as both weapons hit their mark, leaving blood and brain matter blown across the pavement.

At the sound of the gunfire, Chavez and Green cover their heads and turn to where the shots came from. Chavez runs towards the bodies when he sees his partner getting back up and heading towards the stranger, who seems amused by the tragedy.

"Green, stop! Get back!" Chavez yells out as he watches his partner turn towards him with his gun leading the way. Chavez fires first, sending the bullet through his friend's shoulder. Running over to him to see if he is okay, he yells at the stranger, "Don't move!" The stranger just tilts his head and looks at the approaching police officer.

Just as he gets to the feet of his partner, Green turns and fires, Chavez is sent flying back onto the pavement, convulsing as arterial blood from his throat squirts across the sidewalk.

The stranger walks to his briefcase, and as he is adjusting the dials, Officer Green turns his gun on him. "Step away from the briefcase!"

With the briefcase readjusted the stranger turns and tilts his head to Green who is on the ground wincing from the shoulder gunshot.

He watches the officer squint his eyes, trying to shake cobwebs from his mind, while keeping his gun trained on him.

The stranger walks over to the officer, kneels down, and guides the weapon towards the officer's chest. Green brings both fists to his temples. "Aarghh, my head. Why does my head hurt?"

The stranger points and brings the officer's attention to his partner, who is struggling to stop his neck from bleeding and whispers in Green's ear, "Look what you did."

Chavez is grasping at his neck and his legs are kicking. His movements are slowing down. Green attempts to scramble up with his left arm dead and bleeding; he drops the gun and scrambles to get to his partner. "Chavez! Oh my God, what have I done?"

Deserted Farm, Dry Creek, LA

July 18, 1243 hours

A dark-blue, Ford 350 Transit makes its way between the tattered, unkempt cornfields. Behind it is a large dust cloud, kicking up from its wheels on what is a cloudless day in Southwest Louisiana. Crows scatter across the cornfields, cawing in the wake of the intruder.

Admiral Julian Kay, a middle-aged man with authoritative grey eyes, focused on the road. Doctor Lincoln Stevens is tall man, riding shotgun and wearing a metal headgear with minute LED's flashing on the visor covering his eyes. Doctor Harvey Garret is younger and well-built man with short blonde hair, riding in the back and holding on for dear life.

They slow down, as the fields come to an end, revealing a rundown farmhouse and a very large, equally rundown barn.

The admiral turns to the tall gentleman on his right. "Lincoln, are you sure that equipment of yours is working?"

"Yes, I can even see the energy trail, well it is not exactly an energy field, more like a radio frequency type trail." His excitement is clear despite not being able to see his eyes.

"I am going to trust that you know what that means."

They approach the farmhouse and come to a stop.

The three sit in silence waiting for any signs of movement. Harvey breaks the silence, leaning into the front and putting a heavy hand on the driver's shoulder.

"Admiral, you do remember that we barely escaped with our equipment. Tell me we did not come to a place where we are going to get ourselves killed in a way where they make a movie of it later."

Ignoring him, the admiral glances at the radio, notes the time, and gets out to look around. The entire area is overgrown and eerily abandoned.

"Relax, Harvey, this is just a large, desolate farm on the edge of nowhere, just outside of Dry Creek, Louisiana. What could possibly go wrong here?" the admiral scoffs.

Harvey lumbers out of the back of the van, wiping the sweat from his forehead and giving the admiral a sideways glare.

"Why are we even here?"

The admiral turns to the gentleman wearing the equipment. "Lincoln, can you walk us through it again and why I drove twelve hundred miles to get us here."

Looking at a notepad, Lincoln meticulously flips through the pages until he finds his notes on the original sighting. "Little over a month ago I noticed an energy anomaly.

"What I mean is that I noted a stream of waves being pulled through the sky. With this visual gear I built, I am able to see and interpret molecular wave patterns, and I documented this energy being bent in a stream as if being pulled across the sky."

Harvey walks up to his friend's side. "I thought you built it to be a portable laser that could cut anything."

Looking back up, he scans the skyline. "Yes, Harvey, there is that fun factor; however, I can only do that if I can interpret the molecular level of the object I am cutting." His focus turns to the roof of the barn. "Over there the anomaly appears to come to be funneling into the barn."

The admiral steps away from the two towards the house. "Well let's see if anyone is home, shall we."

The admiral and Harvey tentatively make their way to the farmhouse as Lincoln hurries towards the barn with his head up looking at the energy trail leading into the roof. Walking up to the door, before the admiral can knock, a turkey gobbles causing everyone to jump and look for the bird.

Harvey remains off the porch looking around and continually wiping the sweat from his forehead with a towel.

"How's it this humid? There are no clouds in the sky. Just for the record," pointing back in the direction of the road they just came in on, "those birds back there were scary. That turkey is scary.

"This whole goddamn place is something from the Texas Chainsaw Massacre. I thought we were going to Smallville, not to visit The Children of the Corn."

Just as the admiral turns back to knock, Lincoln is walking backwards yelling to them. "You guys have got to see this! There's like a vortex of these radial energy waves funneling into that barn!" Still looking up he does not notice the turkey until it turns and flies to the ground. Harvey takes a step towards his friend, not taking his eyes off of the turkey. The turkey starts to attack both of them with territorial aggression.

The main door opens and a quiet, but forceful, voice makes even the admiral take a half a step back.

"Get off my land!" the voice snarls.

Unable to see who is doing the talking, the admiral recovers his composure. "Sir, we are not here to hurt you or anything of that nature. We are actually here to protect you."

"Are you the police?"

An odd chill, creeps on the back of the neck of the admiral as he turns to see his companions being circled and attacked by the turkey. He shakes his head and pinches the bridge of his nose. "No, sir, we are not the police. My name is Julian Kay, and those two are Doctors Laurel and Hardy."

"What makes you think I need a doctor?" The force from the question makes him feel like he is being pushed.

Still standing his ground, the admiral attempts to lean into the force that is keeping him away. "They are not that kind of doctors. They are engineering doctors."

"Government, get off my property!" An unseen force sends the admiral through the porch railing and into the dirt. Attracting the turkey's attention, it charges the admiral. The doctors are staring at the admiral and the front door, stunned in disbelief.

"That's it!" With excitement, Stevens stands.

"It is not radial energy or waves; it is a magnetic radial wave." Everyone looks at the tall, electronically-masked man, confused. "I can't believe I analyzed it wrong."

The turkey stops his charge at the admiral, turns and gobbles at the tall doctor. Before he can charge, his legs give out and he falls to the ground. His body starts to contort and flatten out. Astounded, everyone watches the turkey flatten into a thin disc; its skin gives out as its inside explode out over the ground and its blood soaks the ground around it.

"Get off my land," the voice from behind the door again commands in a quiet but forceful tone.

The three gentlemen mentally recover from the tragic scene and retreat to the van. Before opening the door, Lincoln faces the house and yells out to the person in the house.

"We can help. There are forces in motion, we can help each other."

As he gets in the van, the admiral looks at him. "What the hell was that all about? and will you please remove that head gear."

Taking off the equipment and still looking at the house he says, "Just trying to reach through to him."

Never taking his eyes off the deceased turkey, Harvey asks, "Did you guys see what he did to the turkey?"

In unison both the admiral and Lincoln tell him, "Yes, we saw it."

The admiral starts the van and proceeds to turn around, but then slams the van to a stop. He quickly gets out, scanning the house, he makes it to the front door, determined to meet this man.

He knocks again. No response.

Waiting for a count to ten, he knocks harder. Still, no response. Stepping away from the door he walks to a window, cupping his eyes, tries to look inside.

Unable to see into the house he walks around to another window.

Not being able to see inside the house he walks back to the van, shaking his head.

Harvey asks confused, "Did you see what he did to the turkey? What were you thinking?"

Without taking his eyes off the door to the farmhouse, the admiral tells him, "You already know I saw what he did to the bird; however, he could have done that to us, but didn't."

Finishing the turn to exit the farm he looks to Lincoln.

"What exactly, are these magnetic-radial waves?"

1895

Veniero's Pasticceria & Caffe, Manhattan, NY

March 12, 1652 hours

Walking down a street in Lower Manhattan, a reporter comes across a small café. Sitting at one of the small tables outside is a man who appears to be incredibly shaken about something. He's having trouble dipping his biscotti into the sweet cream.

The reporter walks over to see if the man is okay. When the man looks up at him, his hairstyle immediately gives away his identity. "Mr. Nikolas Tesla? Are you doing alright?"

His eyes are having trouble focusing. "I am afraid that you won't find me a pleasant companion tonight. The fact is I was almost killed today. The spark jumped three feet through the air and struck me here on the right shoulder. If my assistant had not turned off the current instantly it might have been the end of me."

Astounded, the reporter says, "Sir, did you say you were struck by an electricity bolt? It is amazing that you are alive. I have followed your work, and I am always impressed at your demonstrations. I have seen you stand in the way of electricity and it painlessly passed through and around you."

A hint of clarity returns to his eyes, and he is able to hold his hands steady.

"This was a much stronger and modified form of electricity, three-point-five-million volts stronger."

Letting out a low whistle, the reporter pulls out a chair.

"May I? I know you stated that you may not be pleasant company, however, you do look like you need to talk to someone."

Nikolas gives him a slight nod of affirmation. Taking out a pad of paper, the reporter offers a smile. "What are your thoughts on Edward Lorenz?"

Perking up, he tilts his head as he leans back into his chair.

"Edward Lorenz is logical when he talks about his butterfly effect theory, and the same concept can be applied with time travel."

Raising his hands slightly, the reporter chuckles. "Jules Verne wrote about time travel and landing on the moon, but that is pure fiction."

"Is it? Allow me to break down a few concepts and you can be the judge." The reporter absently picks up a biscotti and dips it into the sweet cream, his eyes never leaving Nikolas.

"Now imagine that if we could manipulate Earth's magnetic properties, we could accomplish so much, and at the same time, we could destroy everything." Realizing that the reporter was having trouble following, Nikolas points for the reporter to hold on.

"How about this, if I were to ask, what is gravity?" The reporter motions as if he is about to say something, however, Mr. Tesla stops him. "You would refer to Sir Isaac Newton. You would say that gravity is the force that keeps us standing on Earth. But what is the force? You could say the force is gravity, and gravity is the force, but what precisely is it? According to Newton, gravity is the force between two objects.

"So, if I were to push you, we would both go in opposite directions, and it would be gravity that caused the separation between you and my hands. However, we have come to only refer to gravity as that which keeps us here on Earth and why things fall. So, I ask again, what is gravity?"

After a moment's pause, the reporter scratches his chin and studies Nikolas Tesla's eyes.

"I have attended universities, and I am no way near your level of intelligence. But I do understand the complexity of your question."

Leaning in to eat some more biscotti, Nikolas nudges the plate towards his guest then sits back into his chair and crosses his legs. After a moment's pause, he continues on.

"Now, we know that the earth has a magnetic field. We have a North Pole and a South Pole, much like a standard magnet. Perhaps gravity is an electric attraction. The energy from my coils fire off electric discharges, and they always strike to the ground. We know that as human beings we can generate static electricity."

The reporter chuckles.

"My niece loves doing that to her hair and touching people on a cold winter night."

Smiling, Nikolas looks up as if to collect a thought.

"With my transformers, I have used magnets to change the power levels of electricity. So, we know magnetism and electricity work together in nature."

"Whoa," the reporter says raising a hand. "How do we know they work together in nature, when you just said that you used magnets to change electricity?"

"We know they work together or else all lightning strikes would be the same."

"Interesting."

"When I was struck today by one of these electro-magnetic arcs, I was momentarily caught. I saw the magnetic fields around me bend—and I could not move. I saw the very fabric that holds the past, present, and future together.

If we take the butterfly effect and incorporate it to the concept of time travel, then if we were to go back in time and change anything, we could drastically change the present. Same type of problem would exist if we were to travel to the future and then return to our present, which would be our future's past, which leads us to the butterfly effect if the present travels into the past."

Eyes widening, the reporter sits to an upright position. "Did you say you saw the future as well as the past?"

With complete resolution, Nikolas leans towards his guest. “My good man, I have seen the future and the future’s future. We, being the human race, are about to traverse into dangerous territory. But having seen this, it has put me in the butterfly effect conundrum that Mr. Lorenz theorizes.”

With the biscotti gone, they sit and seem to get lost in their thoughts. The reporter lets out a quiet whistle and stands. “Thank you, it has been truly an honor.”

Offering his hands out, Nikolas stands, and they shake hands and the reporter gets a static shock.

“I guess I still have some residual energy,” Nikolas says.

“It is I that should be thanking you. You were correct in that I simply needed to talk to someone. So, I will thank you and return to my work, thank you.”

Gathering his coat, Nikolas turns and walks away. The reporter looks around and adjusts his hat. “Well that was enlightening.” Walking away a thought enters his mind, what was that name of that Jules Verne novel?

2015

SLS Casino, Las Vegas, NV

July 18, 1421 hours

A stout man paces as he watches a large monitor showing Earth's magnetic field flexing, resembling a rubber band. Impatiently, he checks his watch. "I need to eat."

He taps the shoulder of one of the operators of the computer station and gestures to the large monitor.

"The only thing I know that can affect Earth's protective field like that is an immense solar flare. We have not had one large enough to come even close to doing that in almost a decade. When I get back from lunch I better have an answer waiting for me."

The computer operator is determined and confused.

"Director Harris, the field was pulled down, as if it was reaching down to pull something up. The source is terrestrial—not extra-terrestrial."

"Then find me the source."

Turning to exit the room, the door opens and the hallway light floods the room.

Two silhouettes of agents walk in; one is a young, former military gentleman, and the other is a young, attractive woman carrying an electronic pad.

Radiance from the computer screens light the room as soon as the door closes behind them. The young woman approaches the director. "Director Harris, I was told you were in here."

She starts tapping her electronic pad, pulling up a map and acknowledging her counterpart.

Looking up at the director she says, "We completed the math, and although we do not know what caused the magnetic pull on Earth's field, we have narrowed it to an area in Southwest Louisiana."

Stretching his arms out, then resting his hands-on top of his head, the stout man looks directly at the woman.

"Well, we are making progress." Motioning out the door he says, "Walk with me, and you can walk me through why you believe it to be in Louisiana." He walks between the two without further acknowledgement, and the door closes behind him.

The two agents look at each other, and the male agent can see the enthusiasm in his younger counterpart's eyes.

"I appreciate you including me in on this find, even though you have confused the shit out of me a hundred times already on this math of yours."

Looking up at him she smiles, and then her eyes widen in realization that the director has left them standing there.

They hurry to catch up to him.

When they get to the elevator they realize the door to the stairway just closed. Agent Sanchez looks at the door in disbelief, "You've got to be kidding me, we're six stories down."

Abergathy shrugs and they bolt for the stairs.

Just as they catch up to the director, the female agent trips, sending the tablet across one of the landings and sliding past the director's feet. He kneels down and picks up the electronic equipment and turns towards the agent. "You should never run on a stairwell. Are you okay?"

Standing back up and looking embarrassed, she says, "Yes, sir."

Still holding the tablet, he begins to stroll through the information on it. "I consider myself an intelligent man, but I must admit this is way above my head. Now that you are vertical and have caught your breath, you can begin walking me through your findings."

Taking a moment to smile, she accepts her tablet back. "Yes, sir." Tapping on her electronic pad, she brings up a model of the earth's core.

"The earth is believed to have a molten iron core, and because of this it gives it a magnetic field that surrounds the planet, protecting it from interstellar radiation that would, without it, make life impossible to survive."

Raising his hand, he stops her. "First of all, what is your name?"

"I apologize. It's Kristen Abergathy, sir."

"Second, I mentioned that I am a reasonably intelligent man. Tell me something I do not know."

They walk up the remaining flight of stairs while Agent Abergathy rambles nonstop regarding her findings.

When they reach the top, they are winded. "Sir, Agent Miguel Sanchez here. If I can ask, why did we take the stairs and not the elevator?"

"Agent Sanchez, as agents, exercise does us all good, and besides I don't trust elevators. Now I understand that being here in Las Vegas, this is as close of a location that you can get. Do you think you can pinpoint a location if you were to go to Louisiana? As it would appear, you are the only ones that have even been close to getting a location."

"Yes, sir, absolutely!" Abergathy says, trying to hold back the excitement that is showing in her eyes as she smiles to the point of being giddy.

With a slight smile and a stern tone in his voice, the director turns to Sanchez.

"I expect a full report. And keep this one out of trouble, Agent Sanchez. You both can fly out tonight."

Trying to keep her enthusiasm in check, Abergathy says, "Thank you, sir. You won't be disappointed."

Shaking his head, the director turns and opens the exterior door and the Las Vegas sun and heat hits them like a brick wall.

"I love this part. It lets you know that you are alive. Now I need to eat. My blood sugar is getting low." Without looking back at the agents, "I expect complete status updates."

Roy's Catfish Hut, Kinder, LA

July 18, 1838 hours

The admiral and the two doctors are sitting in a corner table. The admiral is moving his oysters around his plate, lost in thought. Stevens has his nose buried in his electronics, ignoring the salad in front of him, trying to figure out what they witnessed earlier. Garrett is devouring his crawfish half-and-half platter.

"Lincoln, have you been able to make heads or tails of what happened today?" the Admirals asks Stevens.

Garrett takes a break from eating.

"Did you guys see what he did to that turkey?"

"Harvey, for the umpteenth time, yes, we were there too, remember?" The admiral looks disgusted at Garrett. "How can you eat that?"

"I need protein," Garrett says. "We have not eaten anything since breakfast, and according to the Osage Indians, we owe our existence to these mud crawlers. It is believed they retrieved mud from the bottom of the primordial ocean so that the earth could be created. I'm just honoring them."

Tapping away on his tablet, Stevens is amazed.

"Admiral, the information that my equipment collected while we were there is incredible."

Separating his laptop and laying the tablet half on the table, he opens the screen and shows an aerial layout of the farm and streams of waves swirling into the barn.

The admiral looks over at the screen.

"What are we looking at?"

"Think of an atmospheric pressure front, only in this case it is radio and magnetic waves so dense that they're generating a gravitational field.

"And it is funneling into whatever is in that barn," Stevens explains.

With his plate cleared, Garrett sits back and starts back in on the bucket of peanuts and does his best Giorgio Tsoukalos impression.

"So, you are not saying it's aliens, but it's aliens."

Smiling, Stevens looks at his friend. "Your mechanical ape suit should withstand the pressure that these waves are creating."

"First of all, it is not a mechanical ape suit. It is a high-density, gravitational exoskeleton, and I have never tested it without being under the pressure of an intense gravity environment."

Gaining his appetite, the admiral starts eating his fried oysters. Looking at the muscular friend, the admiral pauses.

"Harvey, please walk me through your metal ape suit again."

Forearming his friend, he says, "See what you started." He turns to the admiral.

"I created a gravitational exoskeleton," Garrett says. "All the Kepler planets that the Kepler satellite system have been able to locate are larger than our earth. It is one thing to know they are there. It is another to be able to walk on them. Some of these planets are one point five to ten times larger than us."

Cracking open some more peanuts, he says, "You may think that one point five times larger would not be that bad, however. . ."

Leaning back in the chair and tossing the peanut shells on the floor, Garrett gestures to the admiral.

"How much do you weigh?"

"Two hundred give or take?" the admiral says.

"On Kepler 186, which is slightly bigger than Earth, it would feel like you weighed three hundred thirty pounds. Not so bad, right?"

Garrett says. "However, on planets like Gliese 581, which is estimated to be four times the size of Earth, it would feel like you weighed . . ."

Garrett reaches inside Stevens's pocket, pulls out a calculator, and types in an equation, and then turns the calculator around and lays it on the table.

"This is how much you would feel like you weighed."

Leaning and looking at the display, it reads 2,342,560,000.

The admiral lets out a quiet whistle. "Are you serious?"

"Give or take a few thousand pounds. Either way, our physical design would be crushed under that kind of gravity pressure," Garrett adds. "The gravitational exoskeleton is capable of withstanding that kind of pressure, allowing you to be able to move around. But it has only been tested under extreme gravity pressure. I don't know what would happen under Earth's gravitational pull."

Stevens points out, "As you so eloquently keep reminding us of what that man did to the turkey, your suit is the only thing that can withstand that kind of pressure."

Feeling both sets of eyes barreling down on him, Garrett shakes his head. "I need to use the restroom." Wiping his mouth, he slides away from the table. He turns to his friends like he was going to say something but instead walks away mumbling.

Stevens leans in on the table and with a lowered voice says, "Admiral, why are we looking for this guy? Don't get me wrong; I'm excited to finally find something like this anomaly. I mean we managed to keep our lives and our equipment. Life is good."

"I understand your concerns. A few months ago, I was working for a NASA division, and I saw a series of reports on some strange happenings all over the place. A longtime friend and I began to dig deeper. There were reports of high-tech equipment being delivered, and then the same report showing it being delivered someplace else. Strange sighting reports were being sent to the local newspapers—only never going to print.

"He found me one night, scared out of his mind, telling me he might have gotten caught looking into some of these reports.

"And he believed he found something. He died in a car accident less than twenty-four hours later. I have lived in the world of special operations for most of my life. I have done things for this government I am not proud of. I have also done things I am very proud of, none of which I can talk about."

Turning to look out the window the admiral continues, "I have seen things that cannot be explained by a rational mind and dealt with people whose sole purpose is to keep it quiet. Those same people will stop at nothing to accomplish their goals. When NASA opened space to the private companies in 2009, this company has done everything in its power to stop them from being successful. Companies have been ruined and people have disappeared."

Taking a moment to take a drink, the admiral looks around to see if the conversation has caught anybody's attention.

"It's through those files my friend found that I was able to find you two. I don't want anyone else to go missing in the name of space exploration."

The two sit in silence as Garrett returns to the table.

"Why is everyone so solemn all of a sudden?"

"The admiral was just telling me of an agency that is preventing space exploration from privateers." Stevens sits up, adjusting his silverware.

Getting excited, Garrett sits up to explains, "You're talking about Project Cadmus. Some say it was formed in 1963, but others say it was formed in 1947 after the Roswell crash and that they're the ones really responsible for the assassination of JFK. I mean seriously, how can a single-shot, six-point, 5mm Carcano carbine rifle fire all those shots that fast? And why was the motorcade rerouted at the last minute so that it would drive right past the book depository? Are these the same people who we are now on the run from? If that's the case we are in some serious trouble.

"Some say, and I'm not saying I believe it completely, that they were the machine behind anyone associated with President Nixon getting out of office, even the president himself."

The admiral looks at Garrett with confusion.

"Harvey, why do you call them Project Cadmus, and who are these people you're talking about?"

"In the DC Universe, Project Cadmus is a private agency whose purpose is to control the Justice League."

Trying not to laugh, Stevens forearms his friend but ends up pushing himself against the window.

"This is not your comic book universe, this is the real world."

"Conspiracies have talked about them for years, whether you want to call them Project Cadmus or Men in Black, they're the same. I already had a hunch that these people are the reason we had to get our stuff and get the hell out of Dodge."

The admiral takes a deep breath. "Whatever we are going to call this organization they are dangerous people. Are you going to see if your exoskeleton will allow us to talk to this guy?" Looking to Stevens, he says, "And Lincoln, if you were able to find this anomaly, you know that they are not far behind us."

Dr. Garrett grabs another handful of peanuts and leans back in his seat.

"Yeah, I'll give it a go. Even though I will warn you that I am not so sure how it will handle."

The admiral raises his glass. "Alright then, to a successful day tomorrow."

Watching the admiral and Garrett drink up, Stevens gets worried.

"Admiral, we've been tracking this guy for a few weeks now. How do we know that he has not already drawn attention from others?"

"We don't. All we can hope for is that we can convince him, and we can get out of here before . . ." gesturing to Garrett, ". . . Project Cadmus shows up."

Garrett laughs and coughs up some of the peanuts, catching them in his hand. Leaning back in the booth, he lifts his glass.

"I'll drink to that."

Stevens, unfazed by his friend's laughter, pokes at his salad. "All kidding aside, just how dangerous are these people?"

Garrett leans in and lowers his voice.

"If they had anything to do with JFK, or even with Nixon, then they are some really dangerous people."

The admiral stares down at his plate, thinking about his friend getting killed the year before in the car accident. He looks up at his traveling companions. "Let's just finish eating, and we can prepare for tomorrow."

Houston International Airport, Houston, TX

July 19, 0156 hours

A black Hawker Siddeley HS-125 jet taxi's the runway. Inside the small jet, Agent Sanchez sleeps on the couch as Agent Abergathy analyzes information on her tablet. Just as the plane takes off, Agent Sanchez shifts position and cracks open an eye towards to his partner.

"You know, you should really get some sleep."

"Oh, shit!" Abergathy flips her stylus onto the deck of the plane. "I thought you were sleeping," she says as her hand lands on her chest as if to verify a heartbeat.

Smiling and closing his eyes, he puts a forearm across his eyes and settles in.

"This is the first plane I have been on that didn't have cargo nets," Sanchez says. "This puddle jumper is beyond my imagination. How did you score us this ride?"

"I simply suggested to our so-called travel agency that when this year is over the FAA will prohibit this plane to fly."

"Why's that?" Sanchez asks with wide-eyed curiosity. "This plane is freakin' awesome!"

Abergathy turns her attention back to her tablet.

"It does not have stage-three-noise-compliant engines."

"Santo Cielo. You have got to be kidding me. You're a genius," Sanchez says as he reclines, resting his arm over his eyes. "This plane is as quiet as a happy kitten. The FAA should be listening to C-130s, then they will have something to complain about."

Over the loud speaker the captain jokes, "Keep it down back there . . .

"The skies are clear, so the remaining leg to Alexandria will be smooth sailing, and we will be landing in an hour."

Sanchez murmurs to his partner while settling further into the couch. "Wake me when we land, and seriously, you really should try and get a little shut eye."

The jet shifts due to turbulence, sending Abergathy's stylus rolling back onto the deck again.

"Smooth sailing, huh?" Looking back at her partner, she says, "Do we have a plan once we find whatever is causing the earth's magnetic field to flux?"

"Our job is to see if we can find the source of the field anomaly with that fancy math of yours, observe it, and report on it. This is your first time in the field, so let's not get overzealous. Now, try to get some rest. You heard the captain, wheels down in an hour," Sanchez answers as he closes his eyes, taking his own advice.

Allen Acres Bed & Breakfast, Pitkin, LA

July 19, 0232 hours

It is an eerie, country-quiet night as the admiral wanders into the kitchen of the rustic bed and breakfast. Opening the refrigerator, an elderly voice startles the admiral.

"You ain't supposed to be in here."

Standing up, the admiral looks around for the voice in the darkness, the light from the refrigerator blinding him from seeing the owner of the voice.

"I was hungry and didn't want to wake anyone."

The voice appears behind him, just under his arm, closes the door, and extinguishes the only light in the room.

"Don't change no fact that you ain't supposed to be in here." The admiral takes a step back and looks towards the refrigerator.

"My apologies, ma'am. I meant no disrespect."

The light in the kitchen is switched on, causing the admiral to shield his eyes. At the doorway is the young brunette who checked them in last night. He turns back to acknowledge the voice of the elderly woman. Not seeing anyone standing by the fridge, he scans the room, and when he does not see the owner of the voice earlier, he uses his hands to calm himself and takes a breath.

"Are you alright, Mr. Kay?" The woman in the doorway asks. "You know guests are not supposed to be in the kitchen."

Still collecting his composure, the admiral gives her a warm smile.

"I did not want to wake anyone. My apologies."

Walking over to shoo him out of the kitchen, the young lady waves her wrist, motioning for him to step back.

"You already apologized, and you don't strike me as someone who repeats himself. Now what can I fix you to eat?"

"Just looking for something to drink, ma'am," the admiral answers as he takes a few steps around the counter, attempting to create some distance from where he last heard the voice.

"Please, my name is Sheryl. You say ma'am and I'm looking for my mother."

Masking his unease, he says, "Alright, Sheryl, as long as you call me Julian."

Looking up at him with her large brown eyes, she says, "Sounds like a deal, Julian. Now what can I get you to drink?"

"Iced tea would be great, thank you." Watching Sheryl turn around, his attention is drawn to her slim, but shapely, figure.

The elderly voice he heard earlier whispers behind him, "She a good girl and know how to cook."

"I am sure you are correct," the admiral mummers, not wanting to turn to acknowledge the voice.

Holding a pitcher of sweet tea and a glass, Sheryl turns towards the counter as the light from the opened refrigerator puts a glow around her hair.

"Did you say something? I hope sweet tea will be fine." Their eyes lock, and a glimmer of a spark holds the gaze.

Garrett walks into the kitchen wearing a Justice League of America tee shirt and rubbing one of his eyes. "Awesome. That would hit the spot."

Not taking her eyes away from the admiral, Sheryl nods at Garrett. "No problem, sir," she says and pours her new guest a glass.

The sexual tension between the admiral and Sheryl is interrupted by a reverberation that shakes the house.

The admiral reaches over the counter and pulls the young lady to the counter top, spilling the tea.

Garrett dives to the ground, covering his ears. After the ringing in the admiral's ears subsides, he realizes he's still holding the owner of the bed and breakfast down on the counter.

"My apologies, ma'am—I mean, Sheryl. Instincts take over sometimes." Looking around the room, he says, "That was a sonic boom. Why are jets flying so low to the ground? And they are prohibited from breaking the sound barrier below a certain altitude."

"I'm okay, thank you." Straightening herself up, Sheryl starts cleaning up the tea. "Dr. Garrett, is it? Would you still like a glass of sweet tea?"

"What the hell was that?" Garrett gets up on one knee, craning his neck around. "I felt that through my bones." The house begins to stir as guests make their way around the bed and breakfast. Stretching his jaw, trying to pop the pressure from his ears, Garrett gets back to his feet. "That would be awesome, ma'am, thank you."

The admiral leans back on the sink counter and crosses his arms as his right hand rubs down his chin. Looking back towards Sheryl, he says, "You don't seem too taken back by the sonic boom."

Handing the glass to Garrett, Sheryl shrugs. "That has been going on for a few months now. We have already contacted Fort Polk and they have been in contact with Port Arthur. Both say that it's an atmospheric-pressure something or other."

Rushing in the kitchen, Stevens is wearing his electronic headgear.

"That was not an atmospheric pressure anomaly! Well, technically it was, but it was not naturally caused."

"What in God's name!" Dropping the glass exchange with Garrett, Sheryl grabs her chest in shock as she sees the tall man rushing into the kitchen wearing a metallic, blinking headgear.

The glass shatters to the floor as Garrett slaps his forehead.

Keeping his arms folded across his chest, the

admiral closes his eyes and shakes his head.

"Lincoln, do you sleep in that thing?" he says to Stevens and raises a hand to let Sheryl know it is okay. "Sheryl, pay no attention to the tall robotic doctor."

She turns to get a small broom. "What kind of doctors uses that fancy equipment?"

"I could tell you all sorts of things that even I don't completely understand, but we are men of science," the admiral assures her.

"I was just going back over today's information again, since I couldn't sleep," Stevens says, "when that sonic boom knocked me out of bed." He walks past the admiral to the long side of the counter top, where he turns to the counter top and gives a quick nod of acknowledgement to someone standing next to the admiral. "Ma'am." Turning to the counter top, Stevens spreads out a map.

Looking up at Sheryl, Stevens continues to spread out and flatten the map. "Excuse me, ma'am."

The admiral takes a step away. "Can we go over this information when the sun comes up? Sheryl, if you will excuse us, we will bid you good night." He scans the kitchen again for that elderly voice and where Stevens saw something.

Stevens looks up. "Oh, okay." He collects the paperwork on the counter.

The admiral presses the shoulders of both of his friends as he ushers them out of the kitchen.

Garrett looks back at the pitcher of tea.

"But I didn't get any tea, and who were you talking to, Lincoln?"

"Never mind that. Harvey, you will survive, and, Lincoln, you can talk about the boom later, I promise, but right now we need to get some rest . . . and some air."

Hawker Siddeley HS-125

July 19, 0250 hours

An alarm sounds in the pilot house as the co-pilot acknowledges it and adjusts the sensitivity of the scope. On the screen a contact appears a few miles on the flight path to Alexandria. The pilot slows the plane down and puts in a call to AEX.

"AEX, this is HS-One Two Five, do you copy?"

"HS-One Two Five, this is AEX tower, we have you on contact."

"AEX, this is HS-One Two Five, need to verify radar contact bearing on our zero."

"HS-One Two Five, this is AEX tower, contact verified and flight path undetermined. Request fuel remaining for go-around."

"AEX, this is HS-One Two Five, 5703 gallons, request go-around flight path."

The co-pilot is still adjusting the radar sensitivity when the contact disappears. A sonic boom cracks the windshield as a jet stream washes just off the portside wing, sending it into a starboard side roll. The jet spirals, losing altitude. Agent Sanchez is sent rolling across the plane and catches the table post latching his arms around it and hooking his legs while yelling absurdities. Agent Abergathy remains belted in her seat, and she grabs her knees to her chest and screams into her lap.

"AEX, mayday, mayday, HS-One Two Five losing pressure . . . caught in a spin . . . altitude dropping."

"HS-One Two Five, copy mayday. Monitor altitude. You can pull out of spin when pressure evens at 2400 feet."

By the time the plane reaches 2250 feet, the pilot is able to regain control of the jet and level it to the horizon line.

"AEX, this is HS-One Two Five, we have regained control. However, we have multiple system failures. Request to make short approach." Checking the radio status, he says, "AEX, this is HS-One Two Five, did you copy last?"

Looking at his terrified co-pilot, he repeats, "AEX, requesting to make short approach, need immediate landing coordinates. And what the hell was that?"

Inside the cabin, Abergathy unbuckles herself and makes her way to the dry bar. With her hands still shaking, she grabs a bottle of Jack Daniels. A moan escapes as Sanchez stands, holding his wrist.

"I hope you are pouring me one of those. You know sharing is caring."

Looking at his bruised and rapid swelling wrist, she opens an ice chest and takes off her shirt to collect the ice for an icepack.

"Here, sit down. Put your arm out on the table, and let's get this thing iced up."

Shocked at the new side of his partner, Sanchez smiles, following her instructions. His eyes have trouble diverting from her bra.

"I am impressed at your field training and, ummm, your confidence."

Sitting across from him at the table, she says, "As long as you keep your eyes up here," pointing to her eyes.

"At least the jet was able to level out. I wonder what happened up there." She pours them a drink.

Setting the icepack on his wrist, Sanchez takes the drink and sips. A shiver shoots up his spine. "Wow, only the good stuff here. Well from the boom I heard through your screaming . . ." She kicks him under the table. "Ow. And the speed and the way we spun out, I say we hit a jet wash."

Getting up, she points a finger. "You stay and keep your wrist on ice. I'm going to go talk to the pilot." She turns and heads to the front of the plane, still reaching out to the sides of the jet for security. Knocking on the cabin door, she opens it up to see the windshield is cracked and multiple lights are flashing. "I may not be a pilot, but I am thinking that this is not a good thing."

Without looking back the pilot acknowledges his passenger.

"Agent, you need to go back and sit down. I didn't turn off the seatbelt light."

"Kristen, please we need you to sit back down." The co-pilot pauses seeing that she is without her shirt.

"Ummm, we know as much as you do, and we're looking for a place to land. We're going to try to make it as close to Alexandria as we can, so right now go back in and buckle up, and tell Miguel to do the same. And put a shirt on. It's going to be a bumpy ride."

Hurrying back into the cabin, she sees her partner lying back, passed out, and the icepack dropped on the deck. His wrist is turning a deep shade of purple right in front of her. Thinking the pain got to him, she looks around the mess-of-a cabin until she finds the first aid emergency kit. Taking a closer look at his wrist, realizing that it is broken, she wraps the bandage around it with the icepack.

Grabbing a pair of pants from the luggage overhead, she ties one leg around his elbow and traps the other leg into the overhead, elevating his arm.

After buckling him in, she makes her way back to her seat and buckles back in, looking out her window into the cloudless starry night.

"Well, girl, you wanted an adventure. You wanted to be a field agent. Let's just hope it is not my last." Seeing her reflection, she realizes that she had forgotten to get a shirt. Smiling she says, "Well at least it is one of my best-looking bras. If I am going to die, I picked a good bra to die in."

The plane shifts again due to turbulence, causing her to grip the table. Breathe in... breathe out.

The turbulence feels like it is attacking the jet. The co-pilot pipes over the speaker system.

"Full disclosure at this point agent. We have lost a lot of our electronic capabilities. We are still about ten minutes out from Alexandria International Airport."

Turbulence hammers the plane, nearly causing the jet to roll.

". . . Captain is doing everything he can to keep us in the air . . ."

White knuckling the armrests, Abergathy yells, "You can stop now!"

"We've lost communication with the tower, so we will be flying in low and . . ."

"That's enough!" she yells.

". . . blind."

Her cell phone rings and instinctively she looks for it, finding it on the floor under the table next to the bulkhead.

"Now is not a good time," she says.

Inside the pilothouse the captain is struggling with the controls, realizing they might not be able to reach the runway.

"Find me something that still works. We need to get in control of the landing gear. And put that hand piece down, you don't need to scare them anymore than necessary."

A metal piece breaks away from the nose of the jet and bounces off of the windshield completing the spider web of cracks.

"Holy cow!"

Dropping the hand piece, the co-pilot mutters, "Was that ours?"

A door slams open to the cockpit and Abergathy grabs everything she can to maintain balance as she hands the co-pilot her phone.

"It's the AEX control tower. Apparently, we are below radar, and they want to know where we are."

The co-pilot just stares at the phone, confused. The captain yells, "Answer the damn phone!" Turning back to agent, he says, "I don't know how you did it, but go back and buckle yourself in, now!"

Deserted Farm, Dry Creek, LA

July 19, 0651 hours

A morning fog settles across the fields as the large van cuts through on the dirt road towards the farmhouse. Garrett looks out the back window, watching the fog stream around the van. "Can this place get any creepier?"

Turning back to his gravitational suit, he notices the admiral and Stevens looking at each other, trying to hide their grins.

"You two are enjoying yourselves, aren't you?" He turns his attention to his suit. He mumbles, "Damn, it does look like a gorilla outfit."

"What was that, monkey man?" The admiral hears a familiar sound and turns into the cornfields as a murder of crows take to the skies.

Garrett is thrown to the back corner of the van as his head whips to the window, watching the crows take flight. "I really, really dislike those birds. A little warning next time, Admiral."

Out the back window, a series of Army Humvees are thundering down the road with the fog obscuring the view of the van. The admiral turns to watch them fly past.

"Well looks like the secret is out, and we're too late."

Stevens taps away on the iPad.

"I still would like to get a look inside that barn, Admiral. I'm not registering any radial-magnetic waves to the levels of yesterday. Whatever was there is gone and it did not leave with those Humvees."

"This is as safe of a distance as we need anyways." The admiral looks in the back of the van at Garrett. "Let's everyone suit up, and that includes you, monkey man."

"Okay, okay, it does look like a gorilla exoskeleton. And if you're going to give me a call sign, I want to be called . . . Beringei."

Stevens nods. "Very nice. Well played."

The admiral looks back at Garrett. "What the hell is a Beringei?"

Smiling, Garrett opens up his suit and adjusts his body into the form-fitting interior. "The Beringei are the largest gorillas in Africa and are on the verge of extinction. And, since both DC Universe and Marvel are already using Silverback as a character name, I thought of the Beringei." The suit closes up. "We should have call signs to hide our real identity."

Tapping away on his computer tablet, Stevens says, "Harvey, you need to get out of your comic book world and into the real world; although, I do like the idea of having pseudo names. You're a genius, Admiral."

Pinching his nose and shaking his head, he says, "Unbelievable. Let's get suited up. We don't know who or what is still here."

The admiral and Stevens walk around to the back of the van. They open the back door to be greeted by a large metallic gorilla.

Stevens smiles. "Beringei, I presume?"

Moving very cautiously, Garrett's suit is computing the earth's gravitational pull. "I don't know about this. This suit may not be able to adjust to Earth's weak gravitational pull."

"Come on! Get out of the van so we can project up," Stevens urges his friend. Garrett, hunched over, slides and grabs the step on the back of the van with both hands. He swings his body out of the van, and in the process the van is thrust forward, and he ends up landing twenty feet behind the admiral and Stevens.

Stevens puts his hand on top of his headgear. "Whoa, you better get a handle on that before you hurt something."

"This is going to take some getting used to," Garrett says. He raises an arm, and as he turns his hand palm up, a crow lands on it. "Seriously?" Seconds later the bird's head is obliterated by the laser from Stevens's head gear.

"Okay, that was gross and really awesome at the same time," Garrett says.

Stevens smiles. "Saved your life."

"Saved whose life?" Getting out of the van, the admiral is wearing a MIT Bio Suit as well as a backpack with carbon tubes connecting it to mechanical gloves.

"That is cool, no pun intended. That nuclear nitrogen pack is truly extra-terrestrial technology," Garrett says. "Where did you get that? That's it! We can call you Admiral A/C."

Pointing a finger at the mechanical gorilla, the admiral chides, "Do it and we'll see how well that suit works on ice."

Throwing both arms into the air, the momentum actually lifts Garrett in the air for a moment.

"Alight, I surrender. We need to come up with something cooler for you."

"Are you almost ready, Lincoln? I am ready to test this suit out." Garrett smiles and tilts his head towards the van.

Stevens steps out of the van wearing his MIT Bio Suit along with a pair of thin boots and gloves that match his headgear.

Shifting in his gravitational suit, Garrett flexes his arms. "Look at us. We could really scare the neighbors, if this ghost farm actually had some."

The trio make their way towards the farmhouse and the barn. The fog is showing signs of lifting as the sun settles in the sky above. After a few minutes of wading through the cornfield, Stevens taps a computer screen on his forearm.

Reaching out he touches the admiral's shoulder and whispers, "Admiral, my boots are not sensing any vibrations of vehicles or any kind of movement other than our own. The coast is clear."

The admiral looks down at his friend's metallic boots and takes a tired, deep breath. Then he looks back to tell Garrett something, only the corn blocks any signs of the mechanical gorilla suit.

"Harvey—where did you go? Dr. Sensory here says the place is abandoned." Admiral tries to keep his voice down.

The admiral and Stevens look up and see a mechanical gorilla flying over their heads.

They can barely hear obscenities as the suit lands with a large thud.

"That was awesome! Holy shit, that was awesome!" Garrett yells. "Yeah, everyone's gone! You two can come out now!" Garrett continues to yell as he begins to gingerly walk around, trying not to launch himself into the air again.

He gets turned towards the cornfields as the admiral and Dr. Stevens step into the clearing. "I told you I was not sure how this suit would handle," Garrett boasts. "It would appear that this totally-awesome suit cannot dummy down to Earth's weak gravity. In this suit, I have super strength. Like Superman, I can leap over tall buildings. Well, I'm like him before he could fly."

The admiral and Stevens walk towards their friend. When the admiral reaches him, he puts a hand on his shoulder. "Harvey, you are no Superman. Did you see anything while you were leaping over tall buildings?"

"Well, actually, I had my eyes closed." Garrett replies while looking down.

The admiral smiles and walks up the steps to the front door. “Now, let’s find out who this guy is?”

The admiral looks through the blackened window, trying to get a glimpse of the mysterious man inside the farmhouse who had chased them away. With no luck he checks the doorknob finding it locked. Looking at his hand, he stretches it out and balls it to a fist then stretches it out again. Examining the poor condition of the wood the handle, he points one finger into a crack leading behind the lock and another finger pointing into the lock itself. The backpack he is wearing starts to quietly hum as ice-cold jets shoot out of the gloved fingers into and behind the lock.

The sounds of ice crackling and freezing cut into the hum of the backpack. After a few seconds, the admiral lets go of the handle, balls a fist and slams it down on the handle separating it from the door.

Garrett shuffles himself behind the admiral and watches the handle drop to the porch. “That is incredible,” he says.

Without looking back, the admiral pushes the door open. “And I didn’t have to leap over tall buildings.

You should go look for Lincoln and see what he is getting in to. Clearly, you’re unable to come inside without wrecking the place.”

“Admiral! Admiral! You have got to see this!” They turn to see Stevens hollering, waving his arms, and running from the barn.

Garrett let's out a laugh. "And you guys made fun of me and the way my suit looks. He looks like a silver-tipped starfish."

Cracking a smile but still maintaining a serious tone, "What is it, Lincoln? What did you find in the barn?" the admiral asks.

Out of breath, Stevens leans forward pukktting his hands on his knees.

"You're going to have to see to believe this. I can't even put it in words."

The three make their way around to the back entrance to the barn. Meanwhile, Garrett looks down and pauses by the blood-stained ground where the turkey met its demise the day before. Looking around, he realizes that they went to the barn without him. Bending his knees, he jumps in the air towards the back of the barn.

Murmuring to himself, "Keep your eyes open, keep your eyes open." Opening his eyes, he watches the barn underneath him as he descends to the ground. Doing some quick math, he realizes that he did not jump high or far enough. "Shit!" Unable to steer, he smashes through the corner of the roof, then crashes down in a three-point stance.

The admiral whips around as Stevens ducks and covers his head. "What the hell was that?"

"That would be our leaping monkey, Beringei," Stevens says as he looks up at the damaged roof.

"Now what is it we have got to see?" the admiral asks. Surveying the interior of the barn, he makes his way over to a horse stall.

"All I see is an empty, worn-out barn."

Excited, Stevens spreads his arms. "That's just it. The interior has to be empty, because the entire floor is a door! I am detecting radio and electronic waves along the entire center of the floor. Something is underneath."

Observing the vastness of the inside of the barn, the admiral makes his way over to Stevens.

"What the hell would require a door to be that large? And can you find us a way to get it open?"

Stevens starts to scan and map the interior walls of the barn as Garrett shuffles his way next the admiral. "What's our starfish doing?" Garrett whispers.

"It would appear that this entire floor is a door, and he is trying to locate a way to open it."

"Does it open in the middle? I mean that would make sense. Rhetorical question, don't answer that." Garrett shuffles to the center and locates an edge in the floor. Sliding his foot along the center edge until it tees off near the entrance of the barn, mumbling to himself, "Holy shit, this is huge."

"There is nothing up here that controls the doors. I have no clue how it opens," Stevens says as he walks up to the admiral. His attention shifts when he notices Garrett standing and observing the floor. "What's he doing?"

The admiral folds his arms across his chest. "I'm not sure."

Stevens yells out across the barn, “Hey, Beringei, there is no way to open these doors from up here!”

Stevens’s jaw drops as his friend reaches into the floor, grabbing one side of the door. The strain of wood cracking fills the barn as the doors lift open. Watching the floor lift, Stevens murmurs, “Impressive!”

Stevens peeks down into the darkness below the floor being lifted, as the admiral examines the doors. The cracking sounds get louder as they hear their friend straining to lift the door the rest of the way. The door starts to push back down, and Stevens and the Admiral take a step back away from Garrett as he continues to strain to swing the doors open.

“Ahhhhhhh! Come on you son of a bitch! Something’s fighting me!” He readjusts his hands and repositions his feet under what he has lifted to be able put his full strength on pushing the door up.

Stevens stands up and snaps towards the entrance of the barn. The LED’s in his headgear are flashing at an incredible speed.

“Admiral, the magnetic-radial waves are back.” Taking a few steps outside he looks above the barn. “Admiral! You need to see this!”

The admiral steps just outside the barn, leaving Beringei to struggle against the giant door, and looks up above the barn. Just then all pressure pushing back down onto Beringei stops. The strength and momentum of Beringei’s pushing sends him flying through the side of the barn flying over the cornfields and out of sight.

Trying to register what is happening as their friend flies into the distance, the admiral and Stevens continue to watch a large object that is hovering above the barn. The barn roof is now open as the object turns 180 degrees.

The admiral can't fight the feeling that the object is watching them. Tilting his head, he watches the object mimic his subtle movement.

The object appears to be solid metal; however, the hull has a swirl, as if in a liquid state with no discernable windows or lighting.

The object tilts up as the doors in the roof and floor close back up. The object shifts forward a fraction, as it appears to become blurry as if heat waves were growing around it.

Then in the one second, it's there, and then gone, generating a sonic boom as it disappears. The sonic boom throws the admiral and Stevens to the ground, knocking them out cold.

Crossroads Regional Hospital, Alexandria, LA

July 19, 1035 hours

Opening her eyes, the room refocuses. In the corner, Director Harris scrolls through a computer pad. Agent Abergathy looks over at him and then back up at the ceiling.

"Please, tell me that's mine."

Looking up, he stands and walks over to her bedside. "Agent Abergathy, you're awake? I do believe that this does belong to you."

Director Harris lays the pad on her bed next to her. "Your level of intelligence is astounding, and from what I hear from the pilot, you know how to think on your feet. Intelligent and resourceful are both sound traits of a field agent."

Turning her attention to the bed next to her and finding it empty she says, "Sir, what happened to . . ."

The director smiles and puts his hand on her arm to regain her attention.

"Agent Sanchez is fine, with the exception of a broken wrist. He is already on a flight back to Las Vegas. We cannot have anyone with a broken wrist out in the field."

"Sir, I am sure what we are looking for and what caused our crash is one in the same." Abergathy tries to sit up.

Putting a hand on her shoulder, he prevents her from sitting up.

"Relax. Lay back down, at least until you regain all of your bearings. We have been looking for this for a year now. It can wait until you fully recover."

Abergathy pushes his hand away from her shoulder and sits up completely. "Sir, I am fine. If that was it, then it has left. I need to find where it was."

Stepping back, he says, "I had a hunch there was some bulldog in you, another good trait for a field agent, tenacity. And I had my own hunch that you were not going to let this rest. So, I already have flown in your new partner. We can't have agents going into the field alone. Agent Carol, can you come here?"

"Sir, I have a partner."

The director grins. "And he was sent home, because you broke that one."

"Sir, I had no control. You know that was not my fault!"

"I know, I know, calm down. Just giving you a hard time. Besides Agent Carol is an outstanding field agent. And she is from around this part of the woods and would be a Yen to your Yang, or Yang to your Yen."

In the doorway an athletic, attractive woman enters the room. "Director?"

"Agent Roynika Carol, come on in. I would like for you to meet Agent Kristen Abergathy.

"She broke her last partner and is need of a new one." He gets a quick, sharp look from Abergathy. "I believe you two will get along great."

The women each take a moment to look each other over then they both turn to the director, as if they were waiting for him to say something further. Realizing that is his cue, he says, "I will bid you two good luck, and remember, I need regular status updates. Meanwhile I have to fly to Memphis. Broken agents always create a lot of paperwork."

Turning to exit, Director Harris stops at the doorway and turns back, looking at Agent Carol. "Make sure you call your mother."

Expressionless, she nods. "Yes, sir, I will."

A heavy pause fills the room as they watch the director turn and leave. Abergathy looks over her new partner. "Agent Carol . . ."

"Please, if we are going to be partners, call me Nika."

"Nika it is then." Smiling and reaching her arm out to shake hands. "You can call me Kristen."

Carol pauses and looks down at the extended hand. "No offense, it's not exactly a phobia, but I have difficulty shaking someone's hand that I just met."

With a puzzled look, Abergathy drops her hand, taking another quick look over. It dawns on her that her new partner is wearing long sleeves and gloves that almost match her skin tone.

On her left side near her collarbone appears to be skin grafting. Thinking the reason for not offering her hand has something to do with a serious accident and that she will let her know when she is ready, Abergathy smiles and raises her hands. "Fair enough."

Carol takes a quick moment to look at the door. "From what I read on the report, as well as your findings," she raises her hands to show no foul, "the director had me skim the file and since I had no idea what I was looking at. It would appear that I am only here to watch your back."

Throwing her sheet off of her, Abergathy swings her feet off the bed. "I'll tell you what, get me out of here, and I will bring you up to speed."

Carol offers her a mischievous grin. "Are you hungry? There is an excellent Cajun restaurant called Roy's Catfish Hut that's not too far from the epicenter."

Changing into her clothes, Abergathy says, "Excellent. Wait . . . epicenter?"

"Oh yeah, you were taking a power nap. With your findings, Port Arthur's and AEX's mysterious radar contact and your near mid-air collision . . ."

Cutting her new partner off, Abergathy walks past her towards the door while finishing getting dressed. "I'll tell you what, you get me out of here, and we can compare notes."

Carol gives her a quick, firm nod. "Well you know the best way to hide is in plain sight. So, let's see how far we can get by just walking out."

With that they walk out of the room with a purpose and not looking around.

Abergathy tries not to laugh as she notices that the nurses at the counter never took their attention away from flirting with the police officers.

Without a hitch, the two agents make it outside. The humidity is heavy as Abergathy comes to an abrupt stop, as if she ran into a wall. Sweat forms across her brow.

"Ugh, is it always like this?"

Shaking her head and smiling, Carol keeps walking. Raising her keys, she disengages the alarm on a black Ford Focus. The chirp chirp of the alarm catches Agent Abergathy's attention. "A black car in this heat?"

"Heat? You're from Las Vegas. C'mon let's go."

Abergathy sticks out her bottom lip and pretends to stomp her feet. "But it's a dry heat."

The ladies look at each other and then start to laugh. Carol opens the door. "C'mon, let's go. I'm hungry. Oh, by the way, nice bra."

Deserted Farm, Dry Creek, LA

July 19, 1539 hours

The Admiral and Stevens remain out cold, lying on the ground in front of the farmhouse. A murder of crows land next to them and begin to turn their heads as they survey the area. A moan escapes the Admiral, sending them scattering.

The caws from the crows cause Stevens to sit up, frantically waving his arms. He looks over to the Admiral, and seeing him still knocked out, he starts monitoring his vitals. The Admiral's blood pressure and pulse rate are elevated. Noticing the rapid movement of his eyelids, Stevens decides to sit back and let him rest.

"What does an admiral dream about?"

(2014)

Cushing, OK

October 10, 1318 hours

A Navy Seals team is gathered around a table playing dominoes when Admiral Julian Kay walks up. One of the men notices someone walking towards them, and recognizing whom it is, he announces, "Attention on deck!"

The admiral motions for them to take it down a notch. "At ease, gentlemen, relax. Where are we at? Petty Officer . . .?"

The leading petty officer who spotted the admiral remains at attention. "Michaels, sir. We were not aware that you would be here or a part of this mission."

Sticking out his chest, the admiral goads the petty officer, "Are you saying I am too old to have any fun, Petty Officer Michaels?"

The other Seals look at each other, trying not to laugh and waiting for their SO1's answer.

Michaels's shoulders relax. "No, sir, it's just that . . . well . . . you missed the fun. We have already detained the individual and some of his equipment."

Raising an eyebrow, the admiral looks around the surrounding area. "Has anyone interrogated the detainee?"

A sense of renewed nervousness and suspicion takes over the petty officer.

"No, sir, we are tasked to stand guard while a team is down below sanitizing the area."

The admiral walks around the table towards the entrance of the large tent when the SO1 steps to stop him from entering it. "Sir, I cannot let you enter."

The admiral turns with an icy glare. "SO1, you have your assignment and I have mine. It would be smart of you to step back and allow me to do mine. Do I make myself understood?"

"Yes, sir, you are understood."

The admiral turns and walks into the tent, closing it back up behind him.

The petty officer quickly turns to his men. "Something's not right here. We would have been told that Admiral Kay was going to be the interviewer."

Putting his domino hand down, a fellow Seal shakes his head.

"Mik, drop it will you? This is Admiral Julian Kay we are talking here. The man is a legend in our world."

"I damn well know who Admiral Kay is, but something is not right." He pauses to gather his thoughts.

"Stay here, finish your game, and keep an eye on the tent. Make sure that nobody leaves that tent until I get back. Is that clear?"

In unison, the remaining Seals all nod and acknowledge, "Yes, SO1."

Inside the tent, Admiral Kay approaches a young and extremely fit man sitting in a chair with his hands tied behind his back. Taking a moment to assess the man, the admiral stands across from him.

"Dr. Harvey Garrett?"

Garrett twists and turns his upper body, trying to work his restraints. "How do you know my name? Nobody here has even asked me my name." Noticing that the man in front of him is not showing any emotions, he puts his large shoulders back against the chair.

"Oh, I see. This is the end. I've heard the stories, and this is where I, my project, and all my research disappear."

"My name is Admiral Julian Kay. Where did they take your equipment, your suit?"

"What do you mean? Why don't you know? Who are you?"

Patting the air with one of his hands, the admiral quickly steps next to the detainee.

"Keep your voice down, I'm here to help you. They're sanitizing your lab and equipment below us as we speak. After that I am sure they will be in here to talk to you."

Garrett starts to try and break free from the restraints.

"What do you mean sanitizing? You mean turn it off? That lab center is an extreme high-gravitational room. It cannot be just turned off. It has to decompress. Idiots!"

Trying to calm him down, the admiral puts a hand on Garrett's shoulder. "Take a breath Dr. Garrett. Where is your suit?"

"They put it in some large, blue, boxy van. We need to stop them from just shutting down my lab. How do you know about my suit?" asks Garrett while still trying to twist his wrist free.

"Never mind how I know about it. What would happen if the lab is just turned off?"

Garrett stops everything and looks at the admiral, perplexed.

"It would be like punching a hole in an aerosol can, only like a million times worse."

Turning away from Garrett, the admiral gets up to leave.

Garrett squirms feverishly in the chair. "Wait, you can't leave me here."

The admiral ignores the doctor as he reaches the entrance, raises his arm, and points a finger towards the zipper. Crackling sounds of ice fill the tent, and the zipper and the surrounding area begin to ice up. The ice spreads out to cover the entrance.

Garrett sits quietly in disbelief as the admiral turns back towards him. "You are not going to put me on ice? Are you?" he asks.

The admiral, still ignoring him, walks around him and pinches the bindings around the Garrett's wrists. Then with a quick pinch-and-pull motion the restraints break away.

"Now, let's get to the van."

Standing, he rubs his wrists, trying to warm them up. "What about my lab?"

Opening a flap in the back of the tent, the admiral looks down. "It is too late for your lab. We just need to get as much of a distance from here, as fast as possible."

Outside the tent, Petty Officer Michaels is running back to the group yelling, "Get in there and restrain the admiral!"

Behind SO1 is a small group of MAs. The Seal team jumps up and one of them reaches for the zipper to open the door. He snaps his hand back; the temperature of the zipper is at sub-zero and nearly freezes the tips of his fingers.

Another Seal takes out his knife and thrusts it into the flap. The knife hits firm and slides through the Seal's hand cutting his palm open.

Petty Officer Michaels pushes his team aside. "Stand back. What the hell is going on?" Nobody says a word as they stare at the tent entrance in disbelief. Just then everyone hears a vehicle start up. Running around the tent they watch the van that they were supposed to guard speed away.

Before anyone can move to alert someone, a low but intense rumble begins to rock everything. An earthquake begins to rip apart the area, sending everyone and everything to the ground.

Screams of terror can barely be heard over the sub-frequencies of the quake.

Speeding down Highway 18, the admiral and Garrett try to stay on the road as the quake begins to extend, as if trying to prevent their escape. The admiral swerves, struggling to keep the van on the highway and trying to avoid a crack that is curling in front of them. Slamming on the brakes, the van skids and fishtails to a stop. The earthquake settles to a faint rumble.

The admiral remains motionless as he stares at the disaster area, mumbling, "Like punching a hole in an aerosol can."

Garrett, holding his neck, looks back. "I guess they didn't decompress."

Looking down and pinching the bridge of his nose, the admiral shakes his head. "How did you even find a place large enough for your project, as you call it?"

"It was one of the presidential safety bunkers built in the late '70s. These bunkers will always have power supplied to them."

"In the late '70s? And you just happen to stumble across one of these so-called Top-Secret bunkers?"

Garrett raises his hands. "What's the big deal? It wasn't even being used. Hell, I figured they were completely forgotten about."

"Admiral, Admiral!"

A muffled voice from outside the van catches Garrett's attention. Noticing a tall, gangly man with strange-looking metallic headgear and waving his arms that have metallic gloves that are reflecting the sunlight. Garrett nudges the admiral. "Who or what is that?"

Without looking up, the admiral nonchalantly shrugs his shoulders. "Oh, that's Dr. Lincoln Stevens."

Confused, Garrett nudges the admiral again. "Who's Dr. Lincoln Stevens?"

The admiral, turning to give Dr. Garrett his full attention, squints his eyes, unsure if Garrett is trying to be funny. "What do you mean who's Dr. Lincoln Stevens?" Seeing that Garrett has a blank and confused look, he snaps his head to see Stevens yelling and waving his arms outside the front of the van.

"Admiral! Admiral! Can you hear me?"

Dumbfounded, he turns to Garrett to see him wearing the Beringei gravitational suit. Squinting his eyes at him, trying to figure out what is going on, he quickly turns to look back to the front of the van. Stevens is now on the hood, tapping the front windshield.

"Admiral! Admiral!"

2015

Deserted Farm,
Dry Creek, LA

July 19, 1539 hours

Snapping to a sitting position, the admiral holds his head, knocking Stevens back on his butt. The admiral tries to ease his breathing.

"How long was I out?"

Stevens is checking his pulse. "I was monitoring your heart rate and it really peaked up there for a minute. I thought you were going into cardiac arrest. Now I think I am having one."

Still holding his head, trying to clear the cobwebs, the admiral looks over to Stevens, who is still monitoring his pulse rate, and asks, "What time is it?"

"It's almost four in the afternoon. We were out for a few hours. I haven't seen Garrett yet. With that suit he could've ended up in space for all we know."

Standing, Stevens scans the neglected cornfields. "I have to get back so I can analyze the readings on that thing." Stepping back and putting his hands on his hips, he says, "I can't believe we actually saw a . . ."

"Don't say it! You have no idea what we saw," the admiral admonishes. "Think for a minute. Whoever or whatever was flying that thing lives here and stores it beneath the barn."

Turning his head, Stevens opens his mouth as if to say something, then raises a finger and says, "One moment." Turning to face the barn, then looking back at the Admiral, he says,

"That . . . is a very good point."

* * *

Off in a distant niche in the road, obscured by the cornfield, Agent Carol watches the gentlemen through her binoculars.

"Are you sure this is where we need to be?"

Without looking up from her computer pad, Abergathy whispers, "Yes, it is. I can't believe you guys were able to narrow it down to a specific location."

Dropping the binoculars, Carol looks back at her new partner tapping away on her iPad in disbelief. "We don't always trip over ourselves."

"I apologize." Abergathy quickly looks over to Carol. "As soon as I said that, I knew it was worded wrong. What I meant was that I have been working on this algorithm to find this location for months and could only narrow it down to a hundred-mile radius."

The memory of her falling up the stairwell to show the director some information floods her line of thinking. "Wait, what exactly did Director Harris tell you?"

"Oh, relax," Carol says trying to maintain the seriousness of the mission. "We all have our moments of glory."

Looking up from her computer pad, Abergathy steps over to Carol. "Nika, why are we just standing here? Did you really have to slash one of the tires of that van? And who are you watching?"

Carol looks back into the binoculars to study the men regaining their bearings. "Breathe in . . . breathe out. Isn't that what you say? What's with the questions all of a sudden?" She lowers the binoculars and turns her attention from the gentlemen lying next to the barn and sees the genuine curiosity in her partner.

"Since this is your first time in the field. We are here to observe and report, not actually do anything. Second, I popped a tire in order to make sure the owner does not try to leave before the team that is supposed to do something arrives."

Carol takes a moment to look around the field as if she heard something. "Lastly, the reason why we are just standing here is because we have no idea who they are and what they have to do with the magnetic field anomaly you were tracking. I do know that equipment they are wearing is not exactly low-grade equipment."

Carol pauses long enough to study her feet. "Hmmm. What we can do is call the cops on them."

Shocked, Abergathy's jaw drops. "What? Why would we do that?"

Dialing her phone, Carol takes to a knee. "Easy. We may not be in a position to see who they are, but the local LEOs are more than capable to do our work for us."

Giving her new partner an appreciative smile, Abergathy looks over to try and see the two men. “Clever. Remind me to thank Director Harris for partnering me up with you.”

Taking the binoculars from Carol, Abergathy turns her focus to the gentlemen.

* * *

Still craning and massaging his neck, the admiral turns his attention to the barn. “Well, we may not have our superhuman-metal-monkey friend, but we still need to find a way to get under that barn.”

Stevens takes a short step back and looks at the admiral. “What? You’re just writing him off? I was only kidding when I said he could be in space.”

The admiral chuckles. “I know you were. He is a very intelligent man, and as long as we don’t go and leave, he will find his way back here.” Looking at the house, he says, “You know since you could not find a way to get those doors open in the barn, perhaps we can find something out inside the house.”

Stevens looks at the admiral, then back at the house. “That sounds logical.” He reaches up and removes his headgear. When he gets to the steps, he looks back over into the cornfields. “I sure hope Garrett makes it here soon.”

Turning back, he steps into the house behind the admiral, noticing that the door handle is missing. “What happened to the doorknob?”

* * *

Agent Abergathy gasps as she sees the electronic helmet removed. She snaps her head towards her partner, who is busy on the phone with the local law enforcements.

Pulling the phone away for a moment, Carol sees Abergathy's expression. "What is it? What did you see?"

"Ummm, not sure. They went inside the house."

Carol squints at her and waits for a moment. Giving a quick nod, "Good, that will make it easier for the police to detain them." Still eyeing her partner as she watches her look back into the binoculars, she then starts back in on her phone call with the police.

Watching the front door through the binoculars, Abergathy becomes lost in thought, her mind spinning with questions. Dr. Lincoln Stevens what are you doing here? How are you involved with this anomaly? Who is that with you? How can I meet you before the police arrest you?

Just then a phone goes flying over her head towards the house, landing and sliding under the front porch. Dropping the binoculars and looking behind her Abergathy asks, "Why did you do that? How did you do that? That's over a hundred yards away."

"The conversation with the LEOs is over, and I know they are tracking the phone, so I put it where we need them to find it." Carol grins nonchalantly as she walks up next to her partner. "Kristen, just tell me they didn't see that."

"No, Nika, they're still inside. But how could you throw that that far?"

Carol smiles making a throwing motion. "Easy, I didn't pay for it."

Abergathy looks at her with an astounded expression at the Captain-Obvious response. "You know what I meant. That was over seventy-five yards."

Stepping in front of her partner, Carol looks out at the house and takes a crouching position. "Let's just say we all bring something different to the table. Now, let's stay low and out of sight. We can wait for the police to show up. I really hate dealing with LEOs."

Sandlot,
West Dry Creek, LA

July 19, 1456 hours

Out in a distant field, slowly moving out of a small crater, Garrett tries to make his way to firmer ground. His suit is not cooperating in the soft sand. "Well this really sucks," he says as he looks around, realizing that he is standing in a sandlot that looks more like a dried mudslide. "Where in the hell am I?"

Slowly trying to maneuver and walk around, his weight causes him to slip and slide down the hill. He stops when he hears the faint sounds of small engines revving. He scrambles up the hill toward nearby trees.

"Whatever it was, it landed up on the landing!" one of the voices yells out.

The voices and the sound of ATV's are getting closer as he looks around for a place to hide. "Damn, if this ain't a pickle." With a push, Garrett clears the sand slope, crashing through the neighboring tree line.

"Over there!" one of the men shouts.

"What the hell was that?" yells the other.

"Shit! Can this day get any worse?" Garrett mumbles to himself after hearing their voices. With that, he jumps up a little stronger, clearing the sandpit and trees.

Shots fire in his direction, and the bullets careen off of his suit. When he lands again he crashes through the tree line on the opposite side. He can hear the roaring of engines as the men charge towards him.

"D'jou see that?" one of the men hollers out.

"I done believe it," says the other, spinning his ATV to a stop. "My grandma always said the Rougarou exists. I ain't never believed her."

"I know, man, never thought I could actually take one down." Paul looks up the hill towards where Beringei landed. "Now man up, and let's get dis thing."

Revving his engine, one of the men spins his ATV back around. "Aww man, we are so gonna die." Wheels spinning, the ATV's try to gain traction in the fresh crater.

"Look at the sizes of dis impact. This Rougarou is a big one."

Shutting off the ATV, he says, "Damn, we're not going to get traction here. 'Sides we need to 'proach with some stealth." Getting off the ATV, he grabs his gun, checking the ammo.

The other man nods and shut his ATV down and then makes his way over to his friend. Holding his rifle, he tries to see into the tree line. "Alright, let's go."

Doing his best to crouch in the shadows, Garrett watches the local men devise some sort of plan. Taking a deep breath and mumbling to himself, "Well, I can't stay here long. At least they will have a story to tell their grandkids."

He shifts his position, and with a stronger jump, he launches into the air and into the distance. While in the air and looking for telltale markers to where he was at, he mumbles again, "Now if I just knew where I was going, that would be awesome."

"Shoot it! There it is!"

Both of the local men fire off shots as they watch it fly over their heads and towards the lake. As the thing leaves their line of sight, they stand wide-eyed, looking at each other.

"I don't know about you, but I didn't see a thing here today."

"Yup, nothing."

Deserted Farmhouse, Dry Creek, LA

July 19, 1609 hours

In the house, Admiral Kay is rummaging through some disregarded mail as Stevens studies the photos on the wall. He stops and looks over at the admiral.

"I'm not sure what we're going to find in here."

Putting the mail down, the admiral scans the room. "This does seem mute, but at least we are staying out of sight until Harvey finds his way back here."

Looking up he notices Stevens has stopped and is staring at his feet. "What is it, Lincoln?"

Stevens puts back on his headgear. "We have company, two vehicles, driving fast in our direction."

"Those boots told you that?" the admiral questions, amazed at the silver footwear on Stevens's feet.

"These boots, as you call them, are registering the vibrations from the cars on the dirt road." Stevens turns and picks up his tablet.

"Well stay inside and I'll go and see who it is," the admiral orders. "We don't want to freak them out with your silver-tipped starfish getup."

Walking to the door, the admiral steps out to see two police cars pull up.

Two officers quickly get out of the first car.

The officer on the passenger side extends his arm with a wave.

"Sir, we got a call that two men were creating a disturbance."

Making his way down from the porch, the admiral walks out to meet him. "I assure you, officers, there's nothing going on here."

Experience tingles on the back of the lead officer's neck as he steps away from the patrol car and places his hand on the stock of his gun.

"Sir, I am going to need for you to stop right there."

The admiral stops and looks innocently at the officer as the other two officers from the second car approach.

"Whoa, take it easy. I told you there is nothing going on here. Let's not get overzealous."

"Where is your partner?" the lead officer asks, handgun drawn.

The two officers from the other vehicle begin to move and make their way around the admiral to the house.

Before they get to the porch, Stevens steps out of the house with his hands up, forgetting that he is still wearing his headgear.

The two officers nearly trip over themselves drawing their weapons.

The admiral closes his eyes and runs one of his hands through his hair.

"Whoa! Whoa," the Admiral calls out to his friend. "Starfish . . . never mind. Come on down, and join the party." Looking at the lead officer, he says, "We are only here to investigate the weather anomaly from last night. That is what the equipment he is wearing is used for."

Stevens makes his way, still keeping his arms up, next to the admiral.

"That is correct," he lets the officers know. "We got here and nobody was home."

"Check inside, and make sure it's clear," the lead officer orders. The pair quickly moves up the porch and enter the house.

Stevens leans in, whispering to the admiral, "Starfish? Do I really look that much like a starfish?"

"We cannot give them our names," Admiral explains.

Trying to maintain his whispering, "No, no, no. I get that, completely, but what do I get to call you if it comes to it."

The admiral affords him a smile. "Let's hope it doesn't come to it."

Dr. Stevens's boots register a faint impact vibration. Realizing what it could be, he looks out over into the cornfields. "Oh no!"

The admiral's smile quickly fades as he turns to his friend. "What do you mean, 'oh no?'"

Not trying to ignore him, Stevens focuses on the readings from his equipment as another, more solid and with closer impact, vibration registers.

"So not a good time."

Dropping his hands, the admiral turns towards his friend. "Tell me what the hell you are registering?"

The lead officer steps towards the gentlemen and says, "What are you two talking about? Move away from each other!" just as the other two officers that were inside come out to the porch, weapons pointed at the ground.

"All clear?" the lead officer asks.

Before they could respond, everyone looks up as they all hear something up in the sky. Everyone squints to see the sun gleaming off of a large, metallic ball plummeting towards them.

The admiral drops his head and pinches the bridge of his nose. "Tell me that's not . . . Garrett . . . Oh shit!"

The metal ball crashes on top of the front police car, nearly folding it in half, sending glass and dust in all directions. The officers near the car, as well as the admiral and Stevens, are thrown to the ground, twisting and shielding their faces.

As the dust begins to settle, the admiral gets to a knee as the police began to fire at Garrett. Their bullets ricochet off of his suit, sending them in every direction.

Stevens stands, looking directly at the lead officer's gun, and in a split second a red laser shoots out of the visor and tears into the gun, cutting it in half. Stevens turns towards the other officer and cuts the barrel of his gun, causing him to release the gun and fall.

One of the officers on the porch fires off a shot at Stevens, the bullet careening off of his headgear. The admiral snaps around and extends his arm out as a high-pressure stream blasts out of the glove extensions from the backpack towards the officer.

The officer falls back into the wall of the house, screaming in pain. His hands are iced up and turning blue. With no feelings in his hands he can't let go of the gun.

His partner, watching him struggle, raises his gun toward the admiral when Garrett launches himself towards him. The police car goes flying backwards as Garrett crashes through the porch railing and pins the officer against the wall.

Garret looks down at the officer he has pinned. "This is where you drop your weapon and leave."

The officer, scared, nods his head and grabs his partner. They both scramble to their car. The other two officers were already at theirs. The four officers jump into the undamaged patrol car and speed off, kicking up a large dust cloud as their tires spin.

The vehicle screams past the two agents as they duck into the cornfield, covering their faces from the dust cloud.

* * *

Just as the local police leave, the two agents, Abergathy and Carol, are hit by the wave of dust left in the wake of the fleeing police cars. Agent Carol reaches for her phone, and then snaps towards the house, realizing that her phone is under the front porch.

"Kristen, do you have your phone?"

Coughing, Abergathy starts waving her arm, trying to disperse the dust cloud. "My phone went down with the plane, remember?"

Grabbing her arm, Carol pulls her to her feet. "C'mon, we need to gct out of here. This place is going to become a circus soon."

The grip on Abergathy's arm was a little firmer than expected and she winces in pain. "Ahhh. That hurts." She drops back down to a knee.

Carol releases her grip. "I'm sorry. Now you know why I don't like shaking hands. Let's go. We need to leave."

Getting to her feet and holding her arm, they head towards the car. The two agents come to a stop as they nearly run into a man who is standing, motionless, in the way of their escape. The man is wearing mismatched clothing that completely covers his skin. Drawing her weapon, Carol calls out to the man.

"Shit, where'd you come from?"

They see the man stretching his hand out as Carol begins to look strained and confused. The man's voice seems to come from nowhere and everywhere.

"So, you are the ones that I was warned about. Clarisse picked up your transmissions earlier."

Carol begins to struggle against an unseen force pushing her back. Struggling to remain standing, the skin on her arms begins to peel away, revealing mechanical extremities.

Abergathy glances between the clothed man and her partner. She gasps as she sees the biomechanical arms on Agent Carol and the prosthetic skin on the ground. “Nika? What’s going on?”

Looking intently at the clothed man, Carol ignores her partner, and with all her willpower, she launches through the intense, unseen force being put on her.

The man, being momentarily distracted at the reaction of the younger agent, quickly turns and emits a high-pressure wave that hits Agent Carol’s mid-torso, separating her from her prosthetics. Her body is sent flying through the cornfield as her limbs drop to the ground.

Blood coats the ground and the tops of the degraded corn, leaving a gruesome trail to where her body ultimately lands with a quiet thud.

Without saying anything, the man begins to levitate above the corn and towards the house, completely disregarding Agent Abergathy.

Abergathy stands motionless, her jaw open in disbelief, unable to move. She watches the clothed man slowly move until he is out of sight. Snapping out of the trance, she takes off running towards their car. Stumbling out of the cornfield and falling to her knees, she looks up and notices the car has been evenly flattened from bumper to bumper. Flashes of Agent Carol getting torn apart and thrown into the cornfield invade her thoughts.

Trying to control her breathing, she cannot escape the images of blood spraying in all directions as those mechanical arms and legs fall to the ground.

Abergathy's stomach catches and she vomits. She slowly recovers her composure and stands back up. Stepping away from her lunch, she walks around what is left of their car.

A couple of crows caw and land near the vomit, startling her and sending her falling backwards. Lying on her back, she stares into the cloudless sky. Clearing her mind, she watches the crows fly around in a circle. When a realization hits her she quickly sits back up and turns her attention in the direction of the farmhouse. Dr. Stevens would be able to tell me what the hell is going on.

More crows land and gather on the car as they start to fight over the leftovers from the Catfish Hut. Scooting away from the macabre scene she gets back to her feet, brushing the dirt off, and she takes a collected breath. "This is so unreal. It's like Stephen King meets Marvel Universe." She heads back towards the house and breaks into a wide grin as an idea comes out of the blue. I wonder if I can be a superhero? That would be kind of cool.

* * *

Outside the farmhouse, the admiral and Stevens face Garrett, who is still lodged in the wall.

"Don't tell me you're stuck," the admiral scoffs at Garrett.

"I'm just waiting for my adrenaline to calm down. That was awesome! We're like real life superheroes!"

Walking up to the edge of the porch, Stevens is shaking his head and waving an arm in the air.

"Yeah, but superheroes don't attack the police. We were . . . like super villains."

The admiral stretches his arms out towards Stevens and Garrett. "How about none of the above. All I know is that we need to get the hell out of here. They will be back." Admiral Kay hops off the porch. Looking at the crushed police car he runs his hand through his hair. Behind him he hears Garrett pull himself out of the wall. The building starts to make sounds as if the side of the wall is going to rip away.

Garrett is able to turn around slowly, keeping the house intact. He sees the demolished police car off in the distance. "Holy cow, I know I landed hard . . ." Dropping off the porch he walks up next to the admiral, who has stopped and is staring at what is left of the car. "Damn, we're in big trouble, aren't we?"

From back near the house, Stevens calls out, "Guys, if we need a place to lay low, I know a place that even the Army couldn't find." Garrett and admiral turn to look at their friend, and then all three turn and look at the barn.

"Harvey, come with me to get the van. I'm sure your suit needs to recharge. Lincoln, find us a way inside there. We'll be back shortly." With that, the two take off into the cornfields towards the van.

* * *

Back at the niche in the road and the cornfields, Abergathy watches the two men head into the cornfields, towards where the van is.

Then she notices Dr. Stevens take a couple steps towards the barn when he stops and slowly turns completely around as if he is looking for something.

Instinctively she steps back into the cornfield and trips over one of the mechanical limbs of Agent Carol.

A flash memory of watching her partner being instantly tore apart floods her thoughts, causing her to scramble out onto the road. Watching the ground, she collects herself. Breathe in . . . breathe out. C'mon girl, get a hold of yourself. After a moment she looks up to see Stevens walk into the house.

Making her way around the front, she finds the camera that was mounted on the dashboard of the smashed police car. She climbs on the hood and reaches in to remove the camera from its mount. Sitting down on the crumpled hood, she looks back in the vicinity of where the van was, and then back at the house. Unsure of what to do, she takes in a deep breath and closes her eyes.

* * *

The admiral and Garrett make their way to the van, and the admiral notices the slashed tire. He snaps around to try to look into the cornfield as Garrett shuffles his way next to him.

"What's wrong?"

The admiral raises his hand, motioning him to stop. After a moment of nobody moving, he steps back and examines the tire.

Not able to see the tire, Garrett asks, "What was that all about?"

The admiral points his hand towards the tire. "We're not alone."

Garrett raises his arm and lifts a small panel on his forearm. Inside it he reads a power meter. "It looks like I still have a quarter juice left. I believe I will hold out from taking it off just yet."

The admiral walks around to the back of the van, "Well, use your monkey strength and help me change this tire."

Just then Garrett's stomach lets out a loud growl as the admiral is pulling out a tire from the back. Admiral stops, dropping the tire. Garrett looks at him.

"What? I'm hungry. This is supposed to be a farm. I wonder if he has any food in the house."

"Let's get this done so we can move the van, and then we can find some food."

* * *

Inside the house Stevens is examining the walls. Walking into the kitchen, his stomach takes a turn.

"I'm hungry." Opening the refrigerator, he is greeted with empty shelves. The freezer has the same results. "Well, this sucks." Looking around the room, something strikes him as off. Raising his hands out, he looks around as if to get his bearings in the room. "Something's not very Feng Shui."

Walking over the narrow floor to a ceiling cupboard, he opens it and is greeted with stocked shelves of canned food, from fruits to Chef Boy R Dee. "Very nice."

On the floor of the cupboard are bags of flour and sugar, sitting on a small roll away cart. "Now why would he have the bags on a roll away? I can see keeping them off the floor. But why am I talking to myself?" Shaking his head, he leans over to pull on the cart. As he does his head hits one of the top shelves, tipping the shelf and sending the cans tumbling on him and the floor.

Cautiously opening the front door, Abergathy hears the cans fall. Making her way to the kitchen, she watches Stevens scrambles to fix the shelf and put the cans back. Before she can say something, Stevens notices something on the floor. He stops collecting the cans and reaches in and pulls out the roll away. A hatch is revealed in the floor, and he reaches in and opens what looks like a thick, metallic door.

Stevens turns and steps down the ladder and starts to scan the walls.

Mumbling to himself, "Lead and concrete bunker. . . I think this is an old fallout shelter from the 1950s or '60s. This farm is full of amazement."

Just then he hears someone else step off the ladder. Turning around he is greeted by the young agent and takes an offensive stance.

Abergathy throws her hands out. "Whoa, relax. Let's not do anything crazy here." They both cautiously relax their posture, and she slowing lowers her hands.

"It's okay. It's been a long day, and there's something insane going on here. Now I'm looking for answers so I don't go completely insane. And I believe you can help me out with that."

Stevens crosses his arms and leans against the wall, nonchalantly watching the young woman. "And what makes you think that there is something going on here?"

Facial expression and posture drop as Abergathy can't believe him. "Really? You are going to stand there, in a bunker of a rundown farmhouse, wearing some high-tech equipment, and you are going to tell me that there is nothing going on?"

Raising his hands to his headgear, forgetting that he was wearing it, Stevens slumps his shoulders. "I do not know who you are, but I can't help you." He turns to head further into the bunker.

"Dr. Lincoln Stevens!" Abergathy calls out as the doctor freezes and turns back around. "Yes, I know who you are. My thesis is on your work for energy waves and atomic structure. And I saw you remove your helmet earlier."

Reaching up and removing the headgear, Stevens tries to collects his focus. "How do you know who I am? And who are you?"

"Breathe in . . . breathe out, Doctor, I'm only looking for answers, and I am hoping you can help me out."

James Monroe Building, Richmond, VA

July 19, 1307 hours

Inside a large, simply decorated office is an oversized oak desk. Behind it, hanging on the wall, is a shadow box from Afghanistan with a Purple Heart medal. On the front wall is a large television monitor where the national news is covering the reopening of an international bank in East Texas. The reporter is going into detail about the police shoot out that claimed three lives.

Standing with her arms folded and holding a remote is a well-dressed woman carrying an air of authority. Watching the newscast with almost invested curiosity, she tries to ignore her laptop as it alerts her to an incoming email.

After a few more minutes of coverage on the news, she walks around her desk. Scrolling her mail, she clicks on the inbox tab. The e-mail that triggered the alert belongs to the director of the Austin branch of their organization. She opens it and sees that it is a transcript from an interview with the surviving police officer involved in the bank shoot out she was just watching. Giving the reporter another glance, she looks back down to read the e-mail.

Director Carol, I believe that this is something you would find interesting and that this situation warrants further investigation.

Clicking on the attachment, a transcript opens up.

DETECTIVE: "OFFICER GREEN, CAN YOU TELL US WHAT HAPPENED OUTSIDE OF THE BANK ON THE 17TH?"

OFFICER GREEN: "I CAN'T EXPLAIN. FROM OUT OF NOWHERE, EVERYONE WAS JUST YELLING AT EACH OTHER. ANGER AND FRUSTRATION WAS EVERYWHERE. AND ALL HE DID WAS JUST STAND THERE."

DETECTIVE: "HE . . . YOU MEAN OFFICER CHAVEZ WAS . . .?"

OFFICER GREEN: "NO, SOME STRANGE GUY JUST WALKED OUT OF THE BANK. THEN LIKE ALL THE FRUSTRATION AND ANGER I HAVE EVER FELT JUST FILLED ME, AND ALL OF US. THE NEXT THING I REMEMBER IS MY PARTNER BLEEDING OUT, AND I JUST KNOW I WAS THE ONE WHO SHOT HIM."

DETECTIVE: "SO, YOU DO NOT REMEMBER SHOOTING HIM."

OFFICER GREEN: "NO, I WOULD NEVER SHOOT HIM!"

DETECTIVE: "BUT YOU DID."

OFFICER GREEN: "ONE MINUTE EVERYONE IS LAUGHING ABOUT WHAT WAS HAPPENING IN THE BANK. THE NEXT MOMENT EVERYONE IS YELLING AT EACH OTHER. THEN I AM SITTING OVER MY FRIEND TRYING TO STOP THE BLEEDING."

THE INTERVIEW GOES ON, BUT ONE PART OF THE INTERVIEW WAS CIRCLED.

OFFICER GREEN: "THE UNKNOWN SUBJECT MESSED WITH A BRIEFCASE SHORTLY BEFORE ANGER AND FRUSTRATION OVERWHELMED US."

Director Carol reaches over and dials the Austin division. After a few rings, she can immediately tell she is on speakerphone.

"Good afternoon, Director Rodgers."

A thick Texas drawl from Director Charlie Rodgers booms through the receiver. "Vicki! I presume ya're calling because ya viewed the e-mail."

"And you would be correct. My question is..." Director Carol taps the up and down arrows on the keyboard, scrolling the transcripts. "Why do you think this warrants our involvement?"

"Let's just call it a hunch. I'm going to assign this to Agent Yukiko Nomi. I believe she is ready for the field."

Director Carol quickly sits upright. "Are you sure? No signs of rejections? She and my daughter were very close once. I think we should observe her longer before she goes in the field."

"Easy there, Vicki. That is why I am giving you the courtesy heads up. I am going to pair her up with Little John. He'll look after her. She's been doing, and will do, just fine in the field. Trust me, this is what I do."

Director Carol tightens the grip on her phone at the thought of being talked down to. "Well, we just happen to have Sydney in the area. I will give him the heads up."

"Sounds like fortuitous timing. I'll send 'em on their way. In the meantime, tell your daughter I said hi and to call me. I would really appreciate an update on her biomechanics."

"Of course, Charlie, I will let her know as soon as I hear from her. Talk to you soon."

Pausing to relax her grip she hangs up the phone and walks over to her window, overlooking I-95.

After a few moments of watching the traffic, she purses her lips and flexes her hands, trying to ease her annoyance. “Give me the courtesy he says, hillbilly asshole.” That makes her smile for a second before she straightens her shoulders and makes her way back to her desk and picks up the phone.

Logan Farm Hams, Alexandria, LA

July 19, 1423 hours

Sitting in a small booth, Director Harris eyes his brisket poor boy sitting in front of him when his phone rings. Looking at the number calling, he shakes his head and looks back at his sandwich again. Thumbing his phone, he quickly brings it to his ear.

"Victoria! How's life in Virginia treating you? Did Roynika call you?"

"Sidney, how've you been? Keeping your blood sugar up, I hope. And no, I have not heard from her lately."

Shifting his sandwich around, he takes a deep breath. "So, what brings this honor?"

"There's a situation that needs looking in to in Katy, Texas. I figured since you're already in the area that you could oversee the operatives that Charlie is sending down."

"Five O'clock Charlie? This must be serious for you to bring the Austin division in on this."

"He's the one who brought this to my attention, and you know he hates it when you call him that."

Director Harris pinches a piece of his sandwich as he tries not to laugh. "It's all in good fun, he knows it."

"With that aid, have you been watching the news and know what happened with the shooting and bank robbery that happened earlier this week in Katy, Texas?"

"I am going to say no on that one. I have been a busy."

"Well, get your nose out of those technical toys of yours and read a paper once and in a while, and then you will know what's happening here on Earth.

There was a bank robbery, and when he went to leave, he somehow managed to get the police to kill each other. We need to find out what kind of technology he or they were using."

"Well this is interesting. I get to play field agent. I am excited about this." He takes a sip of his drink.

"Speaking of field agents, who's the agent you paired my daughter up with? You know how I don't think that agents should be paired up with operatives. It's unsafe, uncontrolled, and unsecured. The only reason I agreed to let you team her up is because she was already in the area visiting her grandmother."

Leaning back in his chair, he can't seem to take his eyes off of the sandwich in front of him. "I know, Victoria, you don't need to worry. Agent Abergathy is one of the brightest, sharpest minds I have ever seen." Running his free hand through his hair, he says, "Roynika's looking good. She seemed to have gained an acceptance for her prosthetics. I am supposed to hear back from them here shortly. She was supposed to call you?"

Director Harris detects a change in Victoria as

her voice gets softer.

"No, I have not heard from her yet today. It has been a long road and tensions a little . . . anyways; she has realized the advantages she now has. She only wishes now that the medical center can make improvements on skin."

"Well you can relax. What time am I to meet these two that Five O'clock is sending me?" Before Director Harris can say anything else his phone chimes. Taking the phone away he looks at it as the icon showing he has a received a message pops up, you are good.

"Read the files, and they will meet you outside the bank at 0900. Oh, and Sydney, if you are still in Alexandria, you should try the ham sandwiches at Logan Farm Hams. You won't be disappointed."

A huge smile forms on his face. "That sounds like a wonderful idea. I will have to do that. Talk to you soon, and I will update you as soon as I have one.

Concrete Bunker, Dry Creek, LA

July 19, 1948 hours

Walking down the concrete tunnel, Garrett is devouring cans of Chef Boy-R-Dee while Admiral Kay is walking ahead. They come across a door that looks more like a hatch to a ship than a door.

Garrett looks around to find a place to put some of the empty cans. He goes to set the empty cans along the edge of the hallway when the admiral looks back.

"Really, you are just going to set them there."

"What? You were the one who didn't want to just sit and eat for a minute. No, we just had to immediately drop down the scary tunnel. Like this afternoon was not exciting enough for you. What's with you Spec Ops people anyways? And I need the protein."

Just then the door opens up. Stevens, smiling, says, "Will you two keep it down? Some of us are trying to rest." He pushes the door open, and he notices the cans that Garrett had set down. "Really, you are just going to set them there."

"That is what he said." Garrett gestures to the Admiral. "I had no place to put them." Lifting his chin and sticking out his large chest and with a British accent, he says, "Now, will you invite us in, and perhaps I can find a proper place to dispose of them. Or are you going to have us answer questions of three?"

Trying not to laugh, Stevens steps aside and gestures with both arms.

"By all means, gentlemen, please come in. Welcome to the laboratory. So, where have you guys been? And, Harvey, you are going to go insane when you see what all is in here."

Just as the admiral steps across the knee knocker into the room, he says, "We were not the only ones here today. We had to move the van. We located a huge and very well-hidden power station installation. Of course, that was . . ."

Stevens goes to raise a finger as if to say something, but before he can, Garrett sees all the equipment.

"You have got to be kidding me! A real-life Bat Cave!"

Making his way to a series of video monitors, one of them showing the hallway they just entered, he says, "This is how you knew exactly what the admiral said." On the other screens are all viewpoints of the farm. "This rundown farm is wired for sound!"

Stevens, trying to contain his own excitement, pulls his friend's attention away from the monitors. "You have got to see what is over here."

Rubbing his temples, the admiral lifts his voice and says, "Gentlemen! We need to focus here. The police were not the only ones here with us this afternoon. One of the van tires was slashed."

Stevens stiffens. "I . . . umm . . . may have some insight on that."

Garrett steps back, opening another can of

ravioli, and watches his friend squirm. "Oh, this is going to be good."

Agent Abergathy steps out from behind a switchboard. "Perhaps I should be the one to cover this part." All attention turns to her as she feels the weight of their stares. She raises her hands defensively. "Too soon?"

Stevens motions her to stand next to him. "Everyone, this is Kristen Abergathy, or as some would call her, Agent Kristen Abergathy."

After a moment for everything to register, Garrett speaks first. "I can't believe you have brought in the people we have been running from. And now they know who we are."

"She recognized me earlier when I took my headgear off outside, and they're not looking for us." Stevens shrugs innocently.

The admiral steps up raising a hand. "Wait, she recognized you?"

"Yeah, of course it had nothing to do with her agency. She was, or is, working on her master's degree, and I was, or rather I am, the subject of her thesis." Folding his arms across his chest, he rocks back on his heels.

Disregarding Stevens, the admiral keeps his attention on the young woman. "Clearly, you're not hurt, whose blood is that on your shirt?"

Both of the doctors do a double take looking at her shirt, and their expressions take on a deep concern.

Abergathy looks up at the admiral as her throat gets caught.

"Shortly after your Marvelesque run-in with the police, my partner and I ran into someone—or something—in the cornfields. There was a man, I think, he waved his hand and something ripped her apart. I mean one minute she is trying to grab him and the next thing I saw were these mechanical arms and legs laying on the field, blood flying everywhere, and her body hurling into the cornfield."

Stevens and Garrett look at each other, and Admiral Kay pinches the bridge of his nose while looking at the floor. "You gentlemen are not even the least surprised or even taken back by this?" Abergathy says incredulous. "This thing just waved and something ripped her apart!"

Stevens softly notes, "It was a gravitational wave."

"You should see what he can do to a turkey." Garrett adds.

The admiral runs his hands through his hair. "Can you describe him?"

Taking a moment Abergathy looks at each of them with growing curiosity. "No, it was like had had his entire body . . ." Looking over the admiral's shoulder, her eyes open wide with fear as her jaw drops.

The admiral notices this and quickly turns around as he is greeted with a gravitational wall that is slowly pushing him backwards.

The man walks slowly towards everyone, and in a low voice that seems to be coming from everywhere he says, “What are you doing here?”

Nobody moves to say anything as the admiral notices a break in the clothing. The man’s skin is eerily similar to the ship they encountered earlier.

The clothed man warns them again. “I told you yesterday to leave.”

“Sir—” Abergathy instinctively reaches out only for her hand to hit something unseen. “Sir, whatever you are doing here is affecting the earth’s magnetic field . . . That’s what brought my team here.”

“The field is fully functional and intact. You and your team can leave now!” The man turns away from the four as the gravity wall lifts.

Garrett steps up waving a hand. “Wait a minute! We are not part of her team!”

The man whips around, and as he extends his arm in their direction, the admiral extends his. Both arms appear to be reaching for each other, and as a gravitational pulse is thrown towards the four, a stream of compressed nitrogen shoots out of the mechanical gloves on the admiral’s hand. The compressed gas connects with the man’s hand causing him to instantly go motionless as the gravitational pulse sends everyone flying backwards, and then it dissipates.

Shaking off the pulse, they sit holding their heads and staring at the man that now looks like a poorly dressed mannequin.

Garrett walks around him getting a better look. "Did you kill him?"

"No, I don't believe I did. I noticed his skin was similar to the liquid metal on the ship from earlier. It must have instantly solidified under the nitrogen, but just in case—and I cannot believe I am saying this—Lincoln, can you please put your equipment on. This way you can monitor his vitals."

Stevens raises a pointed finger and says, "Ingenious," and then heads over to where he left his equipment and hurries to put it on.

The admiral watches him run off. "Lincoln, I am not sure how long he will be motionless, but we need to convince him that we are not a threat, to him or his work."

Turning to Garrett and Abergathy, he points around the room. "You two, see if you can make heads or tails with all this equipment while Lincoln and I talk to our new friend here."

Garrett and Abergathy turn and head towards some of the equipment. She leans in grabbing his arm. "What is this ship from earlier?"

"Did you really think we look, how'd you put it, Marvelesque? You do know the DC Universe is way more realistic."

Stopping to stare at the muscular doctor, Abergathy's eyes are wide with disbelief. "You guys are tripping me out. I tell you that my partner was ripped apart and that she had mechanical arms and legs. I ask you about a ship with liquid metal and all you want to know is, if you guys looked

Marvelesque. What's with you guys?"

Garrett stops and his face takes on a solemn expression. "My condolences about your friend. I can't imagine seeing that, although, we did see him squish a turkey." He rubs his chin and collect his thoughts. "You said she tried to grab him? So, it was defensive gone bad. Either way, this is someone we want as an ally. As far as the bionics, Johns Hopkins has been working on bio prosthetics for years. And as for the ship, I didn't get a good look at it. I sort of flew past it."

Garrett motions at Stevens. "If you were studying Dr. Starfish's work, then some of this equipment in the Bat Cave here should be right up your alley and keeping your mind busy will take it off what happened earlier."

Closing her eyes, she thinks, breathe in... breathe out. She looks back at Stevens and lets out a subtle laugh. "You guys are freaking off the wall." She begins to look at the equipment then back at Garrett. "Let's start at the beginning. What is your name?"

Her attention suddenly shifts to the video monitors. She can see that several police cars have pulled up to the farmhouse with lights flashing.

"Hey, guys. Looks like the cops are back. Take a look at what's on TV."

The admiral and Garrett make their way over as the police are appearing in most of the monitors.

"Aren't you guys worried that you will get caught?" Abergathy asks.

"Agent Abergathy, earlier this morning the army was all over this place and could not find this bunker," the admiral says. "And if it weren't for Lincoln and his sensory starfish equipment, we would not be standing here now. So, no, we are not concerned with getting found."

Reaching down to the controls, he adjusts one of the cameras to get a better view of the front door to the farmhouse. Nudging Garrett he tells him, "Keep an eye on this." Then he turns back to Abergathy. "We need to talk."

Taken aback she watches the admiral walk away from her. She reaches in her pocket and looks at the camera. "Yes, we should."

Banque Societe Generale de International, Katy, TX

July 20, 0951 hours

Standing next to his silver Ford Taurus, Director Harris looks around the front of the bank, watching customers walk in and out as if nothing happened here. He looks down at his watch as a dark-blue Ford F250 pulls up and parks next to him. Shaking his head, he watches the two unlikely pair get out of the truck. Driving the truck is a large man of Jamaican descent, and the passenger, who had to practically had to jump from the truck, is a petite Japanese-American woman.

He stretches his arms out and then rests his hands-on top of his head as the two approach him. "Agents Nomi and St. Clair, you're late, not a good trait for field agents."

Trying to maintain her giddiness Agent Nomi chimes in. "Sir, we would have been on time, but the Neanderthal took forever picking out a rental car."

A deep, booming voice retaliates, "Listen here, Flea. It's not my fault we had to wait for them to get a vehicle large enough for a real man."

Raising his eyebrows, the director gives the large agent a surprised look. "Little John, is that what they call you? After all these years, awareness of your surroundings is a trait you still have not learned."

Realizing that he had just insulted his supervisor he stammers, "No mon, I mean, yes, sir."

"Relax, big guy, I can give people a hard time too."

"Yes, sir."

Agent Nomi goes to give him a friendly punch except her hand passes through him, denting the truck. "I hate it when you do that."

Chuckling and turning to look at the small dent, feeling proud of himself, he whispers to her, "I knew you were going to try and hit me. Except, please try to remember this truck is a rental."

"Agent St. Clair, I see you are getting more in control of the coils. That is outstanding. Are you still getting the headaches and muscle pains?"

"Yes, sir, I mean as far as the headaches and muscle pains, only rarely. But after thirty years I would hope I am getting used to them. Not the pains but the coils. After all they allow me to be."

A voice inside of Agent Nomi speaks up and only she can hear it, "Bumbling idiot."

Grinning, she crosses her arms, steps back, and keeps her voice down. "This time I would agree with you."

Hearing her, Director Harris turns to her with curiosity. "Who do you agree with?"

"Nobody, sir." Turning to the bank, she says, "So this is the bank that had all the excitement?"

Everyone stands and looks at the entrance to the bank as Agent St. Clair turns and looks at the director. "I'm sure the Feds have been all through this place, what you think we're going to find?"

"We need to have our own investigation, and we need to find who is responsible, and more importantly, what kind of technology they're using. Meanwhile, while you two are finding that out, there are a couple of agents that have not reported—and I need answers there."

Stepping up, Nomi grabs her partner's elbow. "C'mon, Little John, that's our cue. Let's see what kind of trouble, I mean, information we can get." She leads him around the truck and they head across the street.

As soon as they open the doors to the bank, the air conditioning blast them like a Freon wave. Goose bumps cover Nomi arms; she rubs them to warm up, noticing that her giant-of-a partner did not seemed phased by the sudden change in temperature.

"Sometimes I envy you," Nomi tells him.

Looking down at her, St. Clair smiles. "C'mon, Flea."

As he leads the way they navigate around the customers until they make their way to one of the large desks on the side.

A shadow casts over a bank employee as they approach the desk. The employee appears to be shaken, but not by their presence. She leans back, cautiously in her chair and sets her pen down.

Looking up, and with a barely audible voice, she says, “What can I do to help you?”

Nomi holds up a badge. “Department of Homeland Security. We need to talk to the manager.”

The employee weakly nods and picks up her phone. “Ma’am, there are somc people out here to see you.” She hangs up her phone, and before she can gesture to a door it opens, and a large woman approaches the two agents.

Reaching a hand out, she says, “Margherita Vargas. How may I be of service?” The presence of St. Clair stops her in her confident tracks. “Dios mio!” she says as she places one of her hands on her large bosom.

Without acknowledging the extended hand, the two agents stare blankly at her. The voice inside of Nomi interrupts her thoughts, “What on your planet is that?” Avoiding a smirk and ignoring the question, she speaks up, flashing her badge again. “Department of Homeland Security, ma’am. Is there a place where we can talk, privately?”

Unable to take her eyes off of the giant agent the woman nods. “Si, si, if you will follow me,” she says and leads them back through the door and to her office.

As they walk back every employee watches and stares at St. Clair. Looking up, Nomi shakes her head, but before she can say anything, her partner leans down. “I have learned to ignore the gawkers.”

Trying to prevent a smile, Nomi nods. “I understand”

Escorting them into her office, Ms. Vargas sits down behind her large oak desk. “I don’t know what I can tell you that I have not already told the police or the FBI?”

Leaning in, Nomi places her hands on the desk. “We are more curious regarding the missing video recordings. According to the police, this man made no attempt to hide himself behind a mask. If he was wearing some type of facial disguise he would not have a need to collect the recordings. So, we will ask, where are the recordings from the other day?”

The bank manager sits assertively. “I will tell you the very same thing I have told everyone else. The recordings are gone, missing, desaparecido. I do not know what else you want me to say.”

The voice inside Nomi speaks up, “She’s lying. Her sweat pores opened up. We should just kill her.” Wincing at the suggestion, Nomi lunges towards the desk with incredible quickness, backing the manager back down in her chair. “You’re lying!”

The manager shifts her eyes back and forth. The little agent takes on a more serious tone. “What is on those recordings? Is it something you do not want anyone to see? Because we couldn’t give a shit if it is remotely embarrassing for you.”

Nomi watches the manager’s reactions and squints her eyes, as if to see through the facial expressions of the large woman.

“No, it’s not that. It’s something else, something that you want to watch, over and over again.” Nomi pries.

A tear begins to fall down her cheek as guilt and terror sweep over her. Ms. Vargas absently reaches into a lower drawer of her desk and pulls out a mini DVD player and a small stack of discs. She stands and slides them across to Nomi. Her hands start to shake as all confidence has gone. "I can't help it, you do not understand—"

Agent St. Clair raises a hand, gesturing her to stop and sit back down. They open up the player and press play.

After a few seconds the small monitor fills with an obscene scene of the bank interior. All of the nerves in Agent Nomi's body flare up, and she slams the lid back down on the player.

Anger and disgust fill Nomi as the voice inside her whispers, "We should kill her now." Handing the player and discs to her partner, she makes her way around the desk effortlessly and with amazing speed, startling the large woman back into her oversized chair.

Before Nomi can act on her inner voice, St. Clair booms out, "Agent! We have the recordings. It is time for us to leave!"

Catching herself leaning over top of the obese woman, Nomi regains her composure; she turns without saying anything and exits the office. St. Clair watches the manager put her head in her hands and start to sob. Shaking his head, he exits the office to meet up with his partner at the entrance to the bank. "What da hell was dat back there?"

Forcefully opening the doors, the intense

heat and humidity absorbs her anger. She takes a deep breath, feeling the heat burn her lungs, as she is able to regain control. In a calmer tone she tells him, "That woman is a disgusting disgrace to humanity."

"I would agree. Now let's get dis back to the room so we can get a clue as to how this man forced all those people to do dose things as well as get the police officers to turn on themselves."

Nomi looks up at her partner; the sun is behind him, and he is creating his own eclipse, making him look even larger. She takes in another deep breath and perks up. "Let's get away from here. I'm hungry." She takes off for the truck with the pep returning in her step.

Shaking his head, St. Clair walks to catch up to his partner.

James Monroe Building, Richmond, VA

July 20, 0912 hours

A short, stout man walks quickly around to the back of the skyscraper. In tow is a tall, fair-skinned woman. Both are impeccably dressed, and as they reach the back sidewalk neighboring I-95 they step inside and immediately are in front of an elevator.

Once inside the woman swipes a badge in the elevator console and without pushing a floor number the doors close. The man checks his watch on his thick wrist and takes in a sharp breath of air.

She looks over to him while still trying to catch her breath. "Grunt, I really wish you would relax. How a nervous Nellie like you ever got to where you are, I will never know," the woman says as they wait for the elevator door to open.

Grunt gives the tall, red-haired agent a sideways glance then turns to look out the window of the elevator. He ignores her rambling and watches the scenery fall in front of him. The elevator stops halfway up the building. As they step out, there is a large set of doors, reading MAINTENANCE. He walks over and punches in a passcode on a control panel as they hear the click of the doors unlocking.

After walking through, they make their way past the A/C plants and electronic-control switchboards until they come across another set of doors.

Without any markings on the door, Grunt again walks up to a control panel and holds his thumb to a clear-lighted touch screen, and the light turns green. The woman repeats, pressing her thumb until the light turns green. A click as the doors unlock. The woman goes to open the doors and looks over to the man.

"With all this technology, why can't the doors open themselves, like in the movies?" Grunt shakes his head and walks past her. Smiling, she watches him fume past her.

"You know, one of these days I am going to get you to say something."

As they make it to the office spaces a young intern steps in front of them. With a flip of some of the pages she is holding she looks up at the two. "Madam would like to see you two in her office."

Grunt gives his partner another sideways glance as they change their direction and head towards their director's office. The woman lifts her hands to her shoulders, shrugging "what?" After putting her hands down, she mumbles as she hurries to catch up with her partner, "I guess it is going to be one of those days."

Turning a corner, she sees the wide oak door of the director's office. Standing in front and staring at his watch, is Grunt. As soon as she stands next to him, he gives her a disgruntled look and knocks on the door.

They look at each other as they hear the director yell out, "What are you two waiting for?"

As they enter they see an imposing woman standing in front of a large television screen. Without saying a word, the director motions them to watch the screen.

On the screen they see the hood of a vehicle pull up to a rundown farmhouse. A man wearing sunglasses and a lightweight windbreaker over a grey and blue, pinstripe, spandex suit walks outside the rundown farmhouse to meet the vehicle.

As they watch what would appear to be a polite verbal exchange, two police officers come into view as another strange-looking man steps out of the house with his hands up. This man is wearing some type of computerized headgear with matching gloves and boots, as well as the same grey and blue, pinstriped suit.

The woman looks back at the director. "Director Carol, what is this, a low-budget movie pitch?"

Director Carol is leaning back on her desk with her arms folded. She points a finger to the monitor. "Just watch, Agent Selenia, and tell me what you see."

With her attention back on the screen she sees the picture go sharply at an angle as a glass and dust cloud fills the screen. They take two steps back from the screen and raise their arms to shield themselves from the debris. As soon as the man with a windbreaker on freezes the police officer's hand the woman takes in an exasperated breath. "Wait, that's the missing nitrogen backpack," Agent Selenia says while waving a hand in the air.

"The one developed for locating water

sources on dry planets." She begins to pace, glancing between the television and the floor. "Who is that wearing it? What is this? Now I see it! Those are the prototype MIT space suits. Where was this taken?"

Selenia is watching the screen when Garrett flies over the camera, through the porch railing, and pins an officer that was about to fire his gun against the wall.

"Didn't see that coming! What is that?" Selenia tries to contain herself. As the scene on the television calms down they see the police officers scrambling off the porch. She turns and faces the director as if to look for answers.

Without saying a word, Director Carol uncrosses her arms and walks around her desk. Sliding paperwork around on her desk, she takes a moment to read the memo that came with the video.

"This was a police cam video that was recorded yesterday at a remote farm in Western Louisiana. As for the three gentlemen at the farm, we do not know who they are or how they came to acquire that equipment."

Taking a moment to look up at her agents, she sees Selenia staring intently, while Grunt's attention has not wavered from the television monitor.

"We have an operative investigating in the area, and we are still waiting to hear from her." Director Carol points back to the screen as the camera view looks as if it is being removed from the vehicle.

Coming into view is the image of a young

woman wearing dirty and bloodied clothing. Then the television screen goes blank.

"As for that young woman, she has already been identified as Agent Kristen Abergathy, out of the Las Vegas branch. Brilliant, but inexperienced mind; she was to be working with our operative."

Agent Selenia taps Grunt on his shoulder to get his attention before turning back to Director Carol. "So, what would you like us to do?"

Opening a cabinet door, the director removes a thumb drive and sets it on a folder, then slides it to her. "Find out who these guys are and as much information on their equipment as you can. The local LEOs have already put out an all-point bulletin for their arrests, and the FBI has already been brought in. So, finding them without drawing attention will be a challenge. Neither the FBI nor the State Police Department has this feed anymore, so they are flying on memory only. That gives us the tactical advantage, let's use that advantage." She sits in her chair and starts to refile the paperwork.

Selenia takes a moment to flip through the folder then looks down at the thumb drive. Nudging her partner, "Come on, we have work to do."

Grunt looks over at the thumb drive and with low garbled, heavy accent he says, "Gud movie," as he heads for the door.

The director calls out as the agents go to exit, "Oh, and if you're late again, this will not be such a pleasant meeting,"

Grunt scowls and gives Selenia a sideways

glance and storms out of the office.

Agent Selenia exits behind him closing the door.

"What? Look at bright side, we get to go to Louisiana. It's miserable there this time of year, you'll love it."

Hilton Garden Inn, Katy, TX

July 20, 1525 hours

Steam billows out of the hotel bathroom as Agent St. Clair walks out with a towel wrapped around his waist and drying his hair with another one. He walks in front of his bed where he looks down at his clothes he laid out when a voice chimes up behind him.

"Hey, big handsome, me love you long time."

"Bumboclaat!" Jumping and whipping around to the voice, he quickly fades from view and reappears. When he reappears the towel that was around his waist has dropped to the floor.

Agent Nomi gets a full-frontal view of her partner. "Ack! Oh my God!" she says as she jumps from the chair she was sitting in to on top of the table.

"You frighten me, Flea! How'd you get here? What'd you doin' here?" He gasps as he reaches down to recover his towel.

Without getting off of the table Nomi covers her eyes and turns to faces the wall. "I am so sorry, Little John . . ." A small smile forms. "Well, I should say, not-so Little John."

He reaches down, grabs his clothes, and storms back into the bathroom. "I can't believe you woman."

Nomi smiles as she peeks and watches him storms into the bathroom.

Not bad, she thinks, looking at his tight physique. "Don't be so uptight; I was just having fun," she calls to her partner.

She notices the circular discolorations that slightly malformed his skin. They do not, however, take away from his physique, which has her thoughts drifting. "Stop it!" The familiar voice inside her snaps her from her thoughts.

"What the hell, you won't let me have any fun."

Out of the bathroom, St. Clair raises his voice. "You call this fun! Sneakin' in my room and givin' me a heart attack, fun?"

Regaining her sensibility, she says, "Come on out, let's talk about this guy and how we are going find him."

Coming out of the bathroom shirtless, having only grabbed his pants, St. Clair looks at her shaking his head. "I still don't know how you got in here."

"That was easy; the rooms are in both of our names. I just asked for a key." Walking up to him, she reaches up and places a hand on one of the darker spots near his shoulder blade. "Are these the coils the director mentioned earlier?"

Recoiling away from her touch, he says, "Yes, now if you don't mind. I would like to finish getting dressed." Picking up a shirt, he side steps around her to the corner of the bed.

A little disheartened, the petite agent backs away and sits back down. "I realize it's personal, but how? Why do you have those coil implants? What are they for?"

Realizing from his perplexed reactions to her, "I mean you made the statement that they allow you to be, and I am curious. You tell me yours, and I'll tell you mine." Nomi gives him a flirting smile.

The voice inside her sets her nerves on edge. "What are you thinking?" Straightening her posture, she shifts and sits in the chair. "It's called trust."

Finishing buttoning down his shirt, he looks at her with curiosity. "Okay, we may need to open some of those little bottles for this; you may not believe everything I tell you otherwise."

Nomi opens a few of the small bottles of alcohol and pours them each a drink. Walking over to the table, he picks up one of them and takes a sip. The alcohol hits him and a shiver hits his spine. Looking at the drink he tells her, "Yeah, this it'll do." He looks over at his partner. "First of all, how much of the Great War do you remember?"

Curling her feet under her body in the seat, she takes a sip of her drink. "If you are talking about World War II, that was a little before my time."

After taking a few steps to look out the window, turning and taking another sip, he looks up at his partner. "Well not for me." Taking one of the chairs over to the window, he sits and looks out through the curtains. "I was born a child of the Depression-era, 1921. My mother was killed when I was very young, and in 1929 the Great Depression hit. My father tried for a few years but could no longer support me and in a drunken rage sent me to the streets. I was thirteen."

Clearly shocked and trying to do calculations in

her head, "Wait, you mean to tell me that you are ninety-four years old?" With effortless movement, she jumps to the bed, sitting with her legs crossed. "No freaking way. You don't look even thirty yet?"

"Thank you, however, you are getting ahead of the story. Now, where was I? Oh yeah, four years later I enlisted into the navy. In 1936, when World War II started and the bread lines relocated to the recruiting offices, I became a Water Technician and got stationed on the Destroyer Escort, DE-one seventy-three, USS Eldridge. Our ships were having trouble making it past the German U-boat blockade. In '43 my ship was reassigned to Philadelphia to undergo a refit. The powers that be were hoping to find a way to get by the U-boats. That's when things got real interesting."

Looking back over to the bed where Nomi was sitting, he finds her squatting on the chair again and pouring herself another drink. "Are you finding this boring?"

Finishing pouring her drink, she settles back into the chair. "No, I was never one for history."

"Well let me try to shorten it up. What do you know about Albert Einstein?"

Looking at him with a deadpan expression, she says, "E-equals MC2, dude, right?" She motions her arm over her head. "Way over my head."

"Fair enough. What about Nikolas Tesla?"

"Oh, the electricity guy," Nomi says. "I saw a show about him on television the other night. It was Ancient Aliens; I love that show."

St. Clair gives her a confused look. "Wait, you

said, that you don't like history, yet you watch the History Channel?"

Finishing her drink, Nomi's expression turns solemn. "It's not the history that interests me; let's just say I have a personal interest in aliens."

Just then a cell phone rings and St. Clair picks it up, looking at his partner with raised eyebrows like they got busted, mouthing, "It's the director." Lifting the phone, he says, "St. Clair here." After listening for a short time, he sets the phone down.

"Pack up. Directive has changed. We're off to Louisiana. That was Director Harris. He says Nika Carol is not answering her phone and neither is the agent she was partnered up with. We're driving up tonight. I suggest we get a power nap."

Frustration flashes over Nomi as she gives him her best pouting face, getting him to smile and shake his head. Heading for the door, she stops, and without looking back, she says, "I miss her, but as much as I miss her . . ." Pointing down at the DVD player, ". . . this asshole needs to be stopped before he does this again."

She turns her head to see that her partner was going to say something, but she raises a hand stopping him. "I'm just saying." She turns and heads out the door towards to her room.

Associated Foreign Exchange, Baton Rouge, LA

July 20, 1302 hours

Stepping out of the Shisha House, a stranger wipes his beard with a napkin and then wipes the sweat that is forming in the midday heat. He walks to his Cadillac Deville taking out a silver briefcase. After looking around and eyeing the sparsely filled parking lot, he walks two doors down into an unmarked corner section of the outdoor mall.

Opening the door, the air conditioning welcomes him. The room is a well-lit office space with a customer service desk to the right. There is a young woman behind the desk helping an older man fill out paperwork. She looks up at the stranger and gives him a quick wave and a smile. The stranger motions for her to take her time.

He sits on the waiting couch, brushing his slacks down, and sets the briefcase next to him. Opening a panel on one of side, he adjusts the thumb locks. Out of the corner of his eye, he watches the facial expressions of the young lady. Watching her as she takes a large, exhausting breath, the older man runs his forearm across his forehead, wiping the early stages of perspiration.

Checking his watch, he looks around the room, noting that the air conditioning was on full blast. He affords himself a small smile and continues to sit with his hands on his lap, watching the door leading to back room.

The young woman is leaning on both arms, her breath becoming labored as the old man has lost all posture and is leaning back in the chair. The door opens and a tall man steps into the main room, dragging his feet, sweating, and massaging his right arm.

With barely a glance in the stranger's direction he leans on the desk next to the old man.

Out from the back room, a tall man staggers out massaging his neck. He notices the man on the couch and gives a polite nod. The sweat is beading up on his forehead, and he wipes it off with his sleeve.

He recognizes that the older man is struggling, attempting to stand, and grabbing his thigh as if to use it as a brace. Helping the man up, he escorts him to the door. Once at the door the taller man opens it as a green-hue wave fills the room, knocking everyone to the ground.

The green hue remains, making the air cloudy and heavy. The stranger stands up and scratches under his beard as he looks around. "This is interesting."

He walks over to the taller man, to watch him struggling to lift his arm for help. Reaching down, he checks the pockets and locates two sets of keys. After examining the keys, he drops the set that has a car key on them. The man on the floor tries, but cannot lift his arms to resist the stranger, and he passes out.

Standing back up, the stranger looks back at the door lodged open; he takes a small step outside.

Looking around he notices and some people are passed out next to their cars. Sounds of vehicles, nearby crashing catches his attention. Scratching just under his beard, he turns back into the office space. "Very interesting."

Making his way past the receptionist towards the back room, he looks around one of the main offices. Seeing a small picture that is too small to be a wall picture, he walks over to it, reaches up to the right side of the picture, and gives it a tug. The picture falls away, crashing onto the floor. The stranger shrugs and continues to look around.

Walking over to the desk, he takes a moment to sit in the chair. Scratching under his beard, he surveys the wooden structural highlights on the wall boarders, giving the room an 80's private eye feel. Pushing himself back up, his thumb presses a lever just under the lip of the desk and on the floor a square door pops up, "Interesting."

Opening it, he pulls out one more bone-like Ingots with strange petroglyphs.

Taking a moment to look them over, he notices they are similar to the ones from the bank. Shrugging, he puts them into his backpack he has hidden underneath his suit jacket.

* * *

Outside on the streets police cars have their sirens blaring as they scream by to get to one of the accidents. One by one, as they get out of their car, they are immediately affected by the green hue. The driver shakes his head as if to clear cobwebs and look at his partner, confused.

His partner is breathing heavy and just smiles, shaking his head.

They make their way to the cars to find everyone in the first vehicle passed out. The older officer attempts to motion for his partner to check the other vehicle, but the muscles in his arms are fatigued and heavy. The other officer understands the subtle gesture and checks the status of the people in that car to find the same, everyone passed out.

With a labored breath the lead officer takes on a worried look. "What da heck is dis?"

The younger officer, struggling to keep his legs under him looks at his partner. "How'd I supposed to know? You've lived here for a while, have you ever seen this?"

Slowly shaking his head, he says, "Nah, never seen nor heard any ting like dis."

Using the car to hold himself up, the younger officer is applying pressure on his eyes to try and clear his thoughts. "This shit is alien man. I kid you not."

With a gasp of a chuckle, the lead officer says, "Regardless, alien or not, get on da radio and call dis in. Oh, and if I were you, I wouldn't mention a word about alien when you call it in, or we'll never live it down."

The younger officer shuffles his feet back to the car. "You don't need to worry about that."

As he gets to the car, his legs give out and he falls to the asphalt, passing out.

With a surge of adrenalin, the older officer forces himself to his partner's side. Kneeling down, he checks for vitals to find he has only fallen asleep.

Feeling his eyes getting heavy as the muscles throughout his body ache, he gets into the car and closes the door. His head begins to clear. Picking up the radio, he calls in the accident and requests paramedics on site.

* * *

Inside the Associated Foreign Exchange, the stranger prepares to leave. As he does he notices the old man is posed holding his left arm, eyes open, and unblinking. The taller man lies asleep as the young lady lies sleeping on her desk.

Stepping out into the parking lot, he hears a crash in the distance of two more vehicles colliding. Making his way to his car and hears a sizzle and a snap sound and turns into the direction,

He notices the electrical substation directly behind the building. Tilting his head, he looks down at his briefcase then back at the substation. Closing the panel, he turns off the briefcase; the green hue begins to dissipate.

"Interesting." He gets into his vehicle, circles, and exits the parking lot.

As he leaves the parking lot he pauses and watches the electrical substation. He turns right to head towards the freeway, and he notices two police cars and an officer motioning for him to slow down and come to a stop.

The officer's breathing appears to be labored, and he is struggling to keep himself standing. The stranger comes to a stop.

With a hand circle, the officer tells him to lower the window. Gripping the car door to keep himself standing, his knees give, but he is able to recover.

"Sir, there has been an accident and Interstate 12 and it is now blocked." Taking a deep, labored breath he pushes himself to a standing position. "If you want, you can turn right here and make a right on Old Hammond, then 'bout a mile down you can make a right on Millerville Rd. That'll take you back to da interstate."

With a nod, the stranger allows the police officer to back away. Then as he is turning the car around, he watches the officer crane and massage his neck. As he follows the directions given to him, sirens fill the humid air and emergency vehicles scream past him, towards the accident.

1989

Base,
Outside Groom Dry Lake, Nevada

March 20, 1435 hours

A seasoned man with thinning hair is sitting at his desk looking over some preparation files when a tentative knocking on his door catches his attention.

"Gerald, I am old, so I really wish you would knock with a purpose!"

Opening a door marked Caretaker, is a short, husky man with youth on his side. "Sir, I apologize, however, well to make this brief, you see, well, we were auditing records, and we found a, or rather in this case, did not find—"

"Can you please get to the point? I am not getting any younger."

Gerald straightens himself, sticking his chin out. "Yes, sir. There are files missing on Project Galileo and other projects."

"For forty years we have managed to prevent this from happening, and we have kept a lid on everything we've accomplished." The Caretaker massages his temples. "Do we know who is responsible and what he or she has?"

Gerald looks down at the clipboard he is holding close to his chest. "It appears to be Robert Lazar. At least he has been unaccounted for today."

The Caretaker quickly raises his head to watch the man with the news. "How do I know that name . . . New guy from Los Alamos, what does he have?"

Flipping through his clipboard, Gerald thumbs the papers, as if he is still looking for the information that was missing. Walking around the small room, he bumps into a chair, nearly knocking it over. He stops to see the Caretaker waiting. "I apologize, sir."

The Caretaker looks at his associate, expecting more.

"Well that is where it gets interesting. The files on the autopsies, photos, and the filming were in the files that cannot be located," Gerald confesses.

The Caretaker stands up too fast, causing him to get light headed, He quickly places his hands on the desk for support to regain focus. After a few seconds, and with a cool strength in his voice, he says, "How did he get that away from the facility?"

Folding his clipboard back to his chest, Gerald takes a step back. "We don't. We are unsure."

"Thank you for the information. I will see how we can recover from this." The Caretaker mumbles to himself, "Colonel Corso would be pissed if he knew about this."

"Sir, it's been over twenty years since he was here. I doubt he would give this news a second thought."

"If this gets out, everyone will give it a second thought."

Noting the finality of his tone, the younger man exits the room. Seemingly frozen, locked in time, the Caretaker eventually sits back in his chair and continues to stare at the phone. After a few more moments of reflections he reaches out to the phone and dials.

A few rings into the call, the Caretaker is just about to hang up when a familiar, strong voice on the other end.

"What can I do for you today?"

"You have always gotten straight to the point, haven't you, Ms. Watkins?"

El Cortez Hotel and Casino, Las Vegas, NV

March 25, 2049 hours

A man wearing a trench coat is holding a newspaper to block the rain. He is thumbing through the directory attached to the pay phone booth. Fumbling around with the pen in his hand he manages to put the quarters in the slot and dial a number. A no-nonsense voice cuts through the chill of the rain.

"KLAS, how may I direct you?"

"Ummm, yeah, I would like to talk to George Knapp?"

"What is this regarding?"

Trying to keep dry, he looks around, watching headlights drive by. "An investigation, please."

"Can you be more specific?"

Leaning into the phone, and in a firm, stage whisper, he says, "No! I can't right now! After a moment of silence, he hears the phone ringing again. A friendlier voice brings his attention back from looking around.

"KLAS, George Knapp, how can I be of help?"

Stomping his feet to remove some of the wetness from his jacket, he says, "Did you get the files?"

"Who am I speaking to? Are you in danger?"

Looking around to see if there is anyone hanging around he says, "This is Dennis, and I can't talk now, but I have some more information you need to get out and let the public know."

"Dennis, I've examined the files you sent, and as much as I am enjoying these phone calls, we need to meet. Is there a place or a number I can reach you?"

After a period of silence, Dennis takes a deep breath. "Okay, but I need to set something up . . ."

An exasperated voice interrupts him, "Can you give me something? I need verifiable information on you before I can meet with you. You and I know Dennis is not your real name, and it has been working for now. But for a face-to-face interview I need to know who you are. Name, background, something."

"My name is Robert Lazar. I am a physicist and a researcher for a testing facility out of Groom Lake. I graduated from MIT and California Institute of Technology. I worked at Los Alamos National Laboratories. That should help you verify who I am. I will contact you tomorrow so we can meet." After another moment's pause, he says, "Mr. Knapp, we are not alone in this universe. We are not even alone on this planet." With that he hangs up.

The rain has lightened up, and he scans the area again. He goes to put the pen in his jacket and misses the pocket and it drops to the sidewalk. Bending down to catch it he stumbles forward and lands in a puddle. Something catches his eye.

Another vehicle takes a turn too fast, loses

traction, and slams into a parked car. Feeling his nerves completely on edge, he looks around one more time then gets into his car and drives off.

Los Alamos National Laboratory, Los Alamos, NM

March 26, 0826 hours

In the parking lot of the facility, Director Siegfried Hecker gets out of his BMW. Walking over to the hood of his car, he lays his briefcase down and opens it. As he is inventorying the contents, an imposing woman with strong features walks up to him while holding out a badge.

"Director Hecker, Director Siegfried Hecker? May I have a moment with you? This is regarding a former employee of yours."

Hesitant, he slides his back against the car, closing his briefcase. Stopping, he watches the woman walking towards him when out of the corner of his eye he notices two gentlemen in suits standing not too far from her. Checking his watch, he looks around only to find nobody else in the area and then looks back at his watch.

"How can I help you?"

Lightening her posture and tone the woman stops just before his car, she says, "This is regarding Robert Lazar..." and she pauses to look around as a car pulls into the parking lot. Closing her eyes, takes a deep breath, and smiles. "Can we walk and talk?"

Gaining confidence, he takes a step, and then pauses as a thought occurs to him, I believe she is allowing me this confidence.

Shaking it off, he looks at the well-groomed, well-dressed woman and smiles. "Absolutely, it is a beautiful morning."

On that note they begin to walk through the parking lot. The other two gentlemen remain behind for a moment then walk towards a black Ford Bronco.

"I apologize, who did you say you were with?"

"Let's not make this about me, this is about Mr. Lazar. He has gotten involved in something, and as a result, he has lost all clearance and himself has become a national security threat."

The director turns pale. "Not again. This can't be happening again. We cannot afford another incident relating to national security leaks." He throws his hands up in the air out of frustration.

The woman takes a step back, "Sir, you need to relax and pay attention. I am not aware about any other concerns."

He stops and studies her strong features. "In 1945 Klaus Fuchs betrayed this company and the country by giving the Russians detailed information of our nuclear program and schematics on the very bombs we ultimately used on Japan." He rubs his hands alongside of his slacks as if he was wiping his hands of the incident. "I do not see Bob doing anything inappropriate like what you are saying. He was one of my most trusted employees. I can't see him doing anything to ruin all he has accomplished."

Straightening her suit jacket, the woman makes her way back to the Bronco.

"I am afraid so. I am only showing you this courtesy in telling you this in case he returns here for further employment."

"This is unbelievable, what has he done?" The director takes a couple steps to catch up.

"I assure you that this is true, however, I cannot mention the things he has done due to national security concerns. You understand."

Looking down, defeated, he rubs the back of his neck. "Uh, yes, yes I do."

"You need to protect the work and all you have accomplished here. I would suggest you erase all records of him in order to maintain the integrity of any project he was working on during his tenure here."

Lifting his head, Director Hecker looks around the parking lot, then back at the woman.

"That is a drastic measure."

"It is a strong recommendation, for your protection."

Director Hecker sticks out his chest. "That is an excellent idea. I will work on that first thing today. I have so much to do." Shaking his head, he says, "We cannot afford this again."

The black SUV pulls up behind them, and before she opens the door she turns to him and says, "Director, the United States government appreciates your help, and I appreciate your help, thank you."

Without waiting for a response, she gets in the car. Standing there he watches it drive away, noting the government license plate. Nodding his head, he adjusts his tie and then turns with renewed purpose as he heads into the building.

Super 8,
Las Vegas, NV

March 30, 2140 hours

Sitting in a dark room, Bob Lazar checks his watch then peers back out the window. After a few minutes of watching cars drive by, he stands and paces as he gets lost in thought. There is a knock at the door, causing him to jump and make a quick dash to look out the window.

Outside, a gentleman is wearing an off-color blazer and is carrying a backpack, as well as a tote behind him. The man glancing between what appears to be a photograph and the door.

Releasing the curtains, Bob gets up and tentatively walks to the door. The gentleman knocks again just as it opens. He looks at the photograph then at Bob. "You must be Robert Lazar." Smiling, he offers out his hand.

Shaking his hand, Bob says, "And you, are George Knapp. Please come in. We should not be talking with the door open."

With his bags in tow, Knapp walks into the dark room while folding up the photo. "I'm not sure we should do this interview in the dark either."

"No, you're right." Turning on the lights, he gestures towards a small table near the window. "If you don't mind, can I ask you what that photo was a picture of?"

Unlatching his tote, Knapp takes out a collapsible tripod. Standing up, he turns and faces Mr. Lazar. Taking the photo from his jacket he hands it to him.

"That is a photo of you at a company picnic in Los Alamos. I talked to one of your co-workers, and he gave me this."

"You went to Los Alamos?"

Knapp raises a hand motioning for him to wait. "Before we go any further, do you have a driver's license and can I see it?"

Taking out his wallet, Lazar shows the reporter his license. "If you already have a verified photo of what I look like, then why did you want to see this?"

After finishing attaching a video recorder to the tripod, Knapp motions to a chair. "Well you may want to sit down for this." Watching Lazar take a seat with his back to the window, he grabs the other chair and sits next to the recorder.

"It would appear that you no longer exist. Meaning there are no records of you graduating from either California Tech or MIT. No records of you working at Los Alamos National Laboratories, despite an employee that remembers you. And to top it off, there is no record of your birth."

He leans back in the chair and takes out and pen and notepad while watching Robert Lazar's expression of disbelief.

"They cannot make me just disappear." Lazar goes to stand back as the reporter holds his palm out to stop him.

"That is why we need to video record this interview," Knapp mentions, matter of fact, as he reaches and turns on the recorder. "Perhaps we should start with your credentials. Who you are, and where do you work?"

Pursing his lips and nodding his head, Lazar pauses as he looks at the video recorder.

"My name is Bob Lazar. I work, or rather worked, at an above top-secret research facility outside Groom Lake, here in Nevada."

"What do you mean by, above top secret?"

Lazar nervously glances between the reporter and the recorder.

"I had a Majestic Clearance, which is thirty-eight levels above the well-known top-secret level. We worked on Project Galileo at S-4 with a small division of researchers, such as myself, who held that clearance."

"How many people worked on the project with you?"

"Twenty-two people."

Knapp glances up from writing. "Twenty-two people on the project?"

Lazar tries to keep his excitement in check, not wanting the reporter to confuse any facts.

"No, twenty-two people total that worked in S-4. This is why I am contacting you. It's just unfair, outright, not to put it in the hands of the overall scientific community.

"There are people much more capable of dealing with this information and by this time would have gotten a lot further along than this small, select group of people working out in the middle of the desert. They don't even have the facilities, to completely analyze what they're dealing with."

"Are you referring to the flying saucers?"

Lazar chuckles and says, "Getting right to it, aren't you? The conspiracies regarding the crash in Roswell may or may not be true. What I do know to be true is the ships they have there are not of this earth. The technologies they are reversing are taking decades to complete."

"Can you give us an example of this technology?"

"Anti-matter reactors that allow the ships to produce their own gravitational fields. The old argument that we can never be visited by an alien race is due to the sheer distance, even at the speed of light."

"What do you mean when you say gravitational field?"

Adjusting his glasses, Lazar straightens his back.

"Around the turn of the century, Nikolas Tesla was interviewed by the New York Times. He talks about an incident where he saw the past, present, and future at one moment. You see, gravity distorts time and space, Einstein theorized this. Just like if you had a waterbed and you put a bowling ball in the middle. It warps it down like that; that's exactly what happens to space. Imagine that you were in a spacecraft that could exert a tremendous gravitational field by itself.

"You could sit on any particular place and turn on the gravity generator and actually warp space and time by folding it. When you shut it off, you'd be a tremendous distance from where you were. However, time would not have even moved because you essentially shut it off."

Lazar takes a moment to catch his breath and push up his glasses.

"I mean it is so farfetched, people. It's difficult for people to grasp, and as stubborn as the scientific community is they'll never buy it, but this is, in fact, just what happens."

"Albert Einstein and Nathan Rosen theorized something along those lines. However, they theorized that the physics would make it impossible to use." Leaning back in his chair, Knapp is proud of his burst of knowledge.

"Well, when you harness gravity, you harness everything. It's the missing piece in physics right now. We really know very little about gravity."

Taking a moment to open a water bottle and trying to register what was just said, all he can do is offer Lazar a water.

"This is all interesting, but how do you suppose they, I mean these ships, are able to harness it, if you will. I mean it sounds all too fantastic to exist."

"The technology to harness gravity not only exists; but, is being tested at S-4. If such technology is beyond human capabilities, it must have come from someplace else."

Reaching out he accepts the water bottle. "This is more than conjecture. There is an element that cannot be found on the periodic chart. The element, called 1-1-5, it is stored in these casings, and these ships utilize this element, creating a magnetic field that is capable of creating its own gravitational field. The government has five-hundred pounds of it, and it cannot be found or manufactured on Earth."

Struggling to keep up, writing in his pad, Knapp raises a finger for him to hold on a second.

"There are a few elements on the periodic table that are man-made. Perhaps it is one of them and it just has not made it there as of yet."

Lazar takes a second to sip his water. "It would be almost impossible, well, it is impossible, to synthesize an element that heavy here on Earth."

Knapp smiles. "At least right now."

"I don't think you can ever synthesize it. You essentially have to assemble it by bombarding it with electrons, atom by atom, and it would take an infinite amount of power and an infinite amount of time. The substance has to come from a place where super-heavy elements could have been produced naturally."

Writing in his pad, Knapp has a feeling of overwhelming dread wash over him. "That type of technology sounds dangerous. If that is just one type of the technology that is being worked on there... What if some of these technologies were to get out and into the wrong hands? How much damage could even one person be able to cause?"

Lazar leans back in his chair. "I am not saying we should just open the gates, but we just need to let people know we are working on such things."

Reviewing his notes, Knapp looks up and stares, concerned. "I'm for the Freedom of Information Act, but even I would be concerned if such technology fell into the wrong hands."

2015

Alexandria International Airport, Alexandria, LA

July 21, 0505 hours

Sitting in the back of the truck, Agent Nomi looks around the parking lot of AEX, "You know, I was researching the USS Eldridge on the drive up here. What did they call it? Project Rainbow?"

Leaning against the truck, Agent St. Clair unfolds his arms and raises his hands. "Don't look at me, I didn't name it."

"Did all that really happen?" Nomi questions him with a disbelieving tone.

St. Clair chuckles. "Which part?"

Nomi kicks her feet harder. "You know, the green cloud, disappearing and reappearing in Norfolk."

"That is where me and some friends of mine, Duncan and Edward Cameron, got off the ship. We jumped off—well we sort of freaked out when we started see my shipmates walking through the bulkheads."

"Wait, that's what you can do," Nomi quips. "You call it phasing."

Turning towards her he grips the edge of the truck bed. "You are getting ahead of the story again. Anyways, when we resurfaced from the water we were picked up by a small group of people that claimed they were waiting for us and that it was no longer 1943, but 1983."

Pure awe and shock take over Agent Nomi. "You traveled in time? Can you do that now, too?"

St. Clair ignores the question. "These coils that have become part of my body are similar to the ones that Einstein, using Tesla's technology and theories, used on the USS Eldridge. Now they allow me to exist, as in not phasing away completely."

"So, the stories about sailors going mad or vanishing are true." Squinting her eyes, Nomi peers at her partner.

St. Clair shrugs his shoulders. "I don't know. I was not there, remember? I was sitting in a lab forty years later."

"What do you know about these two agents we are waiting for? I've never heard of them." Pursing her lips, Nomi shifts her gaze.

"Well Chatter, or Agent Eleadora Selenia, unbelievably intelligent, remembers everything, right down to the smallest detail. We call her Chatter because, well, she never shuts up, unless she's reading or watching something. As for her partner, Grunt, we've never met. I heard about him though. They say he never talks, which is why they call him Grunt."

"What kind of name is Eleadora Selenia?"

Giving her a double take, St. Clair scratches the back of his head. "You know, I'm not sure. I never thought to ask."

Sitting back up and showing her frustration Nomi asks, "Why do we have to wait for them? Why can't we just go after Nika's killer ourselves?"

"Simple, Director Harris told us that we may need the help. We have no idea what we are up against, and I agree—we could use the help." He sets his phone down as he watches Nomi's reaction.

Nomi kicks her feet harder. "So, if I understand this right—and correct me if I'm wrong—we know where, and they know who, and that is why we are waiting for them." Nomi pauses for effect. "You and I can take out anybody."

"All true, but it is more like strength in numbers. Two days ago, two agents went to observe, and one was killed and the other is missing." A tear begins to form in his eye. "I'm going to miss Nika. I was going to see if she wanted to go for drinks when we got back from Houston."

Taking on an endearing tone, Nomi reaches up and lays a hand on his shoulder. "She is too young for you, Little John, and I don't think she's your type."

The inner voice interrupts Nomi's thoughts, "Was, not is, she's dead." Cringing at the voice she grips the tailgate, bending the metal and leaving hand impressions on the edge.

Hearing the metal bending St. Clair brushes his partner aside to get a better look.

"What are you doing? And why do you keep hurting the truck?" Straightening up, he pauses. "What do you mean she's not my type? What makes you say that?"

"Because we were dating before our last mission outside Kandahar."

Nomi looks away and almost gets lost in thought. "Neither of us was never the same afterwards."

"You both fought in Afghanistan? Wow, I am impressed."

Nomi stands up in the bed and walks towards the front. Leaning against the rest window, she crosses arms. "Well don't be, someone gave us bad intel. We had a feeling something was wrong, but we went in anyways. Out of the entire team, they only found enough pieces to put her and me together and . . ."

Raising his hand out in front of him, stopping her from saying more. "My apologies, Flea. Wait, did you say you two were dating?"

The inner voice sets Nomi's nerves tingling all over. "I was wondering if this buffoon was going to catch that."

Ignoring the voice, she makes her way back to St. Clair. "Yes, Little John, we dated. It hadn't gotten to the serious level, but it was moving in that direction." Pausing long enough to calm her nerves, she takes a deep breath before continuing. "We drifted apart after Kandahar while we were recovering with our losses. She was a strong woman, smart and gutsy. I want to know who is responsible for her death, so I can make him pay."

A light, cheerful voice cuts into the night. "Little John! What are you doing here? You big stud you."

The light-hearted voice surprises both agents.

They turn to see a tall redhead and a short, stout man with an Eastern European complexion.

Seeing the giant agent, the tall redhead rushes over and jumps into his arms. "Man, I have missed you. How've you been?"

After a quick, firm hug, he sets her down. "Doing good." He gives her a look over. "Looks like you have been doing pretty well yourself. I heard they partnered you up?" They turn and look at Grunt who is looking up and staring at Agent St. Clair in awe. "You must be Agent Grunt." St. Clair reaches out and offers him his hand.

The only part of Agent Grunt that moves is his arm as he reaches out to shake. St. Clair winces. "Nice grip."

Effortlessly, Nomi jumps from the tailgate to the front corner of the cab. "So, are we going after these guys or not?"

Sticking his chest out, St. Clair ushers a hand out towards his partner. "Chatter, meet Agent Yukiko Nomi, or Flea as I call her."

Agent Selenia smiles and looks at the agent sitting on the bed wall. "Agent Yukiko Nomi, born 1982. Father Japanese, mother American. Paralyzed in a botched attack outside Kandahar, became part of the ASYMB project to restore use of your legs."

With a forced smile, Nomi looks at her partner as the inner voice sets her nerves on fire. "We need to kill her first."

Struggling to maintain the smile, she looks back at Agent Selenia. "It is certainly a pleasure. Chatter is it?"

"I was unable to access the ASYMB program, perhaps you can tell me about it."

"Chatter." St. Clair raises a hand as he notices the muscles on his partner tensing up. Firming up his voice he interrupts Selenia.

Stopping abruptly, Selenia looks at St. Clair. Her eyes open in realization., "She has not told anyone." Looking back at Nomi she says, "I am so sorry, I get carried away."

She turns her attention back to St. Clair, but before she can say something else.

Nomi speaks up. The tension is still in her tone. "So, you guys know who we are supposed to get, right?"

"Yes and no. We have police cam video of the nineteenth when we believe something happened to the agents that were there. There was an altercation with the LEO's, however, we do not see even one of the agents until after the altercation. That agent was, or is . . . her status is still unknown, Agent Kristen Abergathy. She's seen removing the cam from the car. At no point do we even get a glimpse of Agent Carol."

Turning her back to Nomi, Selenia looks at St. Clair. "So, we are not sure if that is who is responsible."

Agent Nomi's inner voice takes on an impatient tone. "You know you can shut her up."

Nomi and St. Clair look at each other as he notices her tensing up. He gives her a faint knowing, smile then looks over at the tall redhead.

"Chatter, did you say you have a video? Perhaps we could all watch it again. We've been in the movie-watching mode as of late." In the corner of his eye he senses what he thinks is a slight grin from Grunt.

"Yes, we do. Grunt's been watching it non-stop on the flight. Speaking of flights, have you guys ever flown in one of the Hawker Siddeley models? Unbelievable ride!" Grunt fishes out of his carrying bag an electronic pad, attached to it is a thumb drive. Selenia pauses long enough to see the iPad being handed to her.

"Now as you watch this, know that we have already identified two individuals. One is an agent out of the Las Vegas Branch, Kristen Abergathy. The other is more of a focus for us, Admiral Julian Kay."

St. Clair stiffens.

Realizing this she, Selenia quickly puts a hand on his chest. "Oh, I forgot you were navy."

Nomi notices the uneasiness of her partner, and she moves silently into a pouncing position on the edge of the truck bed. Nomi's inner voice syncs with her own thoughts, "Now do we get to shut her up?" Before she can act on her impulses, Nomi feels a strong, heavy hand lightly grip her right foot. Looking down she sees Agent Grunt has noticed her silent movements. Their eyes make contact, and a sense of calmness relaxes her. She slowly steps back into the truck bed.

Oblivious to what is going on around her, Selenia continues to ramble. "Anyways, the admiral has stolen ATS equipment. What his game plan is has yet to be determined."

Looking at St. Clair and Nomi she continues, "The agent is an intelligent up-and-comer who is partnered with Agent Carol."

Raising his hand, St. Clair stops her from rambling. "Was partnered. Nika is dead." Everyone watches Selenia's expression drop.

"You weren't told?" St. Clair notes the shocked look on both of the new agents. "Yeah, that's a game changer."

James Monroe Building, Richmond, VA

July 21, 0908 hours

Inside her office, Director Carol leans back in her chair with a remote in hand staring at the television. On the monitor is a paused image of Agent Abergathy as she is removing the camera from the police car. The director sets the remote down, and her assistant walks in the room.

"Ma'am, I have a message from Director Harris." She hands her the note then attempts to quickly leave.

With a rare, soft tone, the director never takes her eyes off of the television and says, "Sheryl, you don't have any kids, do you?"

Turning back, bewildered, she says, "No, ma'am, we are trying though."

"You should, they will bring you the most joy you will ever experience." Looking down at the remote, she absently slides it around. "You should have at least two."

"Ma'am, if I may ask. How many children do you have?"

Straightening up, Director Carol looks at the young assistant then back at the screen. "Just the one." Standing, she gives the remote one last nudge then gives her assistant a warm smile. Taking the note, she gives it a quick read.

CLEAR YOUR CALENDAR
JUST LANDING WILL BE THERE AT 11

"I tell you what, Sheryl," she says without looking up and then checks the back of the note, "go home, take the rest of the day off and go have children."

Turning a few shades of red, the assistant stammers, "Th-thank, thank you, ma'am," and quickly steps out of the office.

Watching the door close, Director Carol smiles then looks back down at the note.

What you are up to, Sydney? Shifting her attention to the monitor, she walks over the paused screenshot. She touches the monitor, tracing the blood on Abergathy's shoulder and cheek.

Director Carol snaps her hand away as if it was burned. She steps back holding up the note from Director Harris and glances back to the screen. "What are you coming here to tell me? And whose blood is that?"

As she drifts in thought, the phone rings. Realizing she had sent Sheryl home for the day, she closes her eyes and takes a deep breath.

Picking up the receiver, she barks, "Director Carol."

"Ummm, ahhh, ummm"

The director recognizes the voice. "Agent Selenia, I've never known you for a loss of words."

"Ma'am, I was just caught off guard. I was not expecting you to answer the phone. Is Sheryl sick?"

"Are you calling me with an update?"

"Yes, Director, we have landed and met with St. Clair and Nomi. We are about to head out to location now. St. Clair is tracking Nika's phone. We will be on location in couple of hours and . . ."

"Call me as soon as you locate my daughter," Director Carol orders.

"Yes, ma'am. Oh, and umm, ma'am, there is something you should know . . ."

Hanging up the phone, the director walks back over to the screen with the remote and begins studying the recording again. Just as she is getting into the recording there is a slight knock at her door and Director Harris timidly peeks in.

The older man puts on a charming smile. "Is the coast clear?"

Shaking her head, she walks over to a small refrigerator and takes out two waters. "Get in here, Sydney. Water?"

He reaches out for a water. "So why are you here?" Director Carol asks abruptly. "And why have you diverted your agents to meet up with mine?"

Taking in a deep breath, Director Harris walks over to the window overlooking Interstate 95.

"You are stalling," she says.

Raising his hands and resting them on the back of his neck, he glimpses over to the monitor. "Vicki, Have a seat."

Anger setting in, Director Carol's posture stiffens up. "What happened?"

"We are not sure as of yet, which is why I diverted the team that you and Charlie sent me to meet with your team."

Trying to contain her emotions, she wrings her hands together, taking a deep breath. "When?"

"Well they were to meet up this morning."

"I asked when. When and now who found her! I warned you against putting agents with operatives!" She tears well up as she weakens in her knees, and she starts to sway. Director Harris makes a quick move to catch her. She throws her fists in his direction.

"This is your fault! I warned you, Sydney. My mother would have never teamed up agents with operatives!"

Deflecting the fists from making full contact, but still allowing the anger to let out, Director Harris notices through the frosted glass walls that people are stopping and then scurrying off.

"We're going to find out what happened, I promise."

The strength is almost completely gone from her legs, and she uses him for support. Director Carol's voice softens. "I knew it! I knew something was wrong. I should have never agreed. My mother would never have allowed this. I have to tell my mother!"

"Victoria, nobody could have foreseen this happening, not even the formidable Director Watkins. It was an atmospheric anomaly that we had localized."

Noticing that she has started to zone him out and has turned her stare to her broken monitor, he slowly backs her up to lean on her desk. As soon as she is steadied on the desk he backs away to look out the window.

"Vicki . . ."

"Leave."

"Vicki . . ."

"Get out! The others will be notified of this."

"Vicki, you know this could not have been foreseen."

"Just leave, please, just leave." Without saying another word, she watches Director Harris come to an understanding and leaves the offices. Just as the door closes a sense of determination washes over her, "My mother would have foreseen."

Concrete Bunker, Dry Creek, LA

July 21, 0946 hours

The air conditioning has started talking its toll as Agent Abergathy keeps cupping and blowing into her hands. Standing off to the side, she watches Garrett type away on the computer and keeps an eye on the monitors. To his left is an ever-present can of Chef Boy R Dee. Looking to her right, she watches Stevens analyzing the thing responsible for killing her partner. Walking over to Stevens she stops a few steps shy and looks around, not seeing Admiral Kay.

Shrugging her shoulders, she continues to walk to Stevens's side. "So, what's the story with Silver Surfer here?"

She and Stevens turn in the direction of Garrett as he is clapping. "Two points for the newcomer. I have been sitting here trying to think of what to call him, but all I could think of was Captain Atom."

Stevens shakes his head and looks back down to his iPad and continues as if not interrupted. "Kristen, this is unbelievable. I have cross referenced the makeup of his skin and the readings I got from the ship the other day; I don't even trust what I am seeing."

Still hearing Garrett mumbling something about Silver Surfer, he looks up at Abergathy then nods over to his friend, trying to keep his voice down.

"Don't encourage the muscle-bound monkey. We are trying to get him away from the graphic novel universe."

Without looking away from the control monitors, Garrett says, "I heard that."

"You guys are unbelievable. Here let me take a look." She reaches up for the electronic pad. "I need to feel useful."

"How familiar are you with atomic structure?" Stevens asks.

"Just give me the pad there Cyclops." They both hear Garrett muffle a laugh as they turn to see him still at work on the computer. Abergathy looks back up at Stevens. "Please."

"Alright young lady, show me what you know." Stevens hands her the iPad.

From out of nowhere, Admiral Kay yells out, "Harvey! Can you come here?"

"Just . . . one . . . sec!" Garrett picks up speed typing away.

Stevens and Abergathy watch the muscular doctor nearly stumble out of his seat trying to hurry.

Holding the iPad, Abergathy looks back at Stevens. "Why do you guys follow him? I mean I get some of it. He appears to be an honorable man, driven and focused. But you two never question his motives."

"Well, last year he saved Harvey's life, and his life's work," Stevens nonchalantly tells her.

"Earlier this year, I met with both of them, and

they showed me that I too was in danger. And that dangerous people were watching my work. Harvey told me what happened at his Oklahoma lab. And we have been together since."

"How did you guys end up here?" Abergathy asks.

Stevens points to the motionless man in front of them. "Well, that is because of this guy and that ship of his leaving magnetic-gravitational waves across the atmosphere. I started tracking them late last year, and that is what brought us here."

Garret makes considerable fumbling sounds as he knocks over some cans, hurrying to meet with the admiral. Abergathy turns her attention back to Stevens.

"So, you are here because he trusts you and is willing to follow your lead."

"Well, nobody here is really the one in charge. We work together." Pointing to the tablet, he says, "Now Kristen, let's see what you know." Folding his arms, he says, "What can you tell me about this man?"

Moving things around on the tablet, she is astonished. "You got all this information from your headgear. That is, like, wow." Making a few more swipes on the tablet, she absently starts to take a few steps; not realizing the tablet is connected to the headgear. It catches and Stevens is jerked down, and he catches his balance by grabbing on her shoulders.

Covering her mouth, she freezes. "I'm so sorry. I didn't realize this was attached."

Stevens reaches up and detaches the tablet. "No problem, it was my fault. There you go."

Watching him straighten up, Abergathy shakes her head. "Okay, first of all, this is a lot of information." She immediately takes a few steps backwards. "This guy's radioactive!"

"He's not though. I would have detected that."

"I am seeing uranium, more precisely diuranium octoxide. That is a natural form of uranium, but I am also seeing thorium nitrate. These two together must be working to create a clean-power reactor, but what is it powering?"

Stopping she looks up and leans towards the mysterious man. "This is incredible. How is this possible? This man has no other vitals."

"Okay, those elements I saw. But what I do not believe is an atomic structure there that should not be there, especially in this quantity. And as for his vitals, I think they're being blocked."

"You are talking about Element 1-1-5." Abergathy begins to slowly walk around the clothed man. She starts to wave a free hand in the air.

"I can't remember what it's called. It just became accepted to the periodic table." Getting a closer look at the mysterious man, she asks, "Are we sure this is not an alternate sentient life form?"

"No, it is not an alternate sentient life form. Although, I like the way you worded that, so much better than alien. Anyways, Harvey found out who he was yesterday."

Taking a moment to remove his headgear, Stevens takes two long strides to the other side of the man. "I would like to introduce you to Professor Eprem Mildiani. Professor, this in Kristen Abergathy, and, as you can see, both attractive and brilliant."

Smiling and shaking her head, she says, "So who is Professor Mill-Dee-Yani?"

"Professor Mildiani. It was his work on atomic structure understanding that inspired me to study in the field." Stevens raises his hand in theatrical fashion.

"Did he look like this when he was inspiring you?" Abergathy asks.

Dropping his hand, Stevens gives her a deadpanned look. "No . . . smart alec. He did not, which is why I need to know how this happened."

* * *

Inside another room of the bunker, Garrett and the admiral stand in awe over the vastness of the room. Garret notices the large computer console and what appears to be an oversized boat docking pad.

"So, this is where he stores that ship when he is not traipsing around the globe."

"Well it is one of the places," the admiral notes without much excitement.

"What do you mean one of the places?" Garrett turns and asks.

The admiral smiles, "Think about it," motioning to the other room. "He is here and where is the ship?"

Garrett looks at the door then up at the giant hatch of a ceiling. "That is a good point."

"You mentioned earlier about him traipsing around the globe, but what did you mean by that?"

"Well I figured since we are dealing with Project Cadmus or rather an unknown, highly organized, highly funded organization that I would check with MUFON to see if they had anything."

Garrett taps his fingers together trying to keep his enthusiasm in check.

The admiral holds his hand out, motioning for him to slow down. "Slow it down. First, who or what is MUFON?"

"Mutual UFO Network, an organization that has been tracking and researching anything and everything that has to do with aliens since Roswell—" Seeing that the Admiral was about to object, he says, "Or anything perceived to have to do with aliens."

"And these people are not a government agency?" the admiral says, rubbing the back of his neck and pacing. "Interesting. Okay, so he was traipsing."

"Of course, it is not conclusive evidence. However, there's photo evidence of it, or something that looks like it." Recognizing the admiral is getting impatient, Garrett focuses his attention to him.

"Alright, he was spotted in Owings Mills, Maryland back in August, Colorado Springs in October, Torrance California in November, and

LA Center in Washington in December. Those are the ones I can almost confirm. This guy is creating quite a stir with the UFO conspiracists and hunters. There was even one spotting on a highway in Colorado in December where it could only be seen on the camera after a shot was taken. And the other locations, one minute it was there then it was gone."

Uneasy and unsure of the new information, the admiral turns to the exit. "Well let's go back in and see if Lincoln and Kristen have made any headway with the professor. I just thought you would appreciate this area that is actually under the barn."

The excitement returns in Garrett's eyes. "This does add to the cool factor. I mean, I love this Bat Cave. If I even had some of this stuff, I wouldn't have been caught."

The admiral chuckles. "Let's go and see what they've found out."

Interstate 165, LA

July 21, 1006 hours

The Ford F250 cruises down Interstate-165. St. Clair notices that Selenia, who's in the passenger seat, keeps looking out her rear side mirror, appearing nervous. St. Clair puts a hand on her shoulder, causing her to jump.

"Relax, what you worried about?"

"Nothing." Selenia lowers the visor to check her makeup. Then she scurries to open her purse and takes out a large compact. Curling towards the truck door, she massages one of her eyes while looking into the small mirror.

St. Clair shakes his head trying to make conversation. "I didn't know you wore contacts. Now that I mention that, I don't really know too much about you."

A smile forms across Selenia's face as she turns to look at him. "You're kidding me, right? Little John, I remember you learning every inch of me."

He tries to hide some embarrassment. "That's not what I mean."

Smiling and looking back into the compact, Selenia says, "Believe me, you would not believe me."

"C'mon girl, give it a shot."

She looks up at St. Clair and says, "How about the fact that I was found on the door steps of St. Andrew's Church in Birmingham, England on a full moon?"

Slowing down, St. Clair pulls off the side of the road. As it rolls to a stop, he turns a look at her. "Well that is mysterious. If you had no parents, how did you get your name?"

Selenia looks around, and not seeing anything on the road she looks at St. Clair with nervous curiosity. "Why are we pulling over?"

"You seem nervous, so we're waiting for Nomi and Grunt. No worries though, Flea'll play nice. I would like to hear about the rest of you while we wait for them to catch up."

"Okay, sounds fair. Wait, why do you call her Flea?"

St. Clair lets out a laugh. "Her size for starters and the fact she can move in quick burst with amazing speed . . . Now you are changing the subject."

Giving an exaggerated wave of her hand, Selenia sighs. "What would you like to know?"

"Well for starters, if you did not have parents, where did you get your name? Eleadora Selenia is a very beautiful, yet unique, name."

Selenia shows a hint of blushing as she watches the sincerity of St. Clair. "The name is Greek and means gift of the sun in the moonlight. I figure since it was a Greek community that found me, what else would you name a baby with alabaster skin and fiery red hair that you find on your doorstep on a full moon?"

Watching Selenia caress her arm as if in a soap commercial, a movement in the passenger side rearview mirror catches St. Clair's eye. "If I didn't know better I believe we have been spotted."

Before he can shift into gear a 2015 Black Lexus GS barely slows down as it passes them. St. Clair catches eye contact with Grunt, and he is immediately filled with a sense of elation as he watches them speed pass.

Inside the Black Lexus, Nomi is driving as if she can feel the wind in her hair. Pulling alongside the Ford F250, sitting off the side of the road, she smiles and slows down a little to get confirmation. Grunt looks out the passenger window making eye contact with St. Clair. As he turns to look ahead Nomi picks up speed again.

"I knew you were English, that accent of yours was always exciting. When did you come to the States?"

"I'm not sure when. I was brought to the States when I was young." She nudges St. Clair "Well what you waiting for?"

"You are absolutely right, let's get going." Grinning, he shifts in gear and steps on the gas, spinning the rear tires as the truck peels out to catch the Lexus.

Selenia screams out. "Whoaaaa! I want to get there in one piece!"

"Relax, Chatter. We are just going to get back ahead of them before they get lost and end up in New Orleans."

Reaching in the center console, St. Clair pulls out an iPad and hands it to her.

"There's an icon labeled Fox and Hound. That's Nika's phone and where we need to be."

She brings up the program, and after a few moments she confides with St. Clair in a dreamy far off voice. "You know I have been clean for four years now; ever since they partnered me up with Grunt. My thoughts have been clear, and I have not even felt any sense of withdrawals."

"I know when we parted ways you was in a bad spot. You know I didn't have a choice."

Gently putting a hand on his hand, she says, "I know, big guy. I know you had to leave." Taking a second to look at him, she continues, "The whole time we knew each other you have never asked about my past before. Why didn't you, and why the sudden curiosity?"

Feeling her gaze, St. Clair gives her a quick acknowledgement glance. "I always figured that your past is your past, and you would tell me when you was ready. But you never said a word, so I thought I'd ask."

"Fair enough," she says as she gives him a subtle shrug then turns her attention back out the window. Her thoughts ramble, causing her to rub a temple and close her eyes. She thinks of the first day she was introduced to Grunt.

"Grunt is a good man, and I know, somehow, that he knows what he does for me. Just sometimes I sense that it is his job to keep my head clear and calm."

Setting the iPad on her lap she looks out the scenery fly past.

Seeing the Lexus as they approach the town of Oberlin, he smiles as he notices they are stopped at a light just passed the twenty-six turn off. Taking the turn, while keeping an eye on the Lexus, he sees them hit the gas and whip into a U-turn. Trying not to laugh, he shifts gear and steps on the gas again. He settles in on the smaller road when the iPad chirps up, letting them know they are closing in on the location. Reaching out he takes Selenia's wrist and softly kisses her hand.

"You good now, we can let the past be the past."

Softly smiling, "You're right, I know. It is just without the medication or Grunt by my side my brain goes into overload, and my emotions go into overdrive."

St. Clair lets out a quick burst of laughter. "Oh yeah, I remember those nights. You knocked a coil loose one time with that vase."

"Yeah, that night is a little fuzzy, even for me." Selenia smiles as the iPad chirps again. "Saved by the chirp, looks like we turn up ahead on the right." As they slow to make the turn off, she sees the Lexus pull up behind them. "And it looks like the gangs all here."

Taking the turn, a dirt cloud immediately fills the air and crows take flight in front of the truck. St. Clair grips and re-grips the wheel. "Whoa, what kind of alternate universe are we heading in? This is something out of an Alfred Hitchcock novel."

* * *

Inside the Lexus Nomi looks shocked as they watch the truck slow then pick up speed, sending dirt and rocks towards her car. “This had better not be payback. That is all I am going to say.”

Bringing the car to a stop to wait for the cloud to settle, she looks over at Grunt. “So handsome, what brings you here? And what can you tell me about that dish you’re with?”

1982

Cannock Chase Forest, Staffordshire, UK

July 16, 1950 hours

It's a cool evening and a full moon is lighting up the forest as Deborah Hinkley is hurrying through the woods. Carrying a bag, she sees her friends off in the distance. Before she can raise a hand and whisper out, a long-eared owl hoots, stopping her dead in her tracks to look around for the owl. Losing a sense of time, she watches the trees for movement or a repeat of the owl.

A light tapping on her shoulder causes Deborah to jump out of her skin and take a sharp intake of air.

"AYY! Bloody hell! You two nearly frightened me out of my britches."

Maddison Wilkshire, the shorter of the two friends, tries to control her laughter and puts her hands on her hips. "So that's what it takes to get you out of those."

"Very funny, Maddi. You should know better than to sneak up on someone, and Meradeth you are not much better egging her on."

Meradeth waves her off, pointing to the bag Deborah is carrying.

"Oh, relax, Debs. Did you bring it?"

Smiling, Deborah steps back and holds up the bag.

With one hand holding the top of the bottle and the other ripping the bag away, revealing a new bottle of English Harbour Rum.

Meradeth puts her arm around Maddi. "We are so out on the piss tonight!"

With a shocked expression, Deb pulls the bottle in close. "Meradeth!"

With that the three look back and forth at each other and hold their breath before busting out laughing, as they take off deeper in the woods laughing.

At a small clearing of trees, they gather to catch their breath. Grasping the top of the bottle, Deborah attempts to open it, the bottle slipping through her grip. Meradeth walks over and reaches for the bottle from her red-faced friend.

"Let me have it, you already look buggered. Are you sure you have not, what do the American's call it, pre-gamed?"

Maddison is wide-eyed and holding her mouth giggling. Deborah does her best to show a shocked expression as she hands over the bottle to her friend. The shocked expression causes Maddi to snort trying not to laugh out loud, making everyone laugh. Holding the bottle, Meradeth manages to remove her shirt, wrapping the bottle in it and using it to help with the grip. Hearing the snap of the seal and the paper surrounding the bottle top, she looks up at her friends to see them gawking at her breasts.

With a genuine expression of shock, Deborah raises a hand to her lips. "Girl you are crackin'."

Maddi looks down at her much smaller attributes cupping them with her hands. "Don't look ladies, it'll be alright."

The three look at each other again and start laughing. After a quick moment they look at each with a somber understanding. Meradeth lifts the bottle to toast, and says, "To the next stage of our lives," and takes a drink of the rum.

"Absolutely!"

"Charge on!"

Handing the bottle to Deborah, she says, "Your turn."

Taking it, she lifts it and looks at her friends. "May we excel at our Uni's and take over the world!" she says and takes a drink of the rum.

"Right oh!"

"Cheers!"

Passing the bottle to Maddison, she says, "You're up."

She takes the bottle as a sense of seriousness takes over. "Ladies, I don't want to do this."

"What are you talking about? We sneak off for a pint from time to time." Deborah looks to her friend.

"It's not the rum," Maddi tells them. "I know we are eighteen now, and in a month or two we are all heading off to our respective universities, but I don't want to split up. I want this night to never end."

"Blimey me." Slapping her forehead, Meradeth shakes her head. "Don't be such a wanker. Why do you have to get all mushy?" Reaching for the rum, she says, "Here, give me the bottle."

Maddi turns her body to shield the bottle. "Hey, it had to be said." With that she holds the rum up and with a mischievous grin she says, "To the bottom of the bottle!" and takes a huge drink.

"That's what I am talking about!"

"You go girl!"

"Help me!"

Meradeth reaches over, and takes the bottle, causing some of it to spill out on the ground. "Don't be greedy," she says and steps back and takes a drink.

Deborah watches her topless friend take a long drink. "You really are a dish."

Bringing the bottle down, Meradeth wipes her mouth with her forearm. "Debs, you are going to make me blush."

Turning visible shades of red, Deborah reaches for the rum. "Don't be cheeky, and just give me the bottle." As they all start laughing.

Maddison walks up next to Deborah while she is taking a drink. "Does this mean we are all going to start snogging now? If so, I think two of us are overdressed."

Quickly bending over, trying to keep the rum in her mouth and not drop the bottle, Maddison snatches the rum away. "Easy peasy."

They all begin to laugh again.

"Help me!"

Meradeth walks up to Maddison and reaches down to grab her hip, pulling them close together.

"Why, Maddi, I never knew. Perhaps it's the rum on a full moon, but I like where your mind's at."

Reaching the bottle around and embracing her friend and allowing her to be pulled closer, Maddison looks up and seductively smiles.

Deborah drops her smile and looks into the forest. "Did you gals hear that?"

Without turning to their friend, Meradeth keeps her attention on Maddison. "Debs, you are ruining the moment."

"Shush! And listen!"

"Help me!"

Goose bumps immediately form on all three ladies. As everyone separates from each other, taking steps back, Maddison tries not to move as she looks around. "Please tell me that was one of your long-eared owls."

"Help me!"

All three snap in the direction of the plea. Deborah steps, crossing between her friends towards the quiet voice. Kneeling, she squints to try and minimize the moon reflections off of the trees when she sees a young figure standing in the distance. "I don't believe it. It is a young girl."

"I can't believe it." Maddison gasps

Meredith scoffs, “What’s a girl doing in the woods at night?”

Taking off in a run, Deborah heads towards the girl, as she appears to be running away from them. Just before she reaches her, she trips on a root and stumbles out on to a dirt path. Looking up she sees the young girl who is standing just on the other side of the path. She turns and looks directly at Deborah, causing her to shuffle back on her butt away from her.

The young girl’s eyes are completely black with no trace of white as she leans towards Deborah.

“Help me!”

The girl turns and runs into the forest. Deborah is unable to move as she watches the young girl effortlessly maneuver through the forest.

Her friends catch up to her while she is staring off into the trees. Breathing heavy, Maddison drops next to her friend and places her hand on her shoulder. “What the bloody hell was that?”

St Andrew's Church,
Birmingham, UK

July 30, 0738 hours

An elder gentleman tends to the prayer candles inside an old cathedral. The light of the morning sun beams through the stain glass windows, decorating the large wooden crucifix with brilliant shades of red, blue, and green light. Behind him is a young couple sitting in one of the pews. A woman is trying to hold back tears while her husband is consoling her and providing support. Stepping back from the candles the gentleman clasps his hands, looks up at the crucifix, takes a deep breath, and closes his eyes. After a few moments of listening to the consoling, the older man turns and patiently exits the main hall.

He stands, taking another deep breath, and waits for his eyes to adjust to the bright lights. Hearing muffled, familiar voices, he smiles and heads towards the murmured conversations. Stopping in front of a large window, he looks in to see Sister Katheryn teaching a small group of kids. In a corner of the room is a young girl with dark-auburn locks of hair wearing a ball cap and blackened swimming goggles.

Sister Elli appears next to him. "Monsignor, she really is a gift from the heavens."

In a solemn tone, Monsignor continues to watch the young girl, and says, "You are correct. We truly have been blessed, however, we have reached our capacity to raise her."

Wringing her hands, Sister Elli catches her reflection on the glass. Noticing the wrinkles around her eyes as her reflection seems to surround the young girl. She reaches up to touch the glass and caresses her reflection and the young girl.

"We cannot keep her hidden much longer. We found her outside again last night. She needs to grow, but I cannot see our lives without her."

"You are correct once again. And I am saddened to that realization as well." Closing his eyes he takes a deep breath as he turns towards Sister Elli. "I have made arrangements." Turning back to watch the young girl, he says, "They should be here momentarily."

They are interrupted as a young man is hurrying towards them. With a concern in his voice he says, "Sir, there are some people here to meet with you."

Reaching out, he places a hand on the shoulder of the younger man. "Peter, it is okay. Can you please escort them to my office? I will be there shortly."

"Yes sir, I can do that." Giving the Monsignor a quick nod, he turns and as quickly as he arrived, he departs.

The Monsignor shifts towards Sister Elli. "It is enthusiasm like that that gives me great hope of our future."

"Yes, Monsignor." The sister agrees and gives him a slight understanding smile.

"Can you please work with Sister Katheryn, and take our young Eleadora into the viewing classroom, while I tend to our guests."

"Yes, Monsignor."

Closing his hands together, the Monsignor turns and heads towards his office. Keeping his ears tuned to the conversations in the classroom, he sends up a prayer, "Lord, forgive us for our weaknesses and grant us the strength to recognize them."

Taking a turn down the hallway towards his office, his stomach tenses up, stopping him in his steps. Wringing his hands, he lifts his chin and makes it to his door. Opening it, he sees two women and a man, all dressed in impeccable suits.

"Good morning," he says as he walks around to his desk, feeling their eyes watching his every move.

One of the women reaches out her hand and says, "Good morning, Father Panagos. My name is Angela Watkins."

"It is Monsignor, and you are very prompt with your arrival."

With a slow, humble nod, Angela withdraws her hand. "Please accept my apologies, Monsignor. After I was informed, I knew we could not waste any time for the girl's sake." She gestures to the younger woman. "This is my daughter, Victoria."

And with a quick motion to the young man she says, "And this is Charles. They will see to her upbringing."

Sitting in his chair, Monsignor looks studies Angela and waits a few moments to let her words sink in.

After watching her and her counterparts check their watches and look around he stands back up.

"I have had the sisters bring her into an observation classroom. Perhaps I can provide you with some insight on God's child."

Offering a warm smile, Angela glances at the two standing with her. "That is an excellent idea." Waving a hand toward the door, she says, "We will follow your lead, Monsignor."

Making their way to the observation room the Monsignor stops with his hand on the door. "I must warn you, she is truly a special child." Opening the door, he escorts them into a small room. On one side of the room is large window, on the other side of the window they watch a small child sitting at a table with Sister Katheryn.

Putting his hands behind him, he faces to the window and watches the young girl. "We have raised her ever since she was gifted to us at our doorstep seven years ago."

Victoria gasps. "She's a foundling? Wow, why would anyone want to abandon such a beautiful child."

Charles steps up closer to the window. "Why is she wearing those goggles? Is she blind?"

"We will come to that in a moment. Right now, I would like to show you the capacity of her intelligence."

Lightly tapping the glass, the sister turns and gives a quick nod. The three agents look at the Monsignor with concerned interest.

Inside the room the young girl is handed a jigsaw puzzle box. They watch her look at the photo for only a moment, then open the box and the dump all the pieces on the table. Without any hesitation, the puzzle starts forming the picture as easy as turning over the pieces, never once going back to the photo.

Victoria drops her jaw in amazement. "That is incredible. Can she do that every time?"

"Yes, however, her knowledge is solely based on visual. If we were to give her a similar size puzzle and not allow her to see the photo, it would take just as long as it would you or I to put it together. She remembers everything she sees or hears; however, she lacks deductive reasoning."

Charles rubs his chin with equal astonishment. "So, she is not blind, Then why the blackened goggles?"

"Well here is why we have reached our limitations to raise Eleadora. She is a very special child and needs more than we can give her."

Reaching up he taps the window three times. Inside the room, Sister Katheryn motions to the young girl. The girl finishes up the puzzle, reaches up, and removes the glasses.

Putting his hands together, the Monsignor looks at the young agent. "You see, my son, those glasses are not really blackened."

Eleadora looks up at what she believes to be a mirror as younger agents take an immediate step back to avoid being seen. Angela and the Monsignor stand fast.

The young girl's eyes stare at them as if she can see through the mirror; her eyes are completely void of any white.

2015

Concrete Bunker, Dry Creek, LA

July 21, 1128 hours

Stepping back into the lab center, Garrett waits for Admiral Kay to close up the hidden access door.

"You know, Admiral, since we are sharing information that the other might find interesting, there is a something I found out last night and just didn't know how to tell you."

"What is it, Harvey?"

"How long did you say you were in the navy?"

Giving him a stern look, the admiral stops and pauses for a moment. "You never asked. I was in the navy for twenty-four years. Why? What did you find?"

Garrett motions like he is putting pieces together. "When we met at my lab site in Oklahoma, there was absolutely zero doubt you were military."

"Can you please stay focused and get to the point," the admiral says. "What do you mean, was no doubt? The uniform didn't give it away?"

"Yeah, well, I went and looked up your record and found no trace of a Julian Kay, officer or enlisted, in any branch of the military."

Waiting for a reaction, Garrett gets puzzled as the Admiral gives him a shrug and turns to walk away.

"I don't get it. Your life was just erased, and you are not the least bit upset or surprised," Garrett says.

"I knew it would be a matter of time before your Men in Black would do that. And two things. One, they did not erase my life, only my history. And two, if they could go into military files and erase my history, just think how easily they could erase yours."

Garrett frantically rushes over to the computer and all the monitors and says, "How would they know about me? Why would they erase my life, or history?"

Stopping, the admiral turns and takes a step towards his friend. "Think about it. My last known whereabouts was driving off in a stolen van with a quirky, muscular lab geek trying to escape capture and an earthquake. If it was the Men in Black that was pulling the strings that day, then it remains safe to say that you have been erased as well."

Turning away, the admiral heads over to Stevens, the professor, and the agent.

Garrett stops to watch him walk away smiling. "Whoa, I never thought about that."

"Sometimes, when you put two and two together, you get twenty-two," the admiral states raising two fingers in the air.

Smiling, but shaken, Garrett stands there watching the admiral and thinking, Sometimes the answer is the bigger, simpler picture. He eyes the computer station then makes a motivated move to find out if the admiral is correct.

Walking over to Stevens and Abergathy, the admiral looks over at the professor.

"How are his vitals?" he asks Stevens. "I would think he would have thawed out by now."

Stevens looks up from the electronic pad. "We're unable to read any type of vitals, however, we're presuming everything is functioning normally, with the exception of not being able to move."

"Have you two been able to diagnose his skin, and why does it look so much like that ship we saw the other day?"

"I did not get a full analysis of it the other day," Stevens says. "However, from what we have discovered here is that they are molecularly similar. I would like to know how this happened."

The admiral and Stevens stare in silence at the professor when Abergathy exclaims "Ingenious!" They look down in her direction with confused expressions. "Thorium nitrate is a soluble powder. It has to be saturated for its reaction property to work." Her excitement is starting to show, she makes her way around the professor without taking her eyes off of him. "And H2O poses all kinds of variables."

Stevens is starting to catch on to the giddiness of the small agent. "Right, distilled water is, well, pure H2O. However, it does not have the connectivity that salt water has."

Abergathy points her hand at Stevens. "Yes, however, salt water will create a calcified residue waste."

"Exactly!" Standing upright Stevens looks at the computer pad. "So, what has the electrical properties of salt water without the waste product?"

Hurrying over to his side, Abergathy reaches over and manipulates the iPad screen.

"Blood plasma."

Waiting for it to sink in she looks up at the admiral, only to see him waiting for them to finish. Abergathy continues. "The electrolytes found in blood plasma could be a cleaner alternative to salinity."

Turning her attention to the professor, she says, "I would wager that he used his own plasma, which still had some of his DNA, and somehow his project became him, or is it the other way around?"

The lights in the bunker dim and then brighten as Abergathy looks up. Stevens and Admiral Kay look over to the monitors where Garrett is leaning back, watching the screens.

The admiral lightly shakes his head. "Well, let's go see who it is today."

The two men make their way over to their friend, and as they look at the monitors, they see a huge man get out of the truck that has pulled up, and out of the passenger side an attractive redhead gets out, looking down at a tablet.

The redhead points over to the house, and the giant walks next to her as he looks over at the screen. Before they move they turn back as another car pulls up. Out of the fancier car a petite woman and a short, stocky man get out and walk over to the other two.

The admiral straightens up and rubs his chin. “Clearly, they are not police. They do move as if they have had training, but I am not seeing military here.” He places a hand on the shoulder of Garrett. “Any ideas, big guy?”

“Yeah, I have an idea, I don’t want to mess with that giant.” They all chuckle, as Abergathy joins them.

Watching the screens, she sees the shorter man making his way from under the porch holding a phone. Her eyes widen, and she takes a small step beck. Watching the three men in front of her, she absently reaches into her pocket and locates the police camera. Struggling to find her voice, “Ah, umm, guys.” When she gets no response, she coughs and clears her throat. “Admiral, I think they are here for me.” All three turn and look at her as she is holding a police dash camera. “You see your Marvelesque performance the other day, well, it was recorded.”

“You knew we were recorded and you did not tell us?” Stevens chides. “Why would you hold that information from us?” turning to leave when the admiral reaches his hand out to stop him from walking away.

The admiral then turns looking at the agent. “You mentioned they are here for you, why?”

“That phone they found under the porch. It belonged to my partner.” she says, pointing back to the professor without looking, “That he killed. So, they are here.” She turns to look at the professor,

"Because he is the one that . . ." She doesn't see the professor where he had been standing, "Where'd he go?"

Garrett whips back to the monitors. "Oh boy, he is going to pull a turkey on them!"

The admiral turns to the lanky doctor.

"How did he leave? Lincoln, I thought you were monitoring him? Harvey, watch for him."

"You got it boss! This is going to be good!"

"Lincoln, see if you and the agent here can find out where he left. We would have heard him leave if he left the same way we came in."

Giving a quick nod, Stevens steps forward and next to Abergathy. Leaning in and whispering in her ear, "Why would you withhold that information from us? From me?" Before she could say something, he walks off to look for that alternate exit.

Back at the monitors, the giant and the redhead walk into the house as the other two are making their way to where the police car was crushed.

Without taking his eyes of the screens, Garrett leans back and asks, "Do you think this group will find anything? We only found an entrance because of Lincoln's project equipment."

Mesmerized at the agents on the screen are moving. "I'm not sure. There is something about this group. I can't put my finger on it." the admiral states.

Garrett folds his arms across his chest and leans back in the chair.

"Well perhaps Kristen can help us out with figuring that puzzle out."

"Lincoln! Agent Abergathy! Need you back here!" the admiral calls out.

Stevens walks up behind the admiral. "I'm right here, you don't have to yell."

Turning, the admiral looks past and around him for the agent. "Where's Agent Abergathy?"

Stevens points to behind Garrett. "I left her here; I can scan the area better alone."

Garrett holds out his hand and counts on his finger. "Okay you lost the professor, and now you lost Mary Ann? Did they go on a three-hour cruise?"

The admiral puts his arms out as they hear a hatch clank. He looks at the other two with instant terror. "Tell me she did not just go out there."

Deserted Farm, Dry Creek, LA

July 21, 2015
1208 hours

Walking out of the house, St. Clair examines the damaged wall again. Through one of the holes he sees Selenia on her phone. He watches her for a moment; unable to make out what she is saying or whom she is talking to. Hearing footsteps, he looks over to the barn. Agents Nomi and Grunt are making their way to the front of the house.

St. Clair turns and almost leans on the broken railing. "This house is shoddy, and there's nothing here. You two find anything?"

"Something destroyed the back end of the roof. The breaks in the wood are still fresh. Other than that, there's not a trace of anyone or anything."

Walking off the porch, the three gather in front. St. Clair takes a few steps, crosses his arms, and turns around looking at the house.

"The admiral and his friend came out of the house. Question is what were they doing here? And why were they in the house?" St. Clair absently thinks out loud.

The two agents cross their arms in imitation of St. Clair and face the house.

"Both of you are jokers. C'mon I know you two found something."

St. Clair shakes his head at them.

Agent Nomi and Grunt glance at each other before Nomi shrugs and steps up, keeping her voice low as not to be over heard. “We both felt it. We’re being watched. However, we cannot find anyone or any equipment.”

Suddenly they all turn to see Selenia ranting as she exits the farmhouse.

“I don’t get it.” She says, waving her arms as she storms out of the house. She motions to the cornfield and to the barn. “They send us out here and what did they expect us to find?” Her frustration shows and she looks off the porch towards Agents Nomi and Grunt. “Did you two find anything, anywhere that can help us?”

The three look at each other then back at the ranting agent on the porch. St. Clair straightens up. “No, Chatter, not a ting, nothing.” The other two agents look at each other with a glimmer of confusion.

Selenia makes her way meeting up with everyone when St. Clair starts to flicker, phasing in and out revealing glimpses of his internal coils and wiring connections. Grunt takes a step back with his jaw dropped, staring at the giant agent.

All four turn as they hear someone approaching. They turn to face a man wearing mismatched clothing covering his entire body. A low, quiet voice reverberates, “Get off my land!”

Everyone looks around, as the voice seems to come from everywhere.

An unseen wave of pressure nudges the agents backwards. The wave continues to affect St. Clair as he struggles to control his coils.

Selenia rushes over to him. “You need to get out of here, like now! We can meet up later, now go!” St. Clair nods as a green hue surrounds him and he vanishes.

Standing firm against the unseen pressure, Selenia yells to the clothed man. “Under the National Security Act, you need to come with us!” The pressure dissipates as the man goes to motion his arm.

Grunt rolls his eyes at his partner then abruptly steps away from Nomi, his attention is drawn to her lower back.

Every nerve in Nomi’s skin feels like they are on fire. “He’s the one who killed your friend!”

She bends her knees and puts one hand on the ground. “You are absolutely correct!”

“Government! Get off my land!” the professor repeats as he swings his arm. An intense gravitational pulse sends Nomi and Selenia backwards and to the ground, unable to move. Grunt was able to withstand the gravitational pressure with some struggles.

Fighting the pressure, he takes a few steps towards the professor.

Abergathy runs out of the house yelling. “Professor! Stop! Don’t do this!” Everyone’s attention turns towards her.

Using the distraction Grunt squints and tilts his head at Abergathy and the professor. The anxiety and stress can be physically seen leaving Abergathy, and both of their postures relax as they slowly drop to their knees and fall back to a sitting position.

The gravitational pressure lifts, as Nomi looks up to see Grunt walk over to the professor. She then notices the young agent sitting on the porch looking like there's not a care in the world. "Grab her and we can get answers. She was there when your friend was killed."

Fighting off the muscle soreness, Nomi springs to grab Abergathy only to hit another unseen barrier. Crashing into it with her full force, she comes to an abrupt stop, causing Nomi to step backwards, lose her footing, and drop to a knee.

The inner voice struggles in a weak whisper, "Okay, I felt that one," as Nomi passes out.

The professor is lying on the ground, and Grunt is standing over him but looking at Nomi. Selenia takes off towards Nomi, but before she reaches her an intense gravity pulse comes sweeping from above, sending both tumbling into the cornfields.

Grunt struggles against the gravitational waves when he looks up to see a large tear-drop ship with a hull that appears to be swirling.

"Awe, shet." Grunt relaxes his body and is swept into the fields after Selenia and Nomi.

Moments later, the admiral, Garrett, and Stevens come running outside looking around, only to find nobody in sight.

They study the area as they make their way to look into the vehicles, dumbfounded. A murder of crows caw as they cut through the dense, humid air.

Garrett throws his arms up to defend himself. "I hate this place."

Looking into the cornfields, he notes the broken stalks, Admiral Kay pinches the bridge of his nose. "We need to get out of here."

Dixie Dandy Shopping Center, Oakdale, LA

July 21, 1216 hours

A green hue develops behind the dumpster of the USA Nails as Agent St. Clair appears crouched down. As the hue fades he stands up and looks around. Taking a moment, he observes the parking lot and the people going about their business.

Realizing that he had gone unnoticed, he steps from around the corner of the building. Seeing the Popeye's, his stomach reminds him he needs to eat. Reaching into his pocket he pulls out his phone. Flashes of the strangely dressed man replay in his mind, causing him to wince and shake his head.

Punching his phone screen, he notices a mom pushing a yellow IGA shopping cart, and her kids are all staring at him. Giving them his warmest smile, he hurries towards the Popeye's, listening to his phone.

"Agent St. Clair! How are things going?"

Looking around he walks into the Popeye's. "Director Harris, we have a problem. I'm waiting to hear from Nomi."

"Wait, you are not there with her?"

Realizing that everyone in the restaurant is watching him, he gives a brief smile then walks back outside.

"Yes sir, Chatter, umm Agent Selenia, suggested I leave because something was interfering with the stability of my coils."

After a moment of pause, Director Harris's voice comes across the phone slow and deliberate.

"Do you know what was causing it?"

St. Clair lowers his voice. "I believe it was coming from a man."

"Say that again? Did you say the interference of your coils came from a man?"

"Yes sir."

After another moment's pause, the director says, "Do you believe that this man is the one who is responsible for killing Agent Carol?"

St. Clair looks around the sky. "I'm not even sure it is a man; but, yes sir." Not hearing anything on the phone, he looks down at the phone to see if there is still a connection. "Sir? Are you still there?"

"Yes, St. Clair, I am still here. Director Carol is putting a lot of pressure in finding this man. She is going to be calling in a lot of favors and big guns on this. So, if we do not want to end up on the front page of some newspaper, we need to subdue this guy and bring him in."

"I will head back out there, sir. But I would rather wait to hear from Flea, I mean, Agent Nomi, to see if it is safe for me."

"Agent St. Clair, you need to man up. Look, I am counting on you," Director Harris tells him.

"I know you have your concerns, but right now we need to focus on bringing that man in."

Turning to head back into Popeye's, St. Clair runs into a bearded man wearing sunglasses, knocking him back a few steps. The stranger looks up at the giant agent with his jaw dropped. Tilting his head, the stranger reaches up and pokes St. Clair's chest.

Scratching just under his beard he smiles and firmly pats the arm of the agent, murmuring to himself, "Interesting and impressive," as the stranger turns and heads to his car.

St. Clair looks at the man trying to figure him out and trying not to crack a smile while watching the man get into a beautiful Cadillac Deville. Hitting him, he recognizes the man as the person responsible for the bank fiasco in Texas.

"Sir! Are you still there?" St. Clair pipes into his phone. "Sir, I am currently looking at the individual that committed that bank robbery in Texas you had us look into."

"He is not our priority right now," Director Harris admonishes. "I need you to get back to Agent Nomi, Selenia, and Grunt and bring that guy in. Understood?"

St. Clair closes his eyes, storing the car's make, model, and license plate. "I understand, sir." Hanging up the phone, he puts it back in his pocket. His stomach growls as he steps back away from the restaurant. "Damn." Then after looking around the surrounding parking lot, he jogs back to the trash can area next to the USA Nails store.

10th Street, Oakdale, LA

July 21, 1256 hours

Turning down 6th Ave., a brown Cadillac Deville slows as the driver studies the buildings. Stopping at the light, he sees that the buildings are a mixture of new and old. A police cruiser crosses in front of him heading north on 10th Street. The driver turns and gives him a quick smile and a nod.

Watching him make his way, the Rush Center sign catches his attention. As the light turns green he slowly makes his way through the light when he notices a Cash Loans store on his right.

Looking over the buildings he notices two more loan companies across from each other, with the one on the right being next to a credit company. Just past the credit company a transformer on an electrical pole causes him to smile. Turning into the parking lot next to Allen Credit, he continues to look around. Across the street is an InstaCash, an Express Check Advance, a Tower Loan, and a Southland Finance Company that is promoting loans. He scratches under his beard.

Talking to himself, he smiles and nods, "Well this holds promise."

A thought comes to him as he gets out of the car with briefcase in hand. "I might just be a while today." Looking up, he locates a transformer on one of the power poles. "Let's see if I can take it up a notch."

The stranger makes his way through a break in between the building and a fence. Standing under the transformer adjusting ear pieces, he holds out the briefcase. Opening the side panel and setting it down, he sets the thumb dials to the setting he used at the currency exchange in Baton Rouge. The transformer immediately reacts to the briefcase, and the entire area is filled with a greenish hue.

Smiling and nodding his head he makes his way to the other side of the fence towards the cash stores. A forceful energy wave sends him into a nearby SUV. The air fills with crackling energy as the green hue takes on a blueish tint. Before he can get moving, he hears multiple car crashes followed by explosions and people ducking to avoid debris, not knowing where the explosions are coming from.

He then walks out onto 10th Street, looking in the direction where the energy wave came from, recognizing the two electrical towers near the World Acceptance Center. He takes a moment to rub under his beard. "Well this could be interesting."

Feeling the amplified energy in his skin, he pulls up a jacket sleeve to see the hairs on his arm sticking up, thinking to himself, "I had better make this quick."

* * *

Everywhere in town, people are opening their doors to see the blueish-green hue in the afternoon sky, only to succumb to instant muscle fatigue. At the police station a few buildings away,

Officers Gennings and Lister are in the parking lot, forcing themselves to get to their cars.

Officer Gennings is using the cars to support him when he looks over at Lister. “What the hell is going on?”

Opening the door to his cruiser, Officer Lister’s legs give out and he stumbles, hitting his forehead on the door edge. “Son of a biscuit!” Still holding on the door, he makes his way into his car. Closing the door, and after resting for what seems like an hour, he murmurs, “How am I supposed to know?”

From inside the car, Officer Lister looks around the station lot to see fellow officers knocked out cold and lying on the pavement or on their vehicles. Across the street the fire department’s sirens are going off and a truck has partially pulled onto the street. The driver and the remaining fire fighters are passed out.

With sweat pouring off of him, he goes to lower the window.

The inside of the vehicle immediately fills with the tinted air, and he closes the window as fast as his muscles would let him.

Studying the air, he watches it gradually dissipate, raising his arm as if to try and feel the alien air.

Adjusting his body, every muscle screams at him. Battling through the pain, he lifts the radio handset. “Anyone out there? This is Lister.”

“Hey, Lister, this is Glen. What the hell is this shit?”

Fighting the soreness again, Lister lifts the handset. "That seems to be the question today." Looking around at the post-apocalyptic scene, "Where you are Glen?"

"I was or rather am over at the Angel Academy Daycare checking on my daughter. Next thing I know most of Oakdale is under some kind of polluted dome."

"Are you not affected?"

"I am hearing the explosions and car accidents, but I can't find a way in."

The air inside the vehicle has cleared away and the strength is painfully returning as he adjusts himself again. "What about the hospital?"

"What about it?" Glen shakes his head.

"Inside or outside the atmosphere?"

"Outside, thank God for small favors there."

Officer Lister expressing urgency, "I need you to come here. You will be fine as long as you keep your windows up and air off."

"Are you nuts? It's like a hundred degrees today!"

"Glen! I need your help! Come to the station! Better yet, I will meet you there, and we can figure something out."

Leaning up he puts his keys in the ignition. "Meanwhile, I need you to get a hold of the station in Oberlin."

Turning the key, Lister sees the air spark in slow motion.

The car's engine ignites the air around it, and in an instant the car blows up sending metallic and glass shards blowing out the windows of the station and setting off the nearby car alarms.

* * *

At the Angel Academy Daycare, Glen is standing outside his car holding his handset listening when he hears another explosion.

"Jon? Jon? Are you there? I have already gotten in touch with Oberlin, and they are on their way." His mind plays out an explosion as a realization hits, and he looks down at the handset in shock. Dropping the handset, he runs his hands through his thinning hair.

Mustering determination, he gets in the car and tears off into the alien atmosphere.

Glen weaves in and out of crashes along George B. Mowad Memorial Highway, he turns onto 10th Street to head towards the police station. He sees the smoke rising up from the station, and he goes to step on the gas when he notices a man wearing a business suit, carrying a backpack walking out of the InstaCASH building. Flipping on the sirens, he slows to a crawl as he approaches the stranger. The man calmly stops in the middle of the street and stands there watching him.

They look at each other, neither one wanting to make the first move. Glen looks around at the alien world around him. He reflects on all of the bodies he saw on the way here, when he realizes this man does not seem affected.

Opening the car door, the energy fills the cars, hitting him like a heavy wave. Immediately feeling the ache in his muscles, he emerges from the car and draws his gun. "Don't move!"

The stranger remains motionless, tilting only his head.

Sweat begins to soak Glen, and his arms get heavier by the second, struggling to hold his bravado. "Drop the backpack!"

The stranger bends his knees, setting the backpack on the ground in front of him. Noticing the arms of the officer struggling and tensing up, he raises a hand, palm out, as if to tell the officer to stop, recognizing fear washing over the officer.

The world around seems to be going in slow motion as another explosion rocks the silence. Through the fog in his brain, he can barely hear the stranger yell, "Don't." His hands twitch, and his focus turns to the hammer of his gun. In the corner of his focus he watches the stranger shield himself and drop to the ground. The hammer of the gun reaches cocked position and for a second everything appears to have stopped.

In a split instant the hammer releases causing the air around him to explode.

Deserted Farm, Dry Creek, LA

July 21, 1242 hours

A green hue forms in front of the farmhouse as Agent St. Clair appears. Examining the area around the rundown farmhouse then back at the vehicles, he notices the tire tracks. Both vehicles are evident to have slid or pushed at least a dozen feet.

Rubbing the top of his head, trying to figure out what could have moved the vehicles, he looks up out into the fields and hollers out, "Flea! Chatter! Grunt!"

While he studies the cornstalks for movement, Stevens walks out of the house wearing his gear. Hearing the door close St. Clair snaps in his direction and squints his eyes, trying to figure out what it is he's seeing. "Stop! Who are you?"

Stevens, trying to be quiet, fumbles backwards into what is left of the wall, raising a metallic hand outward. "Wait! You don't understand!"

St. Clair takes a step towards the strange, gangly man. "What don't I understand?"

Raising his other hand, Stevens slowly side steps off the porch. "I don't want any trouble."

Crossing his arms across his chest, St. Clair looks around the farmhouse. "Hey mon, there is trouble all around here, and it looks like you might just be in the middle of it."

St. Clair makes his way towards the house. “And you need to be answering some questions.”

Stevens begins to frantically wave his arms. “Please stop! I don’t want to hurt you.”

St. Clair lets out a laugh and walks towards Stevens. “Like you could hurt me.”

A laser shoots out of Stevens’s visor, narrowly missing the giant agent and burning though the grill of the Ford F250. St. Clair whips around to see the impact of the laser.

Throwing his arms up he runs to his truck to inspect the burn hole. “Not the truck, mon! Dat’s just rude!”

St. Clair turns back to face Stevens when sparks flare up beneath the truck, igniting the fuel, causing it to explode. The explosion sends St. Clair flying forward to the ground, and Stevens turning away shielding himself from the flying shards of glass.

After a few moments to shake the cobwebs, Stevens pushes on the wall to help him stand and regain his footing. Turning, he watches the giant agent stand back up. Waving his hands again, Stevens tries to maneuver to get around to the side of the house. “That was an accident! I didn’t mean to do that.”

Ignoring Stevens, St. Clair kneels watching the burning truck.

Then facing the man waving his arms, anger takes over him, and he slowly stands, brushing himself off. “You are going to answer for tat and anyting else I can think of.”

Before St. Clair can take another step, they look up to see a large, metallic ball falling out of the sky. Garrett crashes down in a three-point stance behind St. Clair, sending him stumbling forward.

Garrett's eyes open wide, and his arms go up in front of him as the giant agent turns around to face him. "Whoa! Easy there big guy! Let's take it easy. After all, nobody's gotten hurt. We can all just walk away. What's your name?"

"My name is Special Agent John St. Clair, and did you tell my friend she could just walk away, before you tore her apart?"

Confused, Garrett stands upright dropping his arms. "What? Who? What are you talking about?"

Stevens, while still making his way to the side of the house, yells out, "Beringei, I think he's talking about Agent Carol, Kristen's friend. You remember, the one that was killed."

Noticing the expression on the giant agent change, Garrett says to Stevens. "Oh shit! Starfish, for a genius, you are a complete idiot!"

St. Clair turns and takes off in a run towards Stevens as Garrett throws his body towards the agent, catching him around the waist.

Before they can crash into the farmhouse, St. Clair phases out of Garrett's hold. St. Clair winces, watching the metallic monkey suit crash into the farmhouse. Before he can regain his composure, a laser shoots though his arm.

Standing strong, Stevens's jaw dropped.

"Wow! I can see your molecular structure. How did that pass through you? Are those Tesla coils?" He asks St. Clair. "That's amazing."

Looking over at him, St. Clair tries to figure out if he is being serious. All of a sudden, the sound of a roaring engine scatters a murder of crows. The large, dark-blue van bursts out of the cornstalks, skidding and spinning to a stop. St. Clair phases in time for the rear bumper to pass through him.

Admiral Kay leans over the passenger seat and yells out the window to Stevens. "Get in! We have to get out of here! Where's our metal monkey friend?"

The driver side window crashes as a large arm reaches in and grabs the admiral by the collar, trying to pull him out of the van. Face to face with St. Clair, the admiral points his right hand towards the agent's shoulder. A high-pressure stream shoots out. St. Clair dodges it and is able to switch hands, still holding on to the admiral. The stream hits the truck, and steam engulfs the truck as well as the Lexus.

St. Clair's attention is momentarily on the steam cloud when the van is lifted and swung around. St. Clair sees Garrett gripping the lower back end and swinging the van. Letting go of the admiral and the door, St. Clair is sent across the dirt field landing hard and rolling across the ground towards the house.

Recovering to a standing position he sees Stevens only a few feet away. He launches himself in his direction, throwing Stevens into the house, knocking the wind out of him.

Breathing hard, St. Clair looks down at the Stevens, who is struggling to regain his breath.

A high-pressure stream shoots through his left shoulder hitting the farmhouse, filling the air with loud crackling sounds as ice forms inside of the wood. With his left shoulder searing in pain from the subzero stream, St. Clair turns in the direction of where it came to see the admiral standing there, poised. Just as the admiral sends out another high-pressure stream of ice, St. Clair dives into a roll, coming out of it standing next to the van.

Garrett takes a swing at the giant agent, and his right arm passes through him and lodges into the side of the van. "You have got to be kidding me!"

Stepping away from the van, St. Clair looks at Garrett in his metallic monkey suit and at the gangly man that is trying to stand up and recover his breathing. Shaking his head, confused, he says, "There's no way you guys could had hurt Nika."

From behind him, Admiral Kay's authoritative voice stops everyone. "Nobody said we did."

Snapping his head, he watches the admiral walking around the van. St. Clair takes another step back, raising his hands out in front of him. "Admiral Kay, this needs to stop."

"We were never out to start anything." The admiral tells him as he walks around to see Garrett. Watching the van shake, he shakes his head at Garrett who is trying to free his arm without ripping the van in half. The admiral looks back at the agent and says, "I'm not surprise you know who I am, but who might you be?"

The agent paces a few steps to the left, away from Garrett. "Special Agent John St. Clair."

The admiral looks around the farmhouse and barn. "Special Agent St. Clair, it would appear we have a similar interest in this farmhouse."

Still being leery of his surroundings, he paces another few more steps. "We are here to find who kilt one of our own."

Their attention turns to the van and Garrett as the van forcefully slides across the open area. Garrett stands there with his arms raised. "What?" Behind him Stevens walks up tapping him on the shoulder before moving between Garrett and the admiral.

Facing all three of them, St. Clair puts his hands out motioning for resolution. "Look here, mon. I know we had a bit of fun dere, but dis doesn't have to get out of hand."

The admiral raises a hand to the side of the doctors, letting them know to stand down. "You are an honorable man, I can see that. Report in what you've seen here, but we need to help a friend, and we will be leaving now."

St. Clair looks at the three men. "Admiral, you know who went and kilt her. Tell me and we'll be good."

"We are not in a position to do that," Admiral Kay tells him.

"I can't let you leave without telling me." St. Clair half smiles and takes a half step back.

The admiral waves an outward hand for Garrett and Stevens to move backwards to the van.

"We are not going to give you an option there, Special Agent St. Clair. We wish you luck."

Seeing them slowly make their way to the van, not knowing what else to do, St. Clair charges the admiral. The admiral extends his arm as multiple streams surround the charging agent. Diving through a break in the streams he is met with one of the large arms of Garrett, sending him flying back and through a weakened section of the house.

Climbing back outside, St. Clair shakes his head and falls to a knee as he watches the rear of the van kick up a cloud of dust. Rubbing his jaw, he starts to laugh when he sees Agent Grunt running out into the open from the cornfield. "You missed all the fun!"

Stopping and looking around, Grunt raises his hands, motioning that he did not know. St. Clair looks into the cornfield for Agents Nomi and Selenia then back at Grunt. "That's right, you already got to have some fun today."

Walking towards what is left of his truck and rubbing his lower back, he looks down at Grunt who has caught up to him. "You don't suppose you can tell me what happened earlier?"

Agent Grunt looks up at him when he stops, his eyes open wide, and he sprints off back into the cornfield. St. Clair stands dumbfounded and smiling. "What a strange little man."

* * *

Deep in the cornfield, Agent Nomi starts to wake up. Feeling her body ache all the way to the bones, she pushes herself up to sit on her heels. Looking up into the sky and closing her eyes, she inhales the smells of the cornfield. Her thoughts are interrupted by the sound of Agent Selenia forcefully talking on the phone.

The inner voice inside of Nomi cuts into her thoughts. "We are going to feel this in the morning and will somebody shut that woman up!"

Smiling, Nomi stands up to adjust her back. "If only we could." She opens her eyes and exhales as she massages her neck.

The conversation gets louder as Selenia makes her way back towards Nomi. Selenia steps into the clearing with her head down and her left hand covering her eye. Blood is trickling from a deep scratch from her left eye across her temple.

"I need help! No, I do not know where I am!" She continues to pace back and forth, listening to the phone. Stopping for a second, she then paces back into the corn stalks.

The inner voice snaps Nomi out of a trance from watching the tall redhead. "If we kill her now, nobody will ever find the body."

Nomi looks down at her scratches and torn shirt. "What is wrong with you? Why are you so violent?"

"She can't be trusted."

"Why do you say that?" Nomi asks, shaking her head.

Selenia gets louder again as she enters the clearing. "Okay, fine." She jumps trying to get a look over the dried-up stalks. She lands wrong, twisting her ankle. "Son of a—Look I need help! I don't know . . . No, neither St. Clair or Grunt is here."

Listening on the phone and holding her ankle, Selenia nods. "Yes, Agent Nomi is here."

Selenia quickly turns towards Nomi, sending her scrambling backwards shuffling away from her. Agent Selenia's left eye is open and completely black with no trace of white. Blood is trickling from her cut as she stares at Agent Nomi. "Help me."

Nomi pounces into a crouched position. The inner voice ignites every nerve in Nomi's body. "Half-breed!"

In a blink, Nomi launches herself at Selenia. Before she can reach her, her ankle is caught by Grunt, who appears from the cornfield and redirects her momentum.

Just as Agent Grunt turns to Selenia, Nomi flies towards him, arms stretched out, with pure anger. Grunt feints back, his shoulders nearly touching the ground. Nomi clears him. Her momentum sends her twisting and tumbling into another section of the cornfield.

Selenia, still holding her ankle, winces in pain. "I'm so sorry, Grunt. I'm glad you're here."

Out of the corner of his eye, Grunt's attention catches Nomi charging. He takes a half step towards her and reaches out and an arm, and his hand catches her forehead. She collides into the hand as if hitting a concrete pillar. Grunt looks into her eyes.

Nomi's body falls limp, and her weight is being held up by Grunt's grip.

Watching what happened, Selenia's jaw drops.

* * *

Out by the truck, St. Clair hears rustling coming from the cornfield. Taking a few steps away he watches for movement. Grunt steps out of the dried stalks with Selenia and Nomi right behind him. As soon as Nomi sees St. Clair she runs light footed into his arms.

"Little John! You're back!"

"Easy there, Flea. Good to see you too."

Selenia holds her head down and is shielding her eye as she makes her way to the Lexus. Setting Agent Nomi down, he takes a concerned step to her when Grunt steps in front, raising his hand to stop him. St. Clair looks at him, then over to Selenia, then back to Grunt.

He senses he should let her be alone for now. Giving an acknowledging nod, he looks back at Nomi. "We need to get out of here."

Nomi notices the truck. "Holy shit! Little John, what happened? It wasn't me this time."

Rubbing his jaw, "I had a run in with the admiral and his two cohorts." Taking a glance over to the Lexus, he watches Grunt walk up to Selenia.

Nomi catches him watching. "You can't trust her."

Confused, St. Clair looks down at his friend and with a hushed tone says. "What? What are you talking about?"

Nomi gives Selenia a determined but cautious look, and keeping her voice down whispering, "You admitted that you did not know that much about her. Well she's a half-breed."

Selenia's upbeat personality returns, as if a switch was flipped. "If we are going to leave we need to go now."

St Clair nudges Nomi. "We can talk about this later, until then try to behave."

They walk over to join Grunt and Selenia. They all stop and look at the Lexus then back at St. Clair, then back at the Lexus.

St. Clair smiles and chuckles. "You guys meet me at the Popeye's in Oakdale." He steps back as a green hue forms around him, and he disappears.

Selenia looks over at Nomi. "Now that I am getting my wits about me, and now you know a little more about me, can we get a long?"

Agent Nomi gives her a cautious look of curiosity and then forces a smile and nods.

With a quick nod, Selenia opens the car door. "Well alright then, let's get out of here."

Sine' Irish Pub, Richmond, VA

July 21, 1317 hours

Walking down the cobble bricks of Canal Street, Director Harris looks up at an Irish pub. He reaches in his pants pocket and pulls out a coin. Looking down at it, he rubs it between his fingers, and then looks back up at the pub. The voice of Victoria Carol replays in his mind, "I warned you against putting agents with operatives!"

Looking back down at the coin, he puts it back in his pocket and exhales. "What would a good agent do at a time like this?"

Taking a moment to look at the patio entrance to the pub, he goes to walk in when his phone rings. Seeing the M.A.S.H. screenshot he brings the phone to his ear.

"Five O'clock! How are things in Austin?"

"Sydney, what the hell is going on down there?"

"I am in Virginia right now, so I do not know what is going on down there."

"Dammit, I know you are in Virginia. I just got off the phone with the Madam. She is out for your head!"

"Charlie, breathe in . . . breathe out. A young but brilliant agent tells me to do that. I believe it will do wonders for you."

Looking around, Director Harris watches a young couple walk into the patio entrance of the pub.

"Listen up, Sydney! She is calling the twelve cities. Hell, she wanted to dip into the operative pool to go after this guy, who is suspected to have killed her daughter."

Director Harris raises a hand as if he could see him. "Whoa, she wants to do what? She is being rash and not thinking clearly. Tell me—"

"Relax Sydney, I managed stall her for now." There is a quick pause on the line.

"It would appear that we have another issue going on there."

"You are referring to the bank robbery in Katy?"

"Not just in Katy. Cindy is telling me that it happened again, in Baton Rouge, and today a mysterious, unstable energy covered Oakdale. Three loan businesses were robbed."

"Wait, did you say Oakdale?" Director Harris huffs. "When was this?"

"It happened about an hour ago. Twelve people died, including two police officers. Three civilians died yesterday in Baton Rouge, and you know of the three officers in Katy. Cindy has her entire team from San Francisco putting spins on everything."

Director Harris leans up against the wrought iron gate of the pub. He replays his conversation with Agent St. Clair.

"Sir, I am currently looking at the individual that committed the bank robbery..."

"He is not our priority right now. I need you to get back to Agent Nomi, Selenia, and Grunt, and bring that guy in. Do I have myself understood?"

"Shoot, this woman has got everyone confused and is not thinking right," Director Harris says, taking a deep breath. Before he can say anything else, Charlie cuts him off.

"Well, it is not going to get any easier. Expect a call from Cindy. She has pulled all available agents from Adam in Memphis. She even called me to dip into the operative pool to help her out."

"I am not worried about Adam; he and I share the same viewpoint about agents and that they are an invaluable resource."

"Nobody's denying that, but you know operatives have the upper hand. Speaking of which, I thought St. Clair and Nomi were on this."

Rubbing his temple, Director Harris tells him, "I redirected them to find out who killed the Madam's daughter."

"I can understand that." Charlie pauses for a moment. "You need to get back down there and get a handle on this."

Pushing himself away from the gate, he says, "Alright, Five O'clock, I have a flight later tonight."

"I hate it when you call me that, you know that right?"

Director Harris laughs as he disconnects the call. The laughter quickly fades as he exhales.

He checks his watch again then looks back at the pub, claps his hands together, "I should keep my blood sugar up."

Walking into the pub, the smell of the beer fills his sinuses. An attractive, young woman appears in front of him, holding a menu.

"Good afternoon, is it just one, or are you expecting others?"

"That is observant of you, a sound trait for a quality hostess. I will be dinning alone, thank you."

She smiles. "Yes, sir, right this way."

Following her, he intently watches the trays of Guinness being carried to what appears to be a table of VCU college students. The table roars at the arrival of their drinks, and the young hostess reaches his table.

"Will this be alright, sir? And can I get you something to drink to start you off?"

"This will be perfect, and I will have what they are having." He sits and takes out his phone. After connecting it to the local Wi-Fi he brings up the news page.

He scrolls through already endless articles, all talking about a strange atmospheric phenomenon happening throughout Louisiana. He leans back in his booth, shaking his head and checking his watch again, thinking, Cindy, you are amazing.

The Infinity Towers,
San Francisco, CA

July 21, 1123 hours

A disheveled woman paces back and forth in her high-rise apartment, overlooking the San Francisco Bay Harbor. Three pencils are stuck in her blonde ponytail as she reaches and picks up her phone. Taking a moment to gather herself, she scrolls her contact list until she sees a kangaroo icon.

Pressing it she waits for the ring while staring out into the bay. The familiar voice on the other end snaps her back onto land.

"Cindy! I was just thinking about you! How are things?"

"Jesus H. Christ, Sydney Harris! Don't be all jovial on me!"

"Take a deep breath; you don't want to flare up your hyper tension again, now do you?"

Taking a moment to close her eyes, she removes her glasses, throwing them on her couch. "Fuck you, Sydney. There is a serious shit storm going on in Louisiana, and Charlie tells me that you are down there trying to get a handle on it. So that is what he's telling me."

"Cindy—"

"I have had to pull some of my markers with the concrete cowboy in Memphis, because I am the one trying to put a lid on it."

"Cindy—"

Cindy throws her free hand in the air and points at the window as if he was standing there. "Don't try to smooth talk your way out of this. Did you know not only do we have blatant daytime robberies under some type of S-4, Groom Lake, atmospheric conditions, but now we have a Rougarou sighting in the same area?

"To make my job even harder, there has been unexplained craft sightings as well and unexplained booms in the middle of the night breaking windows. If I'm not mistaken, that is supposed to be your area of concern—"

Director Harris cuts her off. "Cindy! Breathe in . . . breathe out. Some of this I know and some I did not."

After a brief pause, her eyes get big. "You're smiling, aren't you?"

"I was just thinking, you are awesome and, of course, not to mention beautiful."

Cindy puts her hand on her ample hip as she shifts her weight. "I know you're aware of the coup de grace, the death of one of our own."

Silence on the phone starts to weigh it down as her burst of energy has worn her down. She presses the speakerphone option and sets it down on a nearby counter. "Sydney? Are you still there?"

"Yes, I am still here. And yes, I know about Roynika Carol. We have an idea of who is responsible. And yes, there's a team in place, but I as I sit here I realize there is a bigger goal for them."

Leaning on the counter, Cindy uses her arm to hold her head up, squeezes her eyes shut, and rubs her temples.

"You know this will give the Madam ammo against you." Her cat jumps on the counter and head butts her in the forehead. "Azrael, you silly cat."

"Is that cat still alive?"

Straightening up she rubs the head of her cat as it plops down to get a massage. "Yes, Sydney, he is still alive. So, what are you going to when the Madam learns you're not going after—?"

"Hopefully we will have resolved with this thief and his technology and she can move to the grieving stage."

"Sydney, you know I trust you, but I don't know if you've got your head above the clouds or up your ass. This could be something that divides us."

"Well, let's hope this ends well."

Ending the call, Cindy walks over to her window. "Here's hoping."

Dixie Dandy Shopping Center, Oakdale, LA

July 21, 1347 hours

Agent St. Clair walks around the USA Nails corner of the building as the sirens of ambulances, fire trucks, and police cars can be heard coming from everywhere. He stands in disbelief at the scenery before him. Watching an ambulance scream by, the wailing of a woman catches his attention. He looks over to the IGA parking lot to see a silver Toyota Tundra burning and a woman crying, protecting her child from the burning truck.

He takes a few more steps, when two Oberlin police cars fly down a crossing main street. A Mamou volunteer fire truck roars into the parking lot towards the Toyota with a paramedic from Ville Platte right behind it.

In the Popeye's parking lot, a man is struggling to get up. St. Clair rushes over to him.

"Sir, can I give you a hand?"

The man grabs his chest as he is laboring to breathe. "Th-Thank-" He winces in pain, and after a few more labored breaths, he says, "Thank you, my friend." Looking up at the giant agent "Whoa!"

St. Clair chuckles. "Take it easy, mon. You're not hallucinating." Helping him stand strong and leaning him against his car, he asks, "Can you tell me what happened here?"

Still in awe with the giant man in front of him, the man says, "Who do you play for? Football? Basketball?"

"I realize I might not look it right now; however, I am with the FBI."

Rubbing his fists in his upper thighs and trying to loosen his leg muscles, the man looks up at his Samaritan. "Whoa, they must be doing some serious recruiting."

Offering a huge grin, St. Clair says, "You have no idea." The sound of another siren passing by catches his attention. "My friend, what happened here?"

"One minute everything's fine, eating lunch and all. Then WHAM! the air is filled with a greenish-blue haze and the quiet sounds of crinkling paper. I got an uneasy feeling and decided that I should probably get back home."

Looking down at the ground, the man holds his stomach. After a few seconds of trying to collect himself, his legs give out, and he drops to the pavement, vomiting.

St. Clair's stomach catches and he quickly turns away. Looking over to the paramedics he yells out, "Hey! We need help over here!"

One of the paramedics looks up and acknowledges him, and St. Clair turns his attention back to the man.

The man is still trying to gather his wits, as he makes it to one knee. "I guess I didn't make it home."

"Help is on the way, take it easy, mon." The man weakens again and spins into his car, regurgitating what was left in his stomach along the side of his car.

St. Clair's stomach catches again, and he turns to walk away, holding the back of his wrist covering his mouth. Stepping away from the car, he almost runs into the paramedics rushing over. They make a motion to help him, but he waves them off, pointing to the man leaning on his car.

Shaking to clear his head, St. Clair walks into the Popeye's. Fishing his phone out of his pocket, he walks up to the vacant counter. "Hello? Is there anyone here?"

An older woman makes her way from the back. Her eyes look tired and her steps are deliberate. "I am afraid, sonny, we're not much up for fixin' anything right now."

"I understand." Looking at her nametag, he assures her, "Mary," and gives her his best smile, "I will take whatever you have already made."

Returning his smile, she says, "You're a charmer ain't ja?" She makes her way to the register. "What can I get ja?"

"Surprise me. I trust you."

Turning away from the counter, St. Clair scrolls on his phone until he reaches the one he wants and presses the call button. He hands the woman a twenty and gives her a wink and another smile. She blushes as she collects the bill.

"Agent St Clair!"

Pulling the phone away from his ear, St. Clair checks the volume. “Director Harris, do you have any idea what is going on?” Out the window he sees the Lexus pull up, and behind it, an Army caravan roll into town. “Sir, the army is here, and it looks like they’re here in force.”

“You must be in Oakdale.”

“Sir, you know about this Armageddon?” St. Clair looks out the windows, astounded at the commotion. “It looks like WWIII went down here.”

“I take it the energy atmosphere has lifted?”

Standing up, St. Clair looks puzzled at the phone. “You must be referring to the greenish-blue haze. No signs of that; however, the aftermath is devastating. Everyone is listless.”

Director Harris pauses as the phone goes silent. “It would appear that I was wrong.”

The phone goes silent again. St. Clair checks to see if the call was disconnected. “Sir?”

“I’m still here. I should have kept you and Agent Nomi looking for the technology. It would seem the same guy you ran into has found a way to increase the power of the equipment he is using.”

Collecting his food, he gives the lady another honest smile and finds a table. At the door Agent Selenia walks in, behind her is Agent Grunt. Looking out the window he sees Nomi watching the aftermath and the Army caravan.

St. Clair turns his attention back to the phone.

"Sir, what about Roynika? I mean Agent Carol. I thought we were to catch and bring in her killer."

"Attention to details. If you remember, I asked you to see if you could find who was responsible. And you did. Now we need to stop this guy who is causing this commotion and recover whatever technology he is using."

Confusion overtakes St. Clair. "Sir?"

"You said you ran into the thief earlier? Well it would seem that after he met you he went and caused the catastrophe there in Oakdale, and he needs to be stopped."

"Hey, Chatter, Grunt, glad to see you made it. That didn't take you long." St. Clair pulls the phone down just before Selenia and Grunt get too close.

Adjusting her sunglasses and giving a quick gesture towards the car, she tells him, "Little John, have you seen her drive?"

St. Clair looks over at Grunt. He could almost sense a smile coming from him. Almost forgetting he was still on the phone, he says, "Director, are you still there?"

"Glad to hear you all are together. Now it is up to you to get everyone on the same page. That is a quality of a good agent."

"Yes, sir." Disconnecting the call, he looks up at Selenia, who is standing there with her arms crossed.

"Looks like we're staying teamed up. There's a guy that caused this destruction, and we need to get whatever technology he is using."

Dismissing St. Clair, Selenia glances at Grunt for an uneasy minute then back at St. Clair.

"Look, I know those are your instructions, but ours is to bring in the admiral and his friends"

St. Clair leans back in his chair. "Well, I saw them take off, whereabouts unknown. And before you can ask, they were kicking up too much dirt to get a license plate number."

He stops long enough to get her complete attention. "Eleadora, since you are here, we could use your help to find out what happened here."

Selenia exchanges glances with Grunt and shrugs. "Okay, we'll assist you. But keep this in mind, we are helping you. We may need your help later, and I expect you to help."

"Yes ma'am, I surely do appreciate this. People here are just starting to wake up."

Adjusting her sunglasses, Selenia's confidence becomes smug. "You can never trust human recollection. If we want to know what happened here, we need to find someone who has not woken up yet." She turns and walks out.

Looking between the food, Selenia, and Grunt, St. Clair tosses Grunt a seafood po'boy and grabs the chicken po'boy for himself. "Here we go."

Sine' Irish Pub, Richmond, VA

July 21, 1551 hours

Finishing up his meal, Director Harris stares at his untouched pint of Guinness. A roar from the fraternity group snaps him out of his daze. Taking a napkin to wipe his brow, he fishes out his phone from his jacket. The waitress startles him, appearing out of nowhere. "You didn't want the Guinness?" she asks.

"I enjoy the aroma. Sadly, I can't indulge."

She reaches for the glass. "I apologize; did you want me to take it away? I can bring you some water?"

"No, no, no, my young lady, but I will take a refill of water."

"Yes, sir. Is there anything else I can get you?"

"That will be perfect, and no, nothing else, thank you." As she goes to leave, his eyes drop to his phone. Scrolling up and down the contact list, he looks at the list when the screen lights up with an image of Al Capone. Setting the phone on the table, he leans in and pinches the bridge of his nose.

Answering the phone, he takes a deep breath. "Ryan O'Connell. How is life in the Windy City?"

A deep, heavy Irish accent booms out of the phone, "Sydney! What the hell is going on?"

"I was just thinking about you."

"More like you were expecting a call from me."

"I stand corrected, or rather, you are correct." Director Harris laughs as he looks around the restaurant. "I trust you have heard from Victoria?"

"You know damn well I did. I just got off the phone with hcr. I have never heard her this upset."

Staring at the glass of Guinness and running his fingertips through the condensation, Director Harris drifts in thought. "She lost her daughter. I am not about to know how she feels. It is just that she is looking to blame someone"

"More like hang, and that is you my longtime friend." Director O'Connell pauses, leaving the phone silent. "Perhaps you can explain to me why I shouldn't launch a full-scale internal affairs investigation on you?"

"I do not know what to tell you, Ryan."

"You can start with why the director of astronomical affairs is assigning field assignments to agents and operatives in Louisiana?"

Director Harris leans back in the booth and rubs the back of his head with his free hand as he cranes his neck and tries to find the right words. "Earth's magnetic field was, or rather is, being influenced by something. I sent two agents to investigate. It turned out the cause was sentient."

"What!"

Pulling the phone away from his ear, he looks around to see if he has drawn any attention.

He then brings the phone back to his ear. "Yeah, that's what I said—only a little calmer."

The waitress returns with his refill. Director Harris motions drawing a checkmark on his palm and receives an acknowledging nod from the waitress as she reaches in a pouch and lays the bill on the table. Turning his attention back to the phone, "Hey, look, Ryan, right now I am working on finding who is responsible for the fiasco in Katy, Baton Rouge, and now Oakdale."

"Sounds like you landed in the middle of a shit storm there."

"Look, if you want to come down here I can walk you through everything. Right now, I am not in a place where I can go into details."

"Well, Sydney, if I don't launch some kind of investigation, then it will be my head in the noose."

"Integrity. That is a good trait for a director/I do not fault, nor will I resist, you with your investigation. I do request you keep everyone away from the agents in the field that are trying to apprehend and solve these mysteries."

After a moment of silence, Director O'Connell chooses his words carefully. "Victoria is calling the twelve cities, so I'm not making promises; however, I will see what I can do."

"I imagine I will see you soon, so until then." Laying enough money to cover the bill and a generous tip, he stands to leave. "I wish you luck. I have to get back in the frying pan."

"See you soon, Sydney, and good luck." The phone goes quiet, and he places it back in his jacket.

Walking out the door, he straightens his jacket and brushes his pants. He takes in the sun and the temperature change as he steps outside. "Good to know you're alive."

His phone starts to ring the X-Files theme song. "Director Harris, how can I be of service this fine day?"

"Sir, something has appeared in the Upper Mesosphere."

"Details, my man, have I not taught you that yet?"

"Sir, that is as detailed as we can get. A small, unknown object appeared from nowhere. We have already cut the Hubble feed."

"Quick thinking is a good trait, get as much information on it as you can and keep me posted. Meanwhile I need you to monitor anonymous terrestrial-energy readings."

"Sir?"

Director Harris leans into the phone. "Listen carefully. You need to monitor lower-atmospheric readings in Southwest Louisiana and Eastern Texas. Let me know if anything shows up, anything that seems even remotely out of the normal."

"Ahhh, yes sir."

Roy's Catfish Hut, Kinder, LA

July 21, 1838 hours

Crunching peanuts and grumbling under his breath, Garrett looks across the table to watch the admiral scrutinizing the menu as Stevens ignores it and stares out the window. Letting go of a handful of peanut shells onto the floor, he cracks a smile.

"Ever get the feeling of déjà vu?"

The waitress chuckles as she approaches the table. "That's funny. I remember you fine gentlemen from last week. I was hoping I would get to see you again."

The admiral smiles and nods. "We're honored that you remember us."

Her smile widens as she shifts her weight. "Let me see just what I do remember." Pointing to the admiral, she says, "Unsweetened tea," looking at Garrett, she says, "a Coke," and gesturing to Stevens, she says, "For you, sir, water."

Leaning back in the booth, Garrett crushes up some more peanuts. "That is impressive."

"Why thank you, it is a gift." Not taking her eyes off of the admiral, she says, "Did y'all know what you want to eat?"

Garret speaks up first. "I'll have the Crawfish Etouffee."

"Very good choice, and for you, sir?" she says, still smiling at the admiral.

"I reckon I will have the shrimp, please," he says, and noticing that she was going to say something, he raises a quick finger and adds, "The large platter."

"Yes sir." Shifting her attention to Stevens, who remains looking out the window, she asks, "And for you sir?"

"Just a house salad for now, with ranch," the admiral answers for him.

"I will put the orders in and return with your drinks." She turns to leave, giving the admiral a quick curtsey and nod.

"I'm not complaining, but why we are still in the area, because I am complaining."

"Two reasons," Stevens says and holds up two fingers. "Reason one, do you remember The Purloined Letter by Edgar Allen Poe? 'The best place to hide is in plain sight.' And reason two, we don't want to get too far away from Professor Mildiani and Kristen."

Garrett leans in. "She's is one of them!"

Stevens quickly turns in to the table, leaning towards his friend, and pressing his finger into the table. "She's a scientist, just like you and I—no more, no less. She wanted answers just like us.

"Now if you will excuse me, I need to wash my face." Shoulder nudging the admiral, Stevens nods to the restrooms.

Admiral Kay lets Stevens out and watches him storm off before he looks back at Garrett.

"You know, the girl was trying to help us," the Admiral lets him know.

"I know; however, she's still an agent of an unknown organization that employs giants that kick our asses."

The admiral runs his hands through his hair. "I'm still trying to wrap my brain around that guy and how things just passed right through him."

"Well wrap your brain around this knowledge," Garrett says while grabbing some more peanuts. "Not only have our pasts been erased, but we have made it on the FBI's Most Wanted list."

"That's fantastic," the admiral says, closing his eyes and pinching the bridge of his nose.

"Now you see why we need to get out of here." Garrett smiles as he disposes the peanut shells. "And now for something completely different. This area is becoming a hot spot for Project Cadmus. Not only are they after us and the Professor, but MUFON is getting all kinds of strange reports that have surely caught their attention."

The waitress arrives with the drinks. "Here you go, gentlemen."

Rocking back on her hips, smiling at Admiral Kay, she says, "If there is anything I can do for you while the food is cooking, just let me know."

"Absolutely, we will do just that, thank you."

The admiral waits until she turns a corner, before looking back at Garrett. "What kind of strange reports?"

"Well, last week the inside of a bank in Houston was turned into a Roman bath house, and outside of it the police re-enacted the O.K. Corral. Three of the four police officers were killed. In Baton Rouge, yesterday, an area became a green, alien atmosphere that caused almost immediate fatigue. People dropped like a prize fighter that finished twelve rounds," Garrett tells him while trying to control his excitement.

The admiral's curiosity peeked. "Was a bank involved yesterday?"

Garrett brushes his hands together dropping some more shells on the floor and smiles. "No, it was a currency exchange company."

"How are they causing people to do that?"

"The local newspaper this morning is calling it an atmospheric phenomenon." Garrett leans back to wait for a reaction from the admiral, then continues, "That is clearly a cover-up article, and you have to be impressed how fast they work hiding the real information."

"Unreal. Of course, who are we to say what is real anymore, and this happened yesterday?" the admiral asks.

Stevens surprises everyone as he firmly places his hands on the table and leans in. Trying to curb his enthusiasm he bends his knees, bringing him to the table level.

"The only thing I know that can cause that is amplified Orgone energy . . ." Motioning his hand to wave off that thought Stevens looks at the admiral. "Set that aside for now. Admiral, you have to hear this gentleman about what happened to him today." He turns his head, and everyone follows his gaze to see a young man with weathered skin and jet-black hair rubbing both of his temples with the palms of his hands.

"What's wrong with him?" Garrett tries to mask his annoyance at being interrupted.

"Hear him out and you will see." Stevens straightens his legs, but still keeps his hands on the table while lowering his voice. "Look, if it's too much trouble, don't. I just overheard them and thought you should hear it."

After a moment of nobody saying anything, Garrett shrugs his shoulders. "Well alright then . . ."

"Relax, Harvey." The admiral wipes his mouth and tosses his napkin on the table. Watching Stevens with curiosity, he says, "What happened today?"

"The guy believes he was abducted," Stevens tells them, letting the statement just hang there.

Garrett finishes off his Coke while everyone just exchanges looks. Setting his glass down, he says, "My curiosity is piqued. Let's go and hear what this man has to say."

The admiral begins to slide out of the booth. "Well Lincoln, lead the way, and we can learn what else happened today."

Upper Mesosphere

July 21, 1840 CST

Waking up, Agent Abergathy massages the back of her neck as she pushes herself up to look around. The room is completely made of some type of metal. There is an eerie silence as the only sound she can hear is her heartbeat.

The walls were mesmerizing, watching them pulse, she stands and gingerly touches the them. It emits a pulsating heat, almost as if it had a pulse and blood flowing.

Flashes of the diuranium octoxide and thorium nitrate pulsating through the ununpentium skin of Professor Eprem Mildiani flood her mind.

She snaps her hand away from the wall with an uncomfortable feeling that she invaded someone's intimacy. Crossing her arms and rubbing her shoulders, scanning the room.

Near the front, she notices waist-high poles that flair out on both sides.

he sees Professor Mildiani leaning back on a standing chair. "Professor? Where are we?"

The professor does not flinch or make a sound. She walks around the room, keeping her distance, trying to get a better look at him. "Professor?"

A voice she recognizes as his appears to be coming from everywhere in the room. "Hello Ms. Abergathy."

Taking a step back and looking around, she straightens up and walks in front of him.

"Professor Mildiani, why did you kill my friend in the cornfield?"

Professor Mildiani looks up, as his shoulders appear to straighten up. "That was not intentional. Her biomechanics reacted different than the rest of her."

He turns to look at Agent Abergathy, causing her to step back again.

The radioactive chemical combination can be seen pulsating through his facial features. He shifts his head as if to study her. "You were not aware of her biomechanics."

"Let's say one minute I'm doing math trying to solve an anomaly affecting Earth's magnetic field and next thing I know I'm in the middle of a Marvel meets X-Files universe." Kristen smirks. "Never would I imagine meeting someone who can kill with a wave of a hand or have been teamed up with a woman with bio-mechanical arms."

After a few minutes passes with no one saying anything, the professor shifts and turns to look at the young lady. "What brought you and your friend to my farm?"

Crossing her arms, Kristen leans back on her heals. "You know why already. Why didn't you kill me as well? Why did you bring me here?"

"You are a person of science and understanding. You are strong willed, and yet have no ill intent." The professor looks straight ahead.

Walking around the room, she notices that there are no corners and no hard edges on the room. "Where are you from?" She asks as she continues to look around the room.

"I am Georgian," the professor notes. "I know accents, and your name, Eprem Mildiani, neither of which are Southern."

The professor shifts his gaze to her. "You misunderstand me. I am from Georgia the country—not the American state. We were traveling here to learn and speak about mineral radiology."

"You are referring to the diuranium and thorium nitrate that flows through you and this room. What I really would like to learn about is the ununpentium—Element 115."

Without saying anything, he brings up an aerial photo of the Louisiana Bayou on a large monitor. As soon as the picture focuses, the professor acknowledges Kristen.

"The Bayou is rich with thorium dioxide and thorium hydroxide. I was speaking at a conference in Tulane, in 2012, when we were asked to look into a rock found by some alligator hunters."

The screen pans and zooms in on an area near Bayou Corne. A large sinkhole comes into focus on the monitor.

Dropping her crossed arms, Kristen steps towards the screen.

"I've heard about this sinkhole. That is where you found the rock."

"We did not find it. I we were asked to study it. It was uncovered after the waters of Hurricane Katrina receded and washed the swamplands away from it."

"What came of that, the rock, I mean?"

"It was 90 percent ununpentium, and approximately the size of a small car."

Walking up to the screen, the agent looks up at the twenty-two-acre sinkhole. "That element is unstable for Earth's gravitation. How could you have found it solid as a rock and one that large?"

"Once again, we did not find it. It was a meteor, and what we did not know is that the area's stability was being maintained by a thorium-ununpentium relationship. We realized later that the Thorium was keeping the meteor and the element stable."

Abergathy reaches up and touches the monitor. "A meteor that size cannot affect a twenty-two-acre area that is still growing. Everyone is blaming the salt miners."

"The gravitational impact of these two elements working together is very powerful." The professor begins to show a hint of enthusiasm. "You saw that. It took two years after we removed the meteor for all the residual energy from the meteor to dissipate, and the earth started to pull the soil towards it. We learned about the relationship once we started to study the meteor and it began to lose cohesion. It was at this time the sinkhole started to form. There was nothing we could do. We realized the relationship between the minerals..."

Turning, Kristen interrupts him. “You keep saying we. Who are we?”

A soft female voice fills the air. “Good morning, Agent Abergathy.”

Dropping her arms, Kristen staggers around looking for the source.

“Who is that? Where are you?”

“My name is Clarisse.”

“I named this ship after my sister,” The professor informs her, as he makes a sweeping motion with his arms.

“This is a ship? What kind of a ship?”

Seconds later a small portion of the wall opens and Kristen gasps at the view. The sun appears to be rising around the earth.

“Breathtaking. How is this possible?”

Clarisse answers, “The American Robert Lazar was correct. The relationship between ununpentium and the radiation of diuranium are able to manipulate gravity and magnetic waves. That allows us to travel vast distances in no time at all, much like the Serbian Nikolas Tesla did in the late eighteen hundred with his plasma experiment when it contacted the electrolytes within his body.

“That is why we thought of using human plasma to help keep the element in its liquid state. It allowed us to mold it to make the hull of this ship. Once we realized the relationship it had with thorium we utilized it along with uranium to try an increase its power.”

Mesmerized at the scene in front of her, Kristen steps back from the view. "This is all so amazing! Have you tried to travel beyond the solar system?"

Sitting back down as the window closes back up, the professor taps away at the controls, and the ship, Clarisse, speaks again, "Our relationship with the earth's magnetic field allows us to move along it like a toy car on a racetrack.

"It could be possible to use it to slingshot into deep space; however, we do not know how it would affect the field."

Kristen places a hand on her forehead. "What's happening? I am getting light headed."

Professor Mildiani rushes to catch her as her knees weaken, and she loses consciousness. Looking at her limp body he tells Clarisse, "We forgot to adjust for the oxygen levels."

Allen Acres Bed & Breakfast, Pitkin, LA

July 22, 0349 hours

It is an oblivious, peaceful night as Admiral Kay stands outside, staring up at the starry night. He tries to recall and recognize the constellations; but the vast number of stars in the night sky, make it challenging.

The heat still sweltering, he wipes his forearm across his forehead, and then takes a sip of tea. Shaking the ice in the glass, he feels something shift in the air. Keeping composure, he keeps his eyes on the glass focusing on his peripherals. The deck takes an ever-slight tilt, causing him to straighten his shoulders.

A deep baritone voice puts his senses on alert. "Good evenin', Admiral."

He turns to acknowledge the greeting. A familiar large hand is reaching out, motioning a sense of calm. "Yu good? We good?"

Shaking his glass again, he nods. "Special Agent St. Clair."

Giving the admiral a questioning look, he says, "You not surprised to see me?"

"No, you, or rather one of your friends, was seen earlier this evening by a friend of mine. We had to give him something to sleep to calm him down."

The admiral takes another sip of the tea.

"I presume that would be that limp noodle, the one the Dr. Garrett called Starfish."

"Lincoln Stevens is a good man, too smart for his own good sometimes."

"He blew up my truck."

Nearly spitting up the sip of tea, Admiral Kay looks at the giant standing next to him.

"Unintentional, I am sure of it."

St. Clair grumbles, "Yeah, he said dat."

Smiling as he looks up at the giant agent. "You don't seem surprised to see me either."

Walking over to the admiral, St. Clair joins him to look up at the stars. "Wow, a beautiful night . . . I saw the van earlier. By the way, that is an impressive fix on the hole in the side. Dr. Garrett, I presume."

"Correct. It seems a little unfair, you know who we are, at least most of us. How about we even up the field?" Smiling, the admiral shifts his weight and looks up at St. Clair.

St. Clair rubs his mouth and chin; his eyes never leave the night sky. "How do you know that I don't know all of you?"

The admiral gives a slight chuckle. "Attention to details. You mentioned my starfish friend, and yet you know my name, and you called Dr. Garrett by his name."

Dropping his jaw, St. Clair shakes his head.

"I keep getting told dat, to pay more attention to details."

They both share a quiet laugh. "Okay, you win this round, Admiral. My partner is Agent Nomi. I call her Flea."

"Wait, she's your partner, not the statuesque redhead?"

"Agent Selenia and I have a . . . well a . . . we were catching up when we got to the farmhouse . . ." He shifts his body to face the admiral. "You saw us?"

"Let's not get ahead of ourselves here." The admiral finishes the tea and shakes the ice.

"You right, that tea looks real good. Let's get a refresher and get out of this heat."

Shaking his glass again, the admiral looks cautiously in the direction of the kitchen, and then tweaks his neck. "Absolutely, and perhaps you can tell me about your military career?"

"You may need something stronger than just tea for dat," St. Clair suggests as they laugh as they enter the house.

As soon as they walk in the kitchen, they see someone rifling through the refrigerator. Backing away from it with his hands full, Harvey uses his foot to close the door. Turning to the counter he sees the admiral and St. Clair. Stumbling back into the refrigerator, he drops a jar of pickles.

St. Clair raises a hand, motioning for him to calm down as the admiral is pinching the bridge of his nose, shaking his head.

"Relax Doctor, this is neutral ground." St. Clair rubs his jaw. "Although, I still owe ya for earlier, but not here, not now."

Walking uneasy, Garrett steps over the broken glass and puts the rest on the counter.

"Admiral?"

"It's alright, Harvey."

Looking them over. "You two were laughing. Tell me that this is not like the Civil War, where the North and the South would meet up the night before. Laugh, share stories, trade coffee for tobacco, and then kill each other the next day."

"Easy mon, let's hope it won't come to dat. For now, let's enjoy some tea." He gives the doctor an honest smile. "And we can laugh and share stories."

The familiar, elderly voice appears directly behind the admiral, sending a chill up his spine. "You ain't supposed to be here."

The other two notice the admiral tense up. Garrett steps back reaching for towels, not taking his eyes off of St. Clair. "Are you okay?" Garrett asks.

Flexing his hands on the counter top, he says, "I'm fine, just had another déjà vu moment."

"Oh, I know, I am expecting Lin..." Taking a quick look at the giant agent, Harvey's eyes darts at a slight movement behind him.

St. Clair catches the eye shift, and before he can say anything a small figure jumps towards his back. Agent Nomi passes right through him and lands on the counter top.

Poising herself on her toes and fingers she shifts her eyes back and forth between the admiral and Harvey. She looks back at her partner. "Are we making friends now?"

"Puppa Jesus, Flea," St. Claire exasperates. "Why do you have to keep trying to frighten me? We are simply enjoying an early morning conversation."

A voice of a young woman interrupts everyone. "What are y'all doin' here? You not supposed to be in here!"

Everyone snaps in the direction of the new voice to see Sheryl standing with her arms crossed. Harvey and the admiral look at each other and smile. "Déjà vu."

Sheryl looks down at the floor to see the broken glass and pickles everywhere. "What have you done? Get, get out, you're not supposed to be in here!"

Fumbling, Harvey drops to pick up the glass. Nomi smiles and leans over the counter to watch him. Sheryl rushes around the counter, waving her hands to get everyone out of the kitchen. "Get, get, get." She pauses to give the admiral a stern look before turning to Nomi, who is still smiling down at Harvey struggling to pick up the broken glass.

The owner swipes her hand at Nomi's feet only to miss. Nomi, with amazing agility, sweeps her feet under her, leaping and twisting onto a counter next to the refrigerator. Sheryl's jaw drops, and her eyes opened wide in disbelief.

Admiral Kay leans in and looks at everyone, then back at Sheryl.

"We apologize, we will move on." He makes eye contact with the agents, motioning them to the exit.

Clair raises his hands, surrendering and smiling he steps back out of the room. "C'mon, Flea, we need to mind her wishes."

Nomi slowly lowers herself onto the floor, stepping down next to. He looks out the corner of his eyes to see the slender legs gracefully slide near him.

Cheryl recovers from her moment of shock to hurry around to Harvey. "Get up, go."

"I truly apologize. I was just looking for something to eat," He apologizes.

Regaining her composure, Sheryl brushes her dress down. "Breakfast is in two hours."

Seeing the admiral standing there watching her, she says, "Shoo, you too." The owner tries to push him out of the kitchen.

He smiles. "Yes ma'am. We do apologize again."

The elderly voice returns by his side, "She's a strong woman."

Struggling to maintain his smile, he nods and raises his hands to show surrender. Then he turns to join Harvey and the agents outside.

Sheryl's voice softens, "Breakfast will be in a couple of hours. I hope to see you there."

* * *

On the back porch, St. Clair walks over to a column and leans his massive size against it, when the admiral steps out to join them. All eyes turn on the admiral as he cautiously looks everyone over.

"Am I interrupting?"

Harvey is pacing with his arms crossed, tapping his chin. "I was just interrogating these two to see if their organization was involved with the resignation of President Nixon."

St. Clair and Nomi give each other confused looks, as Nomi starts to laugh.

He looks at them with mock disbelief. "What? It's a theory I've been working on. Think about every highly-popular president was forced out of office. Lincoln, Kennedy, Nixon, and well someone tried to remove Reagan."

Nomi's eyes dart back and forth, searching her memories. "Oh, what about FDR? Do you think some mysterious organization gave him Polio?"

"There is always that one exception to every rule." Harvey looks down, somewhat defeated.

St. Clair chuckles and waves his hand. "Actually, I was just asking the good doctor here why you three still local and not halfway through Texas by now."

The admiral takes a moment to look at his friend. "We're hoping to locate some new acquaintances."

Nomi chimes up, "You talking about Agent Kristen Abergathy."

Harvey walks over to mimic St. Clair by leaning against a column, making Nomi smile. "Is she one of yours?" He nods to Nomi.

"Yes and no," St. Clair answers as Nomi smiles at Garrett.

Admiral Kay raises an eyebrow at St. Clair. "That sounds a little cryptic."

"Let's just say, she works for one of our divisions, and we can let it go at that...We too would like meet her and ask a few questions."

Harvey shifts his weight and crosses his arms. "Are you sure it is not the other one you are looking for?"

Nomi shifts her feet and pulls them under her as she sits.

Her tone has a bite to it. "Why you protecting him? He murdered someone who is one of us!"

The admiral raises his hands in attempt to calm the air. "We are not aware of anyone murdering anyone else...Everyone deserves an opportunity to tell their side and defend themselves if necessary." His eyes land on the smaller agent, watching her as she appears to be getting lost in a memory.

The tension on the porch is broken as an immense reverberating sound shakes the surrounding area. The agents take refuge on the deck as Harvey and Admiral Kay steady their feet and look at each other.

"Bumboclaat!" Sitting back up and scrambling to his feet, St. Clair grabs his chest. "What ta hell was dat?"

"According to the local Army base and Coast Guard out of Port Arthur, that was a sonic boom." The Admiral smirks. "It is an atmospheric shift or something along those lines. It's all over my head."

St. Clair gives his partner a confused look, as she looks back at him just as confused. "I been around a long time and that ain't no sonic boom. And I am now thinking that that is what Kristen was tracking to get us down here in the middle of this mess. If we didn't have another matter to look into we'd be looking into that."

The admiral walks over to Harvey, then looks over to St. Clair. "As for other matters, I believe we will take the idea and head west. If we come across Agent Abergathy, I will make sure to tell her you're looking for her."

After a heavy pause, St. Clair gives him a subtle nod. "Admiral," goes to walk back inside, nudging Nomi. "C'mon, Flea."

As soon as the door closes behind them, Garrett punches the admiral in the shoulder. "What was that all about?"

"Respect, my friend. Now let's go see if Lincoln is up yet, so we can break the change of plans to him,"

Bose Lakeside home, Jasper, TX

July 22, 0816 hours

The sun is approaching unbearable levels as heat vapors are waving off the rooftops in the small suburban section of town. Pools of mirage puddles vanish as a brown Cadillac Deville pulls up to a moderate ranch-style home bordering the local lake.

Getting out of the car, the stranger looks around to see the dead-end street void of life, he is unable to focus on the homes due to the heat waves. Popping the trunk, he walks around and grabs a series of backpacks in each hand. Giving the street one more look, he heads to the front door.

There were some packages delivered, blocking the door. Tilting his head trying to read where they came from, he cracks a smile and sets some of the bags down to open the door. "This is interesting."

Nudging the door open with his foot the A/C knocks him back a step. Hurrying, he tosses the backpacks just inside the door. One of them lands with a heavy thud, causing him to duck and then smile as he looks back at the bags. Collecting the delivered boxes and feeling the weight, he steps inside and using his hips to shut the door.

Looking down at the boxes, he grabs just under his beard with one hand and behind his head with the other and a wig and beard come off with a little force and tugging.

Underneath the beard are the softer features of a woman as she massages her chin, pulling some remaining glue off of her lower jawline. Setting the disguise down, she takes a knife and opens the boxes.

Inside the smallest box is a neoprene diving suit. She takes it out, holding it up next to her body; she walks over to a mirror. After admiring herself for a few minutes, she tosses it on the bed and heads back out to the other boxes.

Opening one of the larger boxes she sets aside an invoice from Lockheed Martin. She unwraps some of the bubble wrap to reveal rubberized circuit boards. On the boards are taped tabs reading an exaggerated SLOT A and TAB B.

Shaking her head she opens another box to unfurl a fiber antenna mesh. Taking out the mesh, an envelope drops to the counter. Walking over to her recliner she falls into it with the letter in one hand and a glass of ice tea in the other.

She takes a sip as she eyes the envelope. Taking a moment, she looks over at the backpacks stacked just inside the door. Smiling, she forces herself back up to get the heaviest bag and then sits back down. Inside the bag are the gold ingots from the bank. Opening the envelope, she takes another sip and reads the note.

> ***YOU DID WELL AT THE BANK IN KATY. GLAD TO SEE WE HAVE CHOSEN THE RIGHT PERSON FOR THE JOB. NOW SOMEONE WILL BE BY TO PICK THEM UP. UNTIL THEN, ENJOY THE SUIT AND STAY LOW KEY.***

Closing her eyes, she lets time pass. The doorbell rings, startling her. Making her way to the door, a FedEx man greets her with another small package. After signing the electronic pad, she closes the door. A ringing is coming from the package.

Running into the kitchen, she grabs the knife and tears into the box to find an undescriptive phone. She tentatively taps the green telephone icon and says, "Hello?"

A strong woman's voice causes her to pull away from the phone for a second. "We have another job for you."

Allen Acres Bed & Breakfast, Pitkin, LA

July 22, 0853 hours

Back in one of the rooms, Admiral Kay and Harvey examine a map of the Louisiana, Texas. Harvey lets out a loud belch, bringing a fist to cover his mouth just as Lincoln walks out of the bathroom.

"That's disgusting, Harvey. Did you get any on you?"

"No, I did not. But whoever decided that fried chicken goes with waffles was pure genius!"

Letting out a short laugh, Lincoln looks down at the map. "Why are we looking at a map? We already know where the farmhouse is. I felt the sonic disruption last night, so I know Kristen and Professor Mildiani are back."

Without looking up, the admiral has marked the cities and towns that were victims of a mysterious energy.

"Are you guys going to clue me in? I thought we had a plan." Lincoln tilts his head to better see what the admiral is doing.

A news broadcast interrupts the television displaying the admiral and Harvey's faces. The reporter is informing the public that they are wanted not only by the local police but the FBI. The broadcast announces that they should be considered armed and dangerous.

The admiral walks over and turns off the television.

Lincoln takes a step back. "I still can't believe that you two already knew this and weren't going to tell me?"

Raising his hand, Admiral Kay walks back over to the map. "That was my fault. I didn't see the need to stress you out further."

"Well now I am stressed out," he pleads. "We need to get to the bunker with Agent Abergathy and Professor Mildiani and—"

Trying not to raise his voice, Harvey looks up from studying the map. "And what? Hide out until we are old and grey? This organization, these people are powerful and ruthless!"

"What people? Tell me you are not still set on Men in Black, Project Cadmus, Majestic Twelve theory, or whatever you want to call them?" Lincoln questions as he wails his arms around in exaggeration.

The admiral puts down the pen and walks over his friend. "Lincoln, take a deep breath. Agent Abergathy and the professor are not going anywhere. Harvey came up with the idea to catch this guy and stop him from killing people and I do not like the idea of someone running around with something that is killing people. If it is something that is this powerful, we have to get it to the right hands. It is this line of thinking that I found you two and your projects."

The admiral pauses as Lincoln calms down and moves around to the map. "It is a harebrained idea to try to clear our names; but, I'm willing to give it a shot, if at the very least we can save a few people." The admiral explains.

“This guy has to be local. I do not know how or what size of equipment he is using, but I know it can’t be easy to move around,” Lincoln points out.

“The admiral was already thinking he would be local to the area, because it looks like he’s circling around. I was thinking that you could use your starfish equipment to locate him,” Harvey adds.

Lincoln grabs a pen and circles the towns Kirbyville, DeRidder, and Newton. “This is where, roughly, we need to go. Of course, I cannot locate him unless he turns on the equipment. So, it would help if we were in the area.”

“You were able to track Professor Mildiani from Ohio.” The admiral looks at Stevens.

“If it is Orgone energy, it does not leave a lingering trail like the magnetic-radial waves at the farmhouse. Once it consolidates, it dissipates quickly.”

Lincoln waves his hand.

Pinching the bridge of his nose, the admiral walks away from the map. “This guy is escalating, and the more he escalates the sooner he wants to do it again.”

“So, what you are saying is that we have to wait until he starts killing again in order to find him?” Harvey throws his hands up in disbelief.

Finishing drying his hair, Lincoln gives his friend a half-hearted shrug. “Hopefully it won’t come to that, but there is no other way.”

“Well at least we have our projects. This guy won’t know what hit him,”

"Harvey, can you please stay focused here? This is not a movie, and we are not characters in one of your graphic novels," the admiral says while lifting the up the map. He looks over at Lincoln. "How close do we need to be to this energy field for you to be able to detect it? And how close can we get to it without being affected by it?"

"Good questions, both of them. Neither do I have answers too."

Harvey eyes widen. "I did not think of that. Those are good questions."

"Well?" Admiral Kay raises an eyebrow, looking at Stevens.

"Well what? I told you at the restaurant that this capability was purely conjecture and hypothetical. All I can recommend is that we have something distracting our minds if we encounter the energy."

Looking more concerned and less confident, Harvey sits on the edge of the bed. "That's all we need to protect us?"

"It will help, and the suits should deflect the energy."

Folding up the map, the admiral puts it in one of the suitcases. "That's all we can ask for. Now, we need to be out of here and on the road before we get recognized and the police are called."

"Shit. I already forgot about that." Harvey shakes his head. "Hey, I don't have one of those fancy suits. Will I be alright?"

His friend grins. "I don't think you have ever been completely right. There is one more thing . . ." He pauses for impact. "That team of agents, they're right here in this same building."

Harvey smiles with reassurance. "I wouldn't worry about them. The admiral here has a whole respect and understanding thing going on with one them."

Confused he looks over at the admiral looking for details.

Admiral Kay shakes his head. "It's just a mutual understanding. This is not the place for a confrontation. The big guy is an honest man with respect."

"Well this honest respectful man nearly snapped my back," Lincoln quips as he instinctively grabs his lower back.

"You blew up his truck," the admiral notes.

Harvey claps his hands together, laughing. "Boom! You did that?"

Looking over at Harvey, the admiral points and smiles, "Another thing, this man can allow things to pass right through him. And that, actually makes him a character out of one of your comic books."

"I know right, let's just hope he keeps his truce for now. As for his partner..." He shakes his head, grinning.

The admiral snaps a suitcase shut. "Harvey, let's keep focused here. We need to get heading west. The sooner we leave the better chance we have to be in the right area at the right time."

"Fair enough. C'mon Lincoln, let's go check in on our projects. We have a super villain to take down."

Lincoln rubs his forehead as he walks out the door behind his over enthusiastic friend.

* * *

Inside another room, St. Clair is standing by the window. His silhouette is making the room feel smaller than what it is. His cell phone rings, and he answers it with a dire sense of urgency. "Director, were you able to track the car from Oakdale?"

"Agent St. Clair, you should always start a conversation with a greeting, for instance, a simple hello would be great."

Grinning, he massages the shoulder that was ice burnt yesterday by the admiral. "You are correct, sir. Director Harris, how are you this morning?"

"Very well, thank you, and yes, we were able to track the car down, but didn't you say it was a man you ran into and was on the video from the bank?"

St. Clair looks puzzled. "Sir?"

"Well the license plate is registered to a 1969 Cadillac DeVille, which however, is registered to a woman."

"Raas." Lowering the phone, he turns back and starts watching the television. The television is showing a special alert for two of the three men are considered armed and dangerous. He finds himself staring at pictures of Admiral Julian Kay and Dr. Harvey Garrett.

The News report is some reason leaving out their credentials.

Director Harris's voice is muffled on the phone through St. Clair's hand. "Agent St. Clair? Are you still there?"

Gathering his wits, St. Clair looks around the room, "Yes sir, I apologize. It sounds like the car was stolen. Agent Nomi just walked in." He snaps his fingers and points for her to look at the television.

"Excellent, now perhaps the two of you track down all leads and leave no stone unturned."

St. Clair straightens up. "You're absolutely correct, sir. Where can we find this car?"

"Jasper, Texas," Director Harris states. "I will forward you the address."

The door opens again as Agent Selenia walks in, still wearing her sunglasses with Agent Grunt in tow. Nomi gives Selenia a sideways glare and quietly exits the room. As she is leaving, Grunt watches her out of the corner of his eyes and offers her a subtle smile.

"Thank you, I will let you know how it turns out." St Clair says and disconnects the call and tosses the phone on the bed and points to the television. "Hey you two, did you see the news report?"

Ignoring the question, Selenia adjusts her sunglasses and looks at St. Clair. "Was that Director Harris? Does he know where we should be looking for this needle in a haystack?"

"Sure does, we're moving the operation to Texas," St. Clair says.

"Did you see the bulletin on the television? It looks like we may not be the only ones looking for this admiral and his friends." He notices that Selenia does not show any concern or surprise.

"Chatter, who you been talking to?"

Selenia gives her head a quick shake. "What are you talking about?"

"It's a simple question, woman. Who'd you been talking to?"

Crossing her arms and shifting her weight on her hips Selenia scoffs, "I have no idea what you are talking about."

"Why you want to play games! I saw you on the farm talking to someone in the house after I stepped outside, and Flea said you were talking to someone out in the cornfield." Pausing to wait for an answer, St. Clair takes an aggressive step at Selenia pointing his hand. "You already knew the FBI is looking for these guys. You coordinated it with someone else, and that is not how we operate, you know that."

"Look, while we are on this little excursion of yours, we thought the FBI could lend us a hand tracking down these killers."

"When were you going to tell us? And you know they are not the ones who killed Roynika."

St. Clair still points his hand at Selenia.

Grunt steps out from behind Selenia and looks at the giant agent. St. Clair spots him, points his hand right at him, with an added bite in his tone, "Not now."

Grunt gestures both hands up, surrendering, and steps out of the room.

St. Clair looks back at Selenia. "You know they're not the one who killed her."

"We believe you, but they know who did, and that makes them just as guilty." She folds her arms and glances at the television.

"So, you are going to ruin these men." Turning away from Selenia, St. Clair rubs the back of his head.

She throws her hands on her hips just as the door closes to the room. "Why are you trying to defend them?"

"Because I fought against them, and they can no more kill anyone than I could fly. They are only looking for a friend." He squints his eyes and looks closer at Selenia. "Speaking of friends, you do not seem to have even the slightest concern for Agent Abergathy."

Selenia waves his hand away. "She knows who Nika's killer is, and she is probably in cahoots with him too, the admiral, and his cohorts."

St. Clair drops his hands and looks at her with disbelief. "You have become ruthless since we broke up." He looks at the television then back at her. "You were good at keeping tangs from me then, and you are keeping tangs from me now. Who'd you been working with and talking to?"

"That is none of your concern." Noticing a subtle facial flinch, she reaches up to her glasses. "There's something you are holding back."

She removes her glasses revealing her solid black eyes and takes a step towards St. Clair. "There's something you are not telling us"

St. Clair scrambles backwards. "Puppa Jesus! What the hell?"

Selenia takes another methodical step towards him. "You know, don't tell me. As a matter of fact, fight me, try to keep it to yourself."

"What the hell!" Feeling her eyes starting to bore into his, a green aura forms around St. Clair, and he vanishes.

She puts the glasses back on and turns and looks for her partner. "Grunt! Where did you go?"

* * *

Outside the room, at the end of the hallway, Nomi sits on a bench with her feet under her, talking on the phone. "Okay, we'll talk to you soon, Harvey." Disconnecting the phone, she turns and sees Grunt standing there, grinning ear to ear. He turns and quickly walks back to the room.

Nomi looks down at her phone. "Shit"

A green hue fills the corner of the hallway as St. Clair appears. "Flea, we got to get out of here. Like now!" He leans in and keeps his voice down.

Nomi looks up at him with a smile and holds her arms out. "Well, my hero, get me out of here."

"I can't do that. This is a one-ticket ride. Just get, I mean, I'll meet you ta car. We are going back to Texas."

Deserted Farm, Dry Creek, LA

July 22, 1149 hours

A Silver Ford Taurus slowly makes a turn onto a dirt road. A series of broken cornstalks on both sides of the path piques Director Harris' interests, as he comes to a stop.

Getting out of the car and closing the door, he causes a murder of crows to take flight again. He ducks, raising his arms to shield himself from the presumed attack.

Watching them fly across the fields, he shakes his head getting back in the car, and then takes a moment to wipe his forehead. "Get a hold of yourself, it is not a good trait for a director to get weak in the knees."

Further up the path he has to drive around the remains of the Ford F250." I wager that would have been interesting to see." Looking around, he is amazed at the level of damage.

Slowing the car to a stop alongside the dried-up cornfield in front of the house, he gets out, watching for more crows to attack. Pointing his fingers at the footprints and drag marks on the ground, the director starts to walk the open area, following the scuffmarks. Picking up his pace, he steps and slides as if he was listening to some music.

Retracing the tracks, he ends up facing a large hole in the wall of the farmhouse.

"Now that had to leave a mark." He looks back out in front of the house and smiles thinking out loud. "Ever since I saw Boondock Saints, I wanted to that. If I only had opera music it would have been perfect."

Stepping onto the battered porch, the director looks into the living room through the large hole. Making his way through the hole, he notes the dusty shelves, worn out couch, and beat up chairs. Looking around he can't fight the feeling that something is not right.

Counting his fingers with his other hand, he thinks out loud again, "One, the house is very old. Two, the house is extremely run down . . ." After a moment pause, his eyes are drawn to the bookshelf and at a series of books with a lighter dust layer on them. Then it hits him. The house is neat, not clean, but organized neat.

Just as he stands next to the shelf to get a better look at the books, a familiar voice startles him. "Director Harris."

Turning his head to greet the familiar voice, he sees Agent Abergathy standing at the kitchen doorway. With boisterous bounce in his voice, he says, "Agent Abergathy! How are you doing this fine afternoon?"

Cautious with choosing her words, Kristen steps into the room, "Doing fine sir, and you?"

Reaching into his pocket to pull out a handkerchief, he says, "I would be doing better when I can get back to the dry dessert." Director Harris takes a heavy sigh and wipes his brow. "How are you holding up in this humidity?"

Gripping the door frame, turning her knuckles white, she says, “Sir, I haven’t had a chance to call you and give you updates, I mean . . .”

“Relax,” the director tells her, smiling and motioning his hands to calm her down.

“What is it you say, breathe in...breathe out? That is good advice for you right now.”

Taking a deep breath, her grip relaxes, and she affords herself a modest smile.

Director Harris looks down at his watch, then back at the books. “I’ve had to see the value in that over these past few days.” Shaking his head, he chuckles in disbelief. “Hard to believe it has only been three. I need a vacation, and that vacation would not include traveling. Twenty-four hours at a keno lounge, a bottomless drink, and a sign that reads Do Not Disturb. Now that would be a vacation.”

“That sounds like a great idea, sir.”

Motioning with exhilaration, the director puts the handkerchief back in his pocket. “Great, let’s get on a plane, and you can debrief me once we are in the air.” Recognizing her apprehension, he surrenders, “And...we won’t be taking that flight, will we?”

Kristen steps towards the front room. “Sir, I can’t even begin to tell you everything that has happened. Sir, Roynika Carol is dead.”

Age and weariness washes over the director as he leans back against a couch.

"Yes, this we know. It has caused quite a stir. Which..." He points a finger in the air and continues, "...is another reason why you and I must get back to Las Vegas."

"I understand sir, but the phenomenon I found, well, it is..."

"Sentient, I know."

"Wait, you already knew?" She stumbles back a step as her jaw drops.

"I've been enlightened; however, I may not know the details, which is why you must debrief me. I can help," the director reassures the young agent.

"Sir, as much as I want to, I don't know if it is in my place to debrief you."

Director Harris looks around the room, puzzled, as the atmosphere in the room seems to be getting heavier. He motions his hands as if he was weighing the air, when a voice appears to come from everywhere and has him turning around looking for the source.

"Doctor Sydney Harris, astrophysicist from California Polytechnic State University?"

Stunned, Director Harris finds himself staring at a man wearing a variety of clothes in an attempt to cover himself. Watching the man keep his head down and his face out of view, the director shifts his stance and folds his hands in front of him.

"I have not had the nomenclature in quite some time. I see you have me at a disadvantage."

Glancing over at the young agent and seeing her nervousness, He looks back at the mysterious man in front of him. "You know my name, and who might you be?"

"You understand if I do no tell you that just yet."

Rubbing his temples, he tries to contain his impatience. "I have come here in hopes to find answers, I am not fond of riddles."

"I apologize. Young Kristen here told me I can trust you."

The clothed man offers his hand, and the director instinctively reaches out and grasps it with a firm grip. The man raises his head, revealing his metallic facial features.

"Professor Eprem Mildiani."

Feeling the strength behind the grip, the director searches his memory, while never taking his gaze away from the metallic man. "I know the name; however, I cannot recall it at the moment."

"Professor for mineralogy and atomic structure from Georgia. I was speaking at Tulane in 2012, when I was asked..."

The director's eyes light up with instant realization. "We thought you were lost to the sinkhole. I must admit you look quite a bit different than what I remember."

Releasing his grip, the professor puts his hands in his pockets. "Yes, I imagine I do."

Snapping the director out of a daze, Kristen steps in front of the professor. "Sir, now you know why I can't leave just yet."

Without taking his eyes off of the professor, the director agrees, "Yes, I understand. What can I call you? Professor Mildiani was pronounced dead two years ago," the director responds.

"Ms. Abergathy and Clarisse were working on that."

"Your sister, Clarisse, is here as well? I need to sit down."

"No, sir." Catching herself, she looks at the professor. "That is the name of his computer," she interrupts. "Wait, you know who he is? You two already know each other?"

The director lets out a good-hearted chuckle. "Eprem and Clarisse were students of mine, when I taught at Cal-Poly."

Walking around the room, smiling, and shaking his head, the director absently thinks out loud, "It is true to say this is a small world, and it keeps getting smaller. So, Eprem, how is your sister doing? She was one of my brightest students I ever had."

"She passed away a couple of years ago."

Director Harris's shoulders drop. "My condolences. I apologize...So I presume you dove into and buried yourself with your work. I would say doing that could hurt your complexion; however, I remember your complexion being a lot less metallic..."

He affords a momentary smile before he runs a hand through his hair, "What is this element that can cause this... evolution."

The familiar giddiness returns to Kristen's voice. "Sir, would you believe ununpentium."

The director snaps in her direction then looks back at the Professor. "Element 115? I find this...It can't...I'll be damned."

"That's it!" Kristen jumps up and down. "We can call you Praegressus."

Both men look at her, puzzled. The director scratches his chin in thought, and says, "Latin for evolution." He looks back at the professor. "Not bad."

After a moment to organize thoughts, Director Harris brushes some of the outside dirt off of his slacks. "Well Praegressus, what do you think? And, please, I need to hear how you came to evolve in this manner."

Remaining motionless, the professor tilts his head. "Ms. Abergathy was telling me you are a person that can keep this place secret."

Running both of his hands through his hair, the director takes a deep breath. "You see, there, we are in a bit of a pickle. You killed Agent Roynika Carol, an operative of ours."

Kristen interjects, "Sir, what happened was not completely his fault..."

Raising his hand, he stops her in mid-sentence. "I do not want to hear the details of what happened that day; at least, not right now," Director Harris admonishes. Seeing the confusion on the young agent's face, he says, "Relax, what I am going to do is to suggest that you lay low."

Reaching into his jacket he takes out a small flip phone and hands it to her. "I will be in contact, but until then neither of you should go or be seen anywhere. I need to make calls."

Stepping towards the door he smiles and looks back at the professor. "Praegressus, I will be back to learn everything."

The director turns and exits the farmhouse. Just as he makes it near his car, a murder of crows caw and soar past him, causing him to duck and shield himself. After he recovers he opens the car door. "And do something about the crows!"

Concrete Bunker,
Dry Creek, LA

July 22, 1243 hours

Agent Abergathy stares in awe at the ship—the diuranium octoxide and thorium nitrate pulsating in and around the metallic element ununpentium. Crossing her arms, she rubs them to fend off the cooler temperatures.

The large hanger room is extremely quiet with only a hush humming from the ship. She reaches up to touch the ship's hull when she snaps her hand back. Looking around, she spots the professor working in front of a computer center.

"Praegressus, I was just wondering. If your skin has the same makeup as the hull of Clarisse . . ."

"You are going to ask if I am capable of doing the same things she can do. The answer would be that I do not know. I think for now I will stick to levitation."

Recalling the other day when he lifted up and floated above the cornfield towards the barn, "Yeah, that was pretty cool. But have you ever wanted to see if Tesla was correct, I mean really correct, about being able to see, even go, into the future?"

"That is not something I'm interested in, and I am not sure even Clarisse can do that. Nikolas Tesla was years ahead of even us today, with his understanding of electricity and plasma.

"What you are thinking is something I cannot fathom being responsible for knowing."

The professor turns back to the console.

"Okay, okay, but you have thought about it. How about being able to travel in the same manner as Clarisse, here?"

Before the professor can begin to type something in, he looks over his shoulder towards the ship.

"I've thought about that as well. Although there has not been any place I absolutely had to be."

"Fair enough, I can understand that." Abergathy turns back to the ship and continues to rub the chill from her arms. "Do either of you have any idea where Lincoln, Admiral, and Dr. Garrett are?"

The female voice of the ship appears to surround her. "Agent, I have picked up a conversation from the director that was here earlier. It would appear something is going on in Texas that required a sense of urgency. The gentlemen he was talking to mentioned they were getting assistance from a Dr. Garrett. I can replay the conversation."

Abergathy turns and watches the subtle movements of the ship. "Clarisse, your design and overall concept that was Clarisse Mildiani's brilliance, am I right?"

Behind her the professor turns and looks at the agent then up at the ship. "It was her that remembered the American Bob Lazar and what the element was associated with, it was she who wanted to build a ship for the stars."

Walking over to the ship the professor puts a hand on the hull. “After she passed away, Clarisse was only the name fitted for her.”

Kristen turns away from the intimate moment and makes her way over to the computer center. “Clarisse, are you able to bring the conversation up here on the monitor, please?” The screen begins to scrolls to a transcript of the phone conversation.

AGENT ST. CLAIR, HOW IS TEXAS DOING?

DIRECTOR, JUST FINISHED CHECKING OUT THE ADDRESS YOU GAVE US IN JASPER. NO ONE WAS HOME AND NO SIGN OF THE CAR.

WHAT DID YOU FIND?

A WIG AND A BEARD THAT MATCH WHAT I SAW IN OAK-DALE. DIRECTOR, IF THIS WOMAN CAN SHUT A TOWN DOWN, LIKE SHE DID, WE GONNA NEED SOME HELP.

WELL WHAT ABOUT AGENTS SELENIA AND GRUNT?

WE HAD A FALLING OUT AND LEFT THEM IN LOUISIANA.

WELL I AM NOT IN A POSITION TO CALL FOR MORE HELP.

WELL WE RAN INTO SOME PEOPLE THAT MIGHT JUST BE THE BACKUP WE NEED.

ARE YOU REFERRING TO ADMIRAL KAY, DR. GARRETT, AND DR. STEVENS? DO YOU TRUST THEM?

THE ADMIRAL IS AN HONORABLE MAN, AND IF HE TRUSTS THE OTHER TWO THEN WE ARE GOOD ON OUR END.

THEN I WILL TRUST YOU. YOU HAVE BEEN DOING THIS FOR A LONG TIME. YOUR INSTINCTS SHOULD NEVER BE QUESTIONED.

THANK YOU, SIR, I WILL KEEP YOU UPDATED.

CALL DISCONNECTED

She pushes away from the console as if the console suddenly burned her hands. “Clarisse, what happened in Oakdale?”

Clarisse’s voice fills the room again. “At thirteen-ten on the twenty-first of July, a dense electronic field covered the city for forty-five minutes, killing thirteen people and injuring two hundred sixty-five, the source of the field in unknown.”

“They must think it is a person who is responsible for these electronic fields.” frantically pacing, “And they are just going to get Lincoln involved in this.”

Turning back to the professor, she pleads, “I need to warn him. I need to get to Texas! Professor, please, I need your help.”

Elijah's Café, Jasper, TX

July 22, 1346 hours

Closing his phone, Agent St. Clair shields his eyes and squints as he looks around the parking lot. The sun appears to be reflecting off of every surface. In addition, the heat waves are making visibility painful. Looking in the new Ford F250, he watches Nomi have her legs pulled up under her, tapping away on her phone. Shaking his head, he takes a deep breath. The heat sears his lungs, causing him to flicker and phase out for a split second.

Gaining control of his coils, he opens the driver-side door and gets in. Agent Nomi's attention never leaves her phone. Closing the door, he shakes his head. "Flea, what's your story?"

Nomi looks over at him. "What are you talking about?"

"I've seen the way you can move, and you got strength someone your size shouldn't have." He grips the steering wheel. "I thought I knew Chatter."

The inner voice inside of Nomi interrupts her before she can say anything. "You should have killed her when you had the chance."

She disregards the voice. "I still can't believe that she was able to keep that hidden from you. How long were you two f...?"

"Not long," St. Clair cuts her off. "She was always private; I just figured she would tell me when she was ready. Then it got to a point where I didn't even wanna know."

After a few minutes of quiet, Nomi shifts in her seat to face St. Clair. "Do you believe in aliens?"

"Are you talking about that man at the farmhouse?" St. Clair asks.

"No, I mean actual beings from another planet, aliens?"

"I believe the possibility is there, you are talking about aliens like in Roswell?"

"Now who is getting ahead of the story?" she watches his smile and his features soften, when her nerves pinch throughout her body.

"What are you doing," her inner voice snaps her from her thoughts again.

St. Clair becomes concerned as he notices her flinch again. "Are you okay? You seem extra edgy. What happens when that happens to you? I've seen you cinch up a few times since we've teamed up."

Nomi flexes her hand in attempt to ease her nerves. "Chottomatte, I'll get to that." She pokes him as she feels her nerves start to relax.

"Let me tell you about 1974. There was a crash in Mexico that redefined what is believable. It was outside the small town of Coyame, Chihuahua, Mexico. The crash was recovered and relocated, and its passengers were quarantined at Groom Lake . . ."

Noticing that her partner is trying to hold back a slight grin, she shifts her position to face him. "Look, you remember when I was talking about the botched mission outside of Kandahar?"

"I do," St. Clair notes. "You said you and Nika barely got out of there alive."

"Yeah, if it weren't for her mother and the relationship I had with her daughter, I would be paralyzed from the waist down. The main blast blew my lower spine to pieces . . . I got your attention now."

"You got it, girl."

"Out of the bodies of the passengers of the crash in 1974 was a parasite. Took them thirty years to figure out that it lived off of electrical impulses and that it was a symbiont and not a parasite."

Agent St. Clair's eyes open wide. "The ASYMB project, that's what Chatter was trying to find out about."

"ASYMB, or Alien Symbiont, not very creative, not like Project Rainbow, anyways, as a desperate move and without even asking me, they implanted the last living one at the base of my spine."

"Puppa Jesus. That is in you?"

"What they did not know was that it was the symbiont that was in control of the hosts and not the other way around."

St. Clair tilts his head. "So, am I talking to you or the symbiont?"

The symbiont chimes in. "He is a bumbling idiot. Why are you even bothering to tell him?"

Smiling and shaking her head, she continues, "It allows me to use my legs; it also increases my nerve sensitivity, giving me added reflexes, balance, and heightens my strength. What I give it is life and an annoying voice."

"You have managed to keep that secret from Charlie, Director Carol, and the other organization heads?" He tries to hide his surprise.

"Over the last forty years, this is the only surviving symbiont. So, they will never learn what they had this whole time." Crossing her arms, she shifts and leans back against her door. "So, now you know."

St. Clair grips the wheel, trying to comprehend. He lets out a quiet whistle.

The symbiont nudges Nomi's nerves. "Yeah, but can we trust him?"

"You are the only other person to know this about me, and I would like to keep it way," Nomi confides.

"No problem, mon."

Smiling, Nomi looks back out the window. "We are going to need help, you know."

Looking over to her, he fights back a smile. "What are you talking about?"

"You know what I am talking about," she chides. "I can tell you are worried about this. This man, or woman, or whatever it is, is able to incapacitate a crowded bank and even an entire town. We're going to need help. You don't even know what we are dealing with."

"And you do? Or better yet, the admiral and his team know what we are dealing with, and we know who."

"Harvey says Lincoln explained that it could be Orgone energy, whatever that is. I haven't a clue."

St. Clair chuckles and shakes his head, already knowing whom she has in mind. He opens the door and steps out of the truck. Looking around the parking lot, the humidity soaking his clothes to him, he turns back into the truck and smiles at his partner. "I presume they're close by, since you have been texting the good doctor since we left the bed and breakfast. Let them know where we are at."

"You had already planned to team up with the admiral and told Director Harris that we were meeting them." Nomi playfully smirks.

St. Clair shakes his head. "Just let them know where we at. We're gonna need their help."

"Yes, sir," she says as she mocks a salute.

"Funny woman." Stepping back and closing the door, he looks around while wiping his arm across his forehead.

An older voice catches him off guard, causing him to whip around. "Storm's comin', and gonna be a big one too."

Looking down at the man, St. Clair offers him a smile and slight shake of his head.

"Sir, there's scarcely a cloud in the sky."

"My bones are telling me different. Trust me, sonny."

"Yes sir, I'll write that down," he shrugs. "Thank you for the heads up."

He watches the man make his way past him and into the Elijah Café. Getting back in the truck, he startles his partner, who was tapping away on her phone. "We need to get moving. This is not a big town, and that Cadillac has to be here somewhere."

"Well, let's get moving. This truck is blowing hot now," Nomi says. "We should have kept my car."

"You damn well know that car ain't meant for a big man like me." St. Clair puts the truck in gear. "Oh, by the way, an old man said its gonna storm." Nomi looks at him in disbelief as he steps on the gas. "Yup, 'gonna be a big one." They start laughing as they drive out of the parking lot.

* * *

Driving up from Kirbyville, just outside of Jasper on Interstate 96, the admiral and Dr. Stevens notice a few abandoned cars that have died due to the heat or gas limitations. Lincoln appears to be agitated, shifting in his seat every time they pass an abandoned vehicle. Harvey is busy in the back of the van making adjustments and repairs on his suit, while texting away on his phone. The silence in the van is as heavy as the humidity outside.

The constant shifting of the tall doctor causes the admiral to take a deep breath and grip the wheel.

"Lincoln, we'll find her. We know, or at least we believe, that she is with the good professor."

"I know she is. I'm just concerned."

"Tell me again about the energy we are looking for," the admiral says, changing the subject.

"If it is what I think it is, Dr. Wilhelm Reich, in the 1920s, theorized about this energy and the conditions of expansion and contraction on people. He noted how it would affect people all the way down to the autonomic nervous system, even to the cellular and chemical levels. Most of his research was deemed fantasy and he was discredited. Even though modern chemotherapy can trace its roots to this energy. Some say Orgone energy was named after the orgasm which is why parasympathic conditions seems improbable."

Tilting his head towards his lanky friend, the admiral looks confused. "Parasympathic?"

"Yes, it is the creating of a sense of well-being and sexual excitement."

The admiral grips the wheel and exhales to the point of whistling. "Well, all right then."

Harvey chimes in, "That sounds a whole lot more appealing than the violent, negative side."

"We have no idea what side of the spectrum this team is going to use next?"

The admiral cracks his neck as he continues to focus on the road.

"If we can stop this woman, we can clear our names and maybe Beringei and Starfish will become household names." Harvey nonchalantly mentions as he continues working on the suit.

The admiral slams on the brakes and swerves onto the shoulder of the interstate, onto the grass. Both he and Lincoln look into the back of the van at him.

"What the heck was that for?" Harvey hollers out, trying to keep his balance.

"This is not a joke! How many times do we have to tell you that this is not something out of your comics?" Taking a second to regain composure, the admiral looks back out the front window. "There is nothing about this that I like..."

Lincoln jumps in, "This technology appears to be extremely dangerous. People are getting killed, and you're holding back information that could cause us to go in blind."

"Harvey, this is your idea to go after these people and I can see the logic as well as the reason to go after this person." the admiral adds.

"Hey, take it easy you two. I'm new to this excitement stuff. All I now know is that this group of people responsible for the robberies and the killings is actually a woman."

Lincoln sits back in his seat and starts tapping away on his iPad, mumbling to himself.

"There is no..." he pauses to scroll and tap some more "...how did someone..."

"What are you yammering about?" Admiral Kay asks.

"This technology has always been hypothetical, so how can someone create a transportable device of some sort that can create the energy spectrum of Orgone?" He absently questions while staring at the iPad.

Harvey raises a finger. "Perhaps she is using alien technology."

"Come on, Harvey!" The admiral shakes his head.

"Hear me out. This tech does not exist, yet here it is, existing," He explains. "Over the last few days we have seen people that can allow things to pass through them, we have heard of stories about a beautiful woman that can destroy people's memories, and now there is this technology that can create an atmosphere that can get people killed. It is not so far out of the realm of alien technology."

He sits down with a proud look as he watches the admiral think before continuing, "Look, last year you saved my life and my life's work. I trusted you, and now I owe you. We need to meet with this giant agent, which wants to repay me for the hit I landed on his jaw, and his partner. So, you two can establish a plan to stop this woman. Hopefully we can clear our names and recover our records and life will be good."

The admiral waits for a moment, then puts the car in gear. The van steers back onto the highway as Lincoln shifts in his seat again and looks back at the front windshield.

"Harvey, is there anything else you would like to tell us about this." The admiral adds.

"You know, I have been doing my own research on the Hoklonote. I'm thinking that she is actually a Starseed-hybrid child."

The admiral laughs. "Great, this just keeps getting better."

"We're almost to Jasper. Where are they?" Lincoln asks, not taking his attention off of the iPad.

"We can meet up with them at Billy's Bar B Que. I need to eat."

As they enter into town, Lincoln notices a welcome center sign: Welcome to Jasper—The Jewel of the Forest.

"Yeah, right, they find some trees in Texas and they call it a forest."

Harvey chuckles as he looks over at the admiral, who appears lost in thought. "Admiral, I just learned about it being a woman that is responsible."

"It's okay, Harvey, I'm sure once we meet up with the agents we will get a full picture. My main concern is who else is involved."

Billy's Old Fashion BBQ, Jasper, TX

July 22, 1748 hours

The dark-blue Ford Transit 350 pulls into a gravel parking lot of a small set of red buildings. Next to one of them is an oversized smoker with smoke pouring out of the stack. Not wasting any time, Harvey jumps out of the back only to be knocked back into the van from the wall of humidity.

"Holy son of a biscuit!" He shields his eyes as he looks up. A small trace of clouds appears to be building from the south.

Admiral Kay walks around to join him. "Are you looking for a storm to break this heat?"

"This humidity is almost to the point of unbearable," Lincoln adds. "Where are they? We need to get this over with so we can find Kristen."

The admiral steps in front to reassures him. "Lincoln, Agent Abergathy was either with the other agents or with Professor Mildiani. We know now she was not with the agents; therefore, she is with the professor."

Closing the back doors as Admiral Kay locks the van. "He clearly took her to protect her. So right now, we need your attention here and now."

"I got it. I understand. That does not mean I shouldn't worry."

Harvey puts a firm hand on his friends' shoulder as he turns him towards the restaurant. "C'mon, Starfish, you can't tell me that does not smell terrific," he says as he points to the smoker.

As they head towards the doors, the admiral notices that the only vehicle in the lot is a large, brand-new F250. Turning to look around the barren parking lot, he feels the cold air coming from inside the restaurant as they open the doors.

A wisp of a cool breeze cuts through the humidity, turning his attention up to the small gathering of clouds in the distance.

"I guess there is a storm coming to break this heat."

He turns and heads into the air conditioning to see Agent St. Clair talking to Lincoln and Harvey, with Agent Nomi close by.

The large agent sees him walking in. "Admiral, we are glad you gentlemen could make it."

"We figured that it was prudent to join your team. The way I figure, we both have a piece of the puzzle."

"You gentlemen have some kind of idea about this WMD we are up against." Nomi perks up.

"And you know just who may be responsible," Harvey adds as he walks over to her.

Lincoln raises his hands to put a stop to the building excitement. "WMD? Are you kidding me? Let's not get this out of hand here."

St. Clair booms out, “Doctors! Flea! Relax; take a breather. We can mash ideas after we eat.”

Harvey looks up at him and points. “I like your thinking.”

The admiral moves some chairs around. “Why is this place so empty? I’ve heard of this place when I was stationed out of Corpus, only ever heard great reviews.”

St. Clair postures up. “I thought it would be best to work something out with the owner, so that we can discuss this alone.”

“Being a federal agent also helped.” Smiling, Nomi looks up at Garrett.

“So, you two just flash a couple of badges and people are supposed to listen you,” Lincoln says. “Is that how it works?”

The admiral puts a firm hand on his shoulder and leans in to whisper, “Relax, we can get through this and then we can begin to look for Kristen and Eprem.”

He gives a quick nod and moves out a chair to sit down. Everyone else does the same. A sense of unease surrounds the small group.

“Well that was a mood changer,” Harvey lets out a low whistle as he notes the serious look on everyone. “Let’s eat. We all need protein.”

Lincoln and the admiral look at each other and start to laugh, as St. Clair and Nomi look at each other confused. They sit down as an older, seasoned gentleman walks out of the back.

"Good even' all, and welcome to Billy's Old Fashion Barbeque." The man claps his hands together. "Wat kin I start you off wit?"

"I've heard nothing but good about everything you have here. Surprise us." Harvey offers him an enthusiastic smile.

"Sounds excellent!" The gentleman says and heads back towards the kitchen.

They all watch him leave the room, when St. Clair turns back to the table. "What is this technology we are dealing with?"

"From what I have been able to understand, it is an energy that affects people at the nervous system level." the admiral looks over at Lincoln for confirmation.

He nods. "It's called Orgone energy. What I do not understand is how something that only hypothetically exists. How can a team just carry this technology around?"

"Make that one person, and a woman on top of that." St. Clair raises a finger just as Nomi delivers a quick jab in his side, causing him to flinch and Harvey to stifle a laugh.

Nomi shifts in her seat and looks up at her partner with a subtle, concerned expression as the symbiont twinges her nerves. "We can't be a part of this."

Rubbing his side, the giant agent continues without looking at Nomi. "Her name is Dorothy DuFerot."

Lincoln gives his friend a quick look as the admiral leans on the table to get everyone's attention.

"This woman—I have a lot of questions and ultimately concerns here. She targets low-yield, low-risk locations with the exception of the first hit, the international bank. So, she could be literally anywhere. So why the bank, first? Why did she choose a high-risk target? then go after low risk targets. It's backwards. Usually people start with low-risk and then build confidence." the Admiral surmises.

"Rawtid, with all that's been going on, I never thought of that."

"Did you think of that?" Harvey points his hand to his friend.

Lincoln takes out his iPad and turns it on. "No, that does factor in some variables."

"Let's stay focused here," the admiral firms his voice with authority that even catches Nomi's full attention. "I suppose we could ask her when we find her." Looking over at Lincoln, he tells him, "I know you want to get a good look at the technology she is using . . . Another question, why are, or, are the incidents getting larger and more dangerous?"

St. Clair taps a knife on the table, trying to hide enthusiasm. "I did tink of that, and it has me worried. It almost seems like she has no fear and is really enjoying the impact this energy is creating."

"So much is still unknown about the energy, so predicting how it reacts is nearly impossible," Lincoln says.

"However, like most types of energy, it needs to be amplified to be really effective."

"We saw the video from the bank and all there was, was a briefcase. What can amplify to what you are talking about?" Nomi asks.

Harvey leans towards her and whispers, "You have video of her?"

"She was a he then," Nomi says.

"Well since as far as we can tell the bank was the first use, he...or she...did not have the benefit of and external source to amplify the energy," Lincoln interjects.

"What can amplify this energy? Can something be like an antenna array?"

Looking up from the iPad and over to the admiral, "Well not quite; however, it would need to be amped up. An antenna array will only broadcast it with minimal amplification"

St. Clair pushes his chair back, stands up, and walks around the room, when the owner comes out with pitchers of ice tea and water.

The owner looks up at St. Clair then to the admiral. "It will be out soon, don't you worry, sir."

"Not a problem, we appreciate you accommodating us tonight," the admiral says.

"It's not every day we get honored with such an important person."

The owner quickly turns and heads back into the kitchen.

Lincoln and Harvey exchange confused looks as Admiral Kay looks at the giant agent for answers.

"How again did you convince him to secure the restaurant for us this evening?"

St. Clair tries to hide a guilty look when Nomi chimes in, "We told them we were Secret Service and that you were a former vice president."

Harvey tries not to spit up his tea laughing, and even Lincoln breaks out a smile. The admiral keeps looking at St. Clair. "You've got to be kidding."

Trying not to laugh at Harvey's reaction, Nomi continues, "How many people do you think even know who the VP is or were, let alone what they looked like."

Nudging him she says, "Seriously, how many VP's can you name?"

Putting his fist over his mouth he looks at Lincoln for help. Stevens stammers with a puzzled look, "Don't look at me. I can only think of Biden right now."

Watching his counterparts, Admiral Kay raises a wadded napkin to St. Clair. "Impressive improvisation."

Grabbing the back of his chair again, He goes to sit down. "Thank you, Mr. Vice President." He gives the admiral a smile and looks to see everyone trying not to laugh.

St. Clair scans the room to verify that they are alone again. "Okay, I bumped into this guy, I mean, woman a few days ago. She is not a problem; it is the technology that outright scares me."

Lincoln continues to taps away on his iPad, bringing up a map of Southwest Texas and Western Louisiana. "We need to profile this woman if we're going to figure where she will hit next. I am already thinking she is going to stay out of the major cities and stay local."

Nomi's interest is piqued. "Why you say that?"

"Well, Agent Nomi, we believe she is going to stay local, hence the circle she went," Lincoln tells her without bothering to look up.

Harvey adds, "Judging some of these towns, she's more comfortable in the small towns."

"I can see that." Nomi brings her feet up on the seat, lifting her up a few inches. "Now for my two cents. She is enjoying herself. I believe the money is now secondary to what the technology can do."

Everyone stops and looks at the small agent. St. Clair walks around to stand behind the admiral as they both look for her to continue.

St. Clair motions to her. "Don stop on that note."

"You remember how run down the house was, right?" Nomi says. "I wager she now has more money than she has ever had. Since money is no longer an issue."

St. Clair rubs the top of his head. "Brilliant. Okay, my turn. Since money is not a concern," he says, acknowledging his partner, "and she is not going very far," he pauses to acknowledge the tall doctor, "I say she is starting to enjoy herself and wants to go big."

The admiral leans forward to his temples. "People that want to go big usually have something to say, a cause. What is troubling me is that I don't think this technology is hers."

"Now you are talking my language," Harvey practically yells, nearly jumping out his seat. "This is becoming a conspiracy. Is everyone feeling energized now, or is it just me?"

"Admiral, why do you have to feed his imagination?" Lincoln asks without looking up from his iPad and ignoring his friend.

Making his way back over to his seat, the large agent sits back down. "We have to ask her when we find her."

"Well that sounds easier said than done. We may never know where she's gonna be." Harvey says.

"Perhaps not," Lincoln says, not taking his attention away from the iPad. "He's going to want to—"

Everyone in unison says, "She."

"She is going to want to find a small town that can give her the biggest impact." Lincoln pulls up a map shot of the town Beaumont in Southern Texas, setting the iPad on the table.

The map shows the FCC approved antenna towers, which causes Harvey to let out a low whistle. "Five hundred thirty-six towers? Wait, I thought you said antenna towers will act only as a repeater and that the energy would need a boost?"

The admiral sets his drink down. "Lincoln, please keep going."

"Entergy provides most of the electricity for this part of Texas and Louisiana, and all she would have to do is find a substation somewhere. That will boost the energy enough for her to get her desired effect."

Putting the iPad away, Lincoln starts to stand up when the admiral extends out a hand. "Lincoln, relax. She has a thing for daylight. She's not going to do this tonight."

St. Clair gives the admiral a quick tilt of his head then looks back at Lincoln.

"He's right, and besides we've all been on the road all day, and it smells like there is a great meal on its way."

Everyone watches Lincoln slowly look around the room, and before he can protest the food begins to come out from the back.

"We thought we'd start ya'll outwit some out our famous BBQ sliders, beans, and butter'd cobs."

The admiral takes a sip of his tea. "Everything smells great. We thank you, again, for doing this for us tonight."

"Sir, da honor is all ours," the owner says as he returns to the other room.

Everyone begins to dig in to the meal without saying another word about tomorrow. Outside, off in the distance, the clouds let out a quiet roll of thunder.

Eastex Freeway, Beaumont, TX

July 23, 1035 hours

With the winds kicking up, the van rocks and sways to the wind as it makes its way towards Beaumont. Harvey is grinning, gripping the wheel, and trying to maintain control of the van. "This reminds me of storm chasing when I was younger."

In back, Lincoln is tapping away on the iPad again, trying to remain in a seated position, without looking away. "It's only supposed to be a tropical storm, so let's not make it out to be bigger than it is."

Riding shotgun is Agent Nomi, and her phone chirps as she stares out the window, unable to tear her eyes away from the storm clouds. The clouds are shades of grey and almost black as they roll and swirl across the sky. Her phone chirps again.

Harvey slows the van down and takes Eastex Freeway and pulls off the side as they enter Beaumont. He nods to Nomi. "Are you going to check that?"

Nomi sits back to check her phone, reading the series of texts, she shakes her head.

"Well, Dr. Stevens, you may be as smart as you look. The Cadillac was spotted by an intersection camera at the Interstate Ten Frontage Road and Hollywood." Scrolling through the phone, she looks back out the window.

"Of course, if you could see these clouds your idea of a tropical storm might just change."

A flash in the sky changes everyone's attention to the windows.

"A little rain, a little wind, a little Orgone energy, I don't know. How much harm can it be?" Harvey smiles.

Tapping on the iPad some more, Lincoln brings up the weather report. "Look KBMT News Twelve has this only lasting a few hours."

"KBMT? That must be a local station."

Harvey raises a finger as if to say something then drifts in thought before re-raising his finger. "You know I don't think fiber optics run rampant in these parts. You mentioned yesterday that this energy would need something to boost it."

Lincoln continues to tap away in the back, and the van takes on a heavy sway. Everyone grabs something to hold on to. grabs the wheel and maneuvers the van into a Shell gas station just up ahead.

"Lincoln, where's that television station?"

"Already ahead of you. Would you believe Interstate Ten Frontage Road and Hollywood? However—"

Nomi's phone interrupts him with a series of chirps. "The admiral and Little John want to know where we at?" she reports.

Struggling to hold onto the wheel.

"Tell him that we are trying to stay vertical and this wind is not making it easy. Where do they want to meet up?"

"Tell them to meet us at the television station," Lincoln says. "We need to hurry. If she is going where I believe she is going then we do not have a lot of time."

Another gust of wind hits the van, almost lifting it up onto two wheels.

"Harvey, I have an idea, move it next to the building.!" Lincoln yells.

Slowly rolling the van to the side of the building, Harvey puts it in park. The building is shielding the van, keeping it from rocking back and forth. Looking back at his friend, who somehow managed to be still tapping away on the iPad, "Okay, I like your idea for the van. But now how do we get to the television station?"

While Nomi is drastically searching for her phone she dropped when the van nearly tipped, another lightning bolt streaks across the sky, and immediately a crack of thunder follows it, shaking the windows, causing everyone to shield themselves.

The symbiont grabs Agent Nomi's attention by stinging her nerves. "I do not like this. Let them deal with it."

"I can't," she says out loud.

They both look over at the Nomi, who has gone pale.

Harvey reaches out and touches her shoulder. "What do you mean?"

Her eyes dart in his direction. "Nothing, just talking to myself. That bolt was close wasn't it? What's the plan?"

"First, I need to talk to the admiral." Lincoln opens the back door to get out. Hearing the wind gusting, he turns back to his friend. "Meanwhile, we need to project up."

Beaumont Yacht Club, Beaumont, TX

July 23, 1042 hours

Across town at the Beaumont Yacht Club Inc., St. Clair and Admiral Kay watch a silver Ford Taurus pull up next to them. The admiral's phone rings; he grabs it out of his pocket and walks around the car.

Getting out of the Taurus, Director Harris smiles up at Agent St. Clair. "Fine day for a disaster, isn't it?" The sky lights up again, and again, a crack of thunder immediately follows it. They both flinch and shield themselves. "That was a close one. I didn't even get a chance to count that time."

The sky opens and rain pelts the gentlemen as St. Clair points to the Taurus and runs to the passenger side. He and the director both hurry into the car. St. Clair looks up to see that the admiral has jumped back into the truck, still talking on the phone.

Almost on cue the director and the large agent run their hands over their heads to wipe off the water. Director Harris watches the rain in disbelief. "Where did that deluge come from?"

"I was warned yesterday from an old man that a major storm was coming. There wasn't a cloud in the sky." Looking out the window, he sees even darker clouds coming in quickly, covering up the already ominous clouds. "It's sure looking worse for wear out there."

"I got your report last night. I have to say, this Dr. Lincoln Stevens sounds like someone I would like to work with," Director Harris notes.

Still watching the admiral, St. Clair reaches down and adjusts the seat back to give his legs more room. "When we survive today, I will let him know."

"Positive thinking, always a good trait for a field agent." The director smiles as he continues to watch the storm.

St. Clair looks out the window, watching the clouds build. "Were you able to find any truth to the admiral's theory?"

"You mean the one where she is just a pawn and that someone has fed her the technology? Not yet. Director O'Connell is looking into that possibility."

St. Clair snaps his head in disbelief. "Director O'Connell? From Internal Affairs? You think it comes from one of us?"

"Well, this briefcase is not public technology. And from your report of her house I am inclined to agree with the admiral. I also have him looking into who erased their past, and he promises me he will rectify that; however, getting them cleared from the FBI list is out of my hands I am hoping Director Merrick out of Boston can help with that."

The rear door opens as Admiral Kay dives into the back seat. The wind catches the door, nearly snapping it off of its hinges as the admiral catches it on the first bounce back and slams it shut. "It is getting nasty out there."

Looking up at the driver he says, “You must be Director Sydney Harris. Agent St. Clair here told me you can be trusted.”

“I am, on both accounts, or I would like to believe. Admiral, I have to admire the trust you have in your team. I was just telling Agent St. Clair here that I would be honored to work with them one day.”

“Well let’s see when we survive the day first. I’m not comfortable with all these unknowns. For every answer we have there are more questions that come up. All in all, we have no idea what we are going up against.”

Giving his agent a quick look, Director Harris turns back to the admiral. “Do you have a game plan for today to help everyone with that task?”

“It would appear that Dr. Stevens has told everyone to ‘project up’, so he believes there is a sense of urgency here.”

St. Clair grabs the back of his neck, and everyone hears the popping as he adjusts it.

“What does he want us to do?”

Reaching into his pocket, the admiral pulls out audio earpieces, and St. Clair does the same. The admiral notes a confused look on the director face. “Dr. Stevens believes that if we can focus our minds with music we can protect our subconscious from registering and being affected from the energy.”

“Interesting line of thinking.” The director wipes his forehead again.

Finishing up putting in his earpieces, the admiral leans back in the seat. "Your agent here informed me you are the one with the eyes in the sky? If you can, keep all eyes open and keep him updated with status reports. It could be a huge help." Noticing the raised eyebrow from the director, the admiral raises a hand apologetically. "Please."

He gives the admiral a respectful nod. "That I can do."

The admiral taps St. Clair's shoulder. "We better get going."

"Where does Dr. Stevens think we should go?" St. Clair says, finishing up with his ear pieces.

"We need to get to Hollywood, looks like we are going on TV?"

Eastex & Lucas Plaza, Beaumont, TX

July 23, 1058 hours

Back at the van, Agent Nomi is leaning back against the wall of the Shell gas station as Garrett is wearing his mechanical suit, shielding her from the torrent of rain. The backdoor of the van opens, and Lincoln gets out dressed up in his MIT suit and metallic gear.

Muffling her mouth, Nomi tries not to laugh at the two scientists in their space-aged outfits. "You guys look like something from a B-rated sci-fi movie or a weird rock 'n' roll band." Nomi then whispers to Harvey, "I saw him on the recording, but it looks so different in real life."

Without moving, he smiles. "He's our starfish. Hey, why do you think it is happening today? This weather is unreal."

"Yeah, Starfish. There's no way she's doing whatever she's doing in this weather," Nomi adds.

"The admiral mentioned that he's going to want go big. This electrical storm will only amplify the energy all the more."

Lincoln ignores the sarcasm and adds, "Which is why we need to get to him before he turns it on again."

"She hasn't made any demands, and I can't even think of what there is to take in this rat hole of a town." Nomi lets her frustrations show.

"Okay he's a she, I got it! Whatever it is, it has escalated every time it turns it on."

Harvey steps back and turns to his friend, still trying to shield Agent Nomi from the rain.

"Lincoln, relax. To quote Batman: The Dark Knight, 'Some people just want to see the world burn.' We got it. Just tell us what we can do to stop this guy, I mean, woman."

They both remain motionless, watching Lincoln stand up.

With the LED's in his headgear flashing in no distinguishable pattern he rubs his chin and looks around.

"Beringei, we need to get to the television station. I'm sure that is where she's going to set this potential nightmare off."

Nomi gives him a satisfied smile then looks up at Harvey. "Beringei?"

Looking down at her, he gives her a smile. "I'll explain later."

"Well Little John calls me Flea." A huge grin forms across her face.

After a moment for the name to register, Beringei tries to hold back his excitement. "Now we all have superhero pseudonyms."

"Not you too! I knew I shouldn't have mentioned that!" Going to slap his forehead, he forgets about his equipment as his metallic glove clangs against his headgear, causing him to stumble back.

As they laugh as another lightning bolt lights up the sky, and a few seconds later a deafening crack of thunder motivates everyone to somber up.

Harvey slides away from the wall. “You know, every time I have been seen in my suit I have been shot at. How far away is this television station?” He pauses, collecting a thought. “If we can get the briefcase away from her before she turns it on then this will be an easy day.”

Without any warning, a series of relentless compression waves sweep across the town. The air around them becomes strange and unreal with every rapid compression wave. Lincoln is pressed against the van as Nomi has a death grip on Harvey’s suit. The ringing in her ears is unbearable as every nerve in her body is searing in pain.

Lincoln’s sensory equipment is registering to almost the point of overloading the circuits. “Harvey! You need to take down the FCC towers!”

“You’re kidding right? They’re like five thousand of those in this town.” He looks at his friend in disbelief.

The last of the waves sweep across town as the air takes on a purplish-bruised look along with an eerie stillness. They all look up as the rain comes to an abrupt stop. Harvey adjusts the volume on his MP3 player, shaking his head he strains to looks up at the clouds. “These clouds look pissed.”

Walking over to his friend while he watches the ever-darkening and churning clouds, Lincoln taps away on the control panel on his wrist. “This is not good! One lightning strike and the entire area affected by this energy could hypothetically ignite and blow up.”

Shifting in the direction of his friend, with the music still blaring in his ears. "I get it, disable the towers, and we can weaken the energy field."

"Right, and there are only five hundred and thirty-six towers. I will get to the television station; the admiral and Agent St. Clair should already there."

"Five hundred thirty-six, that's so much better." Shuffling away from his friend, Harvey goes to launch himself into the air when he notices Nomi has a full body grip on his leg. "Flea! I need you to let go!"

Lincoln rushes over to her. "Her vitals are in overload! We need to get them out of this atmosphere and fast!" He looks around. "The van!"

Not hiding the sarcasm, Harvey realizes that the energy has not made it inside his suit. Turning down the MP3 player, he yawns to pop his ears. "Great idea, there's no airflow in there!"

Rushing over to the back door of the van he waves for Harvey to hurry. Harvey reaches down and as gently as he can, tries to grip Nomi without crushing her. Wedging his mechanical hand between her and his leg, he manages some separation.

Nomi's head snaps up. Pure anger is making her almost unrecognizable as she throws herself off of his leg and against the nearby wall.

With no time to register a reaction time, she springs off of the wall and flies over Harvey, knocking Lincoln over, pinning him to the ground.

Nomi grabs the base of his headgear and twists her body in an aerial movement, snapping his neck while flipping him face down on the asphalt, his hands landing on the back of his head. Pausing in a crouched pose, she poises herself at mechanical exoskeleton.

Harvey slides himself around to see her crouched over his friend. Before he can understand what happened, Nomi launches herself at him. Reacting, he is able to catch her leg causing her scream. She grabs a hold of the mechanical arm and looks at Harvey. Their eyes meet and her facial features are almost unrecognizable. "Whoa, Yukiko, what has gotten into . . . Oh damn, it is the energy in this atmosphere."

Glancing at the open van door, he pleads, "I hope you don't hold this against me." He then tosses her in. Hearing a loud thump, she crashes into the equipment, nearly tipping the van over. Her screams of anger and pain echo from everywhere.

He slams the back door closed and pounds the top of the van, crunching in the doorframe, preventing the doors from being able to open. Then grabbing the back of the van, he swings the front end into the wall, cutting off any exit from the van.

"And I hope the admiral doesn't hold that against me." He steps back away from the van, watching it and hearing Flea's rage quiet down as if running out of steam.

"Hey, Starfish, it's safe to get up now. I wonder how the admiral and Little John are doing on their end."

I-10 Frontage Road, Beaumont, TX

July 23, 1159 hours

Sitting in the parking lot of the Farmers Insurance Group next to KBMT 12, Agent St. Clair and the admiral sit in disbelief and awe at the color of the air around them.

The television station appears to be vacant when the admiral lets out a low whistle.

"Agent St. Clair, have you ever seen anything like this?"

"Call me Little John, and yeah, well, sort of."

The admiral quickly looks at him. "Little John? As in Robin Hood?"

He chuckles. "Alan Hale was my dad's favorite actor, and I was nicknamed after his roles in the Robin Hood movies."

"I am not sure I know that name, but that will be for another time. Lincoln says this atmosphere could be caused by Orgone energy."

"Don know about that, never heard of that energy. What else does that limp starfish have to say about it?"

Shaking his head, the admiral chuckles. "Don't care for him much?"

"He blew up my truck."

"We covered that already. Anyways, he was telling us that this energy affects the nervous system, and whether it is negative or positive depends on the spectrum being used."

Flashes of Nomi flood St Clair's thoughts and he recalls her words, 'It also increases my nerve sensitivity.' He grips the wheel and looks around the truck. "This is not good. Where are they now? They're in trouble."

"We all are if we can't find this Ms. DuFerot and stop her." The admiral looks at him confused.

"It's Flea, I mean Agent Nomi, and she has a medical thing that affects her nerves. This origami energy will not go well with her," St. Clair stresses.

As if on cue, a Honda Civic crashes into the light pole behind them and explodes on impact, causing the truck to lift for a spilt second.

The admiral jumps out of the truck and rushes over to the fire. Pointing his arms out, high-pressured streams shoot out, freezing the water surrounding the vehicle. The ice builds and stacks as steam pours into the air and over the fire.

St. Clair joins him. He can feel his coils struggling to maintain cohesion as he flickers in and out of phase. "Not very good at putting out fires, are you?"

"It is not exactly a garden hose, and when we make it out of this you need to tell me about your condition as well as Agent Nomi's."

"Yes sir, we can do that."

Behind them a whisper can be heard over the crackling of ice. "Well isn't this interesting."

They both snap in the direction of the voice to see a woman remaining motionless as she is tilting her head towards her shoulder. A slight smile forms on her face as she recognizes St. Clair from the other day. She is wearing a skin-tight, neoprene suit with what appears to be electronic circuits stitched into it.

St. Clair rushes towards her; however, the energy surrounding the woman is making it even more difficult to maintain his coil cohesion. The admiral, still trying to extinguish the car fire, hears the sirens of emergency vehicles coming from the highway.

Stopping right in front of her, he continues the internal struggles.

Her smile grows wider as she steps towards him, reaching her hand to touch his chest. "And who might you be?" she asks as her hand passes through him.

St. Clair vanishes and reappears behind her. With all the focus and concentration, he can muster, his body solidifies, and he grabs her at the shoulders. Struggling at the surprise, she takes out a control unit to the suit. With slight thumb movements across the screen, the energy level surrounding her intensifies, causing St. Clair to yell and drop to a knee.

The admiral hears the yell and looks back at the woman responsible for this energy field and sees the large agent falling to his knees, rapidly phasing in and out.

Hearing the sirens, she turns in the admiral's direction. Seeing the igloo forming over the car crash, she jumps up and down all giddy. "You must be Admiral Julian Kay. M was right." Looking at her phone again, she thumbs the screen again, and a pulse emits from her body causing the admiral to be thrown back into the icy car wreck.

Beside her, St. Clair is trying to stand up. She reaches out and pats him on his shoulder. "Be a good stud, and stay right there. After I kill the admiral I will be right with you." He vanishes. She steps back and crosses her arms. "Well that was rude."

Turning back to the admiral and in a sing-song tone, "Oh Admiral Kay, are you okay over there?"

Holding the back of his head, the admiral regains his composure. "How do you know my name?"

"Oh, I know all your names; yours, Dr. Harvey Garrett, and Dr. Lincoln Stevens. By the way, where are your sidekicks? Are they coming too?"

"You failed to answer my question, Ms. DuFerot. How do you know our names?" the admiral says as he slowly makes his way back on his feet.

Stopping in her tracks, she tilts her head with a curious expression as she hears her name. "Well I am impressed, although, that name is dead to me now. I've been given a new beginning, a new name."

Sirens of emergency and police vehicles interrupt her as they slow their approach to the car crash.

One of the officers jumps out of one of the cars yelling, “What happened here? What is going on?”

“He did it officer! This was his fault!” the woman screams, pointing at the admiral.

The police scramble out of the vehicles and surround the admiral with their guns pulled.

The lead officer begins to yell as the other officers follow suit. “Put your hands up! Get on the ground!”

The admiral’s expression drops as he looks back at the woman who is smiling. “Oh, you got to be kidding me.”

Eastex & Lucas Plaza, Beaumont, TX

July 23, 1211 hours

"C'mon, Lincoln, it's safe to get up now."

An explosion off in the distance catches his attention, snapping his head in the direction he hears a woman scream, "Lincoln!"

Harvey turns to see Agent Kristen Abergathy running past him. Looking around, he notices the atmosphere around them has cleared as if it was pushed aside. Catching his attention, he notices that Professor Eprem appears to be floating towards them. "Professor Eprem! Ummm, what are you doing here?"

"Lincoln!" Kristen continues to yell.

"He's fine, agent. Just got the wind knocked out of him, that's all." Shuffling around towards the agent and his friend, he catches his breath.

Kristen has managed to roll him over, and the break in his neck is apparent. She looks up at Harvey. "What happened? Who did this?"

Fumbling to form a thought he turns a look at the van. Kristen watches him turn, and she notices the crumpled-up van.

She jumps up and runs at the van. "Is this your fault?? hearing movement inside the van, "Who is in the van? Harvey! Did they kill Lincoln?"

Not knowing what to say or do, tears well up as he looks from the van to his friend on the ground. He looks up at the atmosphere that is being shielded away from them; he murmurs, "This was not her fault."

Turning her head back to him, Kristen screams, "Her who? Who is in there Harvey?"

"Look, it's the atmosphere, the energy that caused this. She was not prepared for its effects."

A quiet voice that seems to come from everywhere interrupts them. "What is this energy?"

For a split second they look all around to find the source of the voice before they both turn to Professor Eprem. Kristen tries one more time to open the smashed back door before falling back to Lincoln's side. She caresses his chin as a tear lands on his headgear and trickles down the side.

Two more explosions can be heard off in the distance. Harvey looks back over to Professor Eprem. "Starfish, I mean Lincoln, knows about this energy and is able to analyze it . . ." He looks over to his friend as something gets caught in his voice. "I mean he was able to . . . using that equipment of his . . ." Shifting his gaze to the young agent, he pleads, "Kristen, you know how his equipment works."

She stares back up at him in disbelief. "Your friend has been dead for a second, and you are already trying to part his life's work from him!"

Another explosion only a block away, causing them to turn, Harvey lets out a whistle. "That was close. Look, Agent..."

She jumps ups and tip toes into his clear visor saying, "I can't! It's not right!"

"I apologize, but you need to see the big picture. He was my friend! But the big picture is that we need you to work his equipment or more people are going to get killed . . . Professor, talk to her."

Professor Eprem levitates up about an inch more. "Please call me Praegressus. Professor Mildiani Eprem died in 2012."

Looking at his metallic, pulsating facial features, Harvey nods, saying, "I like it, you may refer to me as Beringei, and this over here is Starfish..." then gesture towards his friend and stops short. After a brief, quiet pause, another series of car-crash explosions interrupt the solemn moment.

"Kristen, Praegressus talk to her tell her."

Praegressus lifts upwards and levitates in a controlled circle.

"This energy, it is causing all this? Energy needs power. Control the power and you can control the energy."

"Are you sure you are not Captain Obvious? I'm not a student in one of your classes."

Watching Praegressus snap in his direction and the pulsating in his skin increase, he can begin to feel his suit registering the gravity weight increase around him. Raising his arms to surrender, he watches the professor levitate around him. "Okay, okay, don't do the turkey trick on me. How do you suggest we control the power? Nothing short of power removal will control this energy."

The clouds flash all around them. Kristen lays across Lincoln to shield him as everyone else looks up. Thunder grumbles, causing her to grip tighter onto his body.

Praegressus maneuvers closer to the ground in front of Garrett. "What is your suit made of?"

"What does that have to do with anything. We need to get Lincoln back to the farm."

"Agent Abergathy and I, will see to Dr. Stevens, right now we need to cut off the power to the energy. You need to focus, what is your suit made of?"

Surveying the energy crackling around them and then looking back at the crumpled van, the suit straightens up as he looks over to the professor, "It is my creation of tungsten carbide and trisodium dodecarbonyl infused steel. I created it to withstand extreme gravitational pressure."

Raising a hand, Praegressus stops him. "Are you positive?"

"Of course, I'm positive. I created it."

Praegressus looks up in the sky at the clouds and the strange atmosphere that surrounds them. "That's not what I am asking."

A lightning streak lights up across the clouds, and seconds later another deafening rumble follows it. Staring up in awe, his expression drops with realization as he looks back at the professor. "Oh, you have GOT to be kidding me."

I-10 Frontage Road, Beaumont, TX

July 23, 1219 hours

"Get down on the ground!"

"Face down!"

Officers are yelling and side stepping with their guns drawn to circle Admiral Kay.

Closing his eyes, the admiral shakes his head while slowly raising his arms. When his arms reach out from his sides a steady mist shoots out towards the police officers. Some of the officers closer to the icy streams shake their heads as if to clear out cobwebs.

The admiral circles and continues to spread out the icy mist. More officers are shaking the cobwebs from their minds and begin to lower their weapons.

Astonished, the woman thumbs at the phone attached to her suit. "That is so not fair. I have an answer for that." An energy pulse emits from her suit and causes everyone to stumble.

The lead officer firms his grip on his 9mm. "What the hell are you doing here!"

Regaining their balance, the other officers join in yelling orders.

"Get on the ground!"

"Hands behind your back!"

The admiral looks at the lead officer and tries to explain, "Officer, this is a misunderstanding. Everything that is going on around us is being generated by..." With a quick movement, he points at the woman and a high-pressure stream hits the woman in the shoulder. Ice forms on and around her shoulder as she drops to the asphalt.

The lead officer yells, "Stop!" and fires his weapon, hitting the admiral in the shoulder of his extended right arm. The admiral spins to the asphalt just as another officer fires his gun, hitting the admiral in his lower, left abdomen. Blood sprays across the ground as the admiral curls in a fetal position.

The woman stands back up, trying to work her shoulder to loosen the ice from it. Two of the younger officers make their way to her when the sky lights up. Everyone stops to look up and see a giant ball of lightning heading in their direction. The officers scramble and run; some hit the deck and shield their heads.

The woman watches the lightning ball. As it gets closer she can make out something or someone screaming, coming from inside the lightning ball. Then she realizes that it is Dr. Garrett.

Mumbling to herself, "What are you doing, doctor?"

Before she can figure where the lightning ball is landing, it hits with an explosion. Less than a mile away sparks and fireworks fill the sky around where it landed. The lightning bolt returns to the clouds, leaving behind its courier.

Without warning the atmosphere starts imploding in no discernable direction. Deafening popping sounds of the implosions cause her and the remaining police officers to cover their ears.

* * *

Harvey unclenches his eyes. His suit circuitry is fried, he is unable to move. Hearing the implosions, he watches the atmosphere clear up. Just as the atmosphere goes back to normal the rain falls, as if catching up for old times. With zero visibility due to the rain on his helmet and the lightning frying his suit, he shakes his head.

"Great, just great. This better have helped the admiral."

* * *

At the television station, the remaining officers are trying to maintain their footing in the high winds and sheets of rain. In the middle of the television parking lot a localized green hue develops.

Despite the low visibility, one of the officers tries to focus on the anomaly, and as soon as Agent St. Clair materializes, the officer throws himself back against his vehicle.

Drawing his 9mm at the giant agent, the officer struggles against the wind. "Where'd you come from? What the hell are you?"

Standing up from a crouched position, He reaches in his jacket and takes out a badge and walks purposely to the officer. "FBI! We appreciate your help here today, but you and your men are going to have to clear the premise. I will deal with this gentleman."

Pausing to scrutinize the badge, the officer gives him a suspicious look before turning towards two other remaining officers. "C'mon! We need to head back and regroup."

The two other officers get in and the car heads towards the I-10 Frontage Road.

Watching them leave, St. Clair turns to see, Dorothy DuFerot, getting in her Cadillac and driving off. "Rahtid!"

Turning his attention to the admiral curled up on the asphalt. Running to his side he looks down at his immobile body. "Mi sarie, Admiral."

The admiral shifts to turn his face away from the torrent of rain, mumbling, "Will you speak English, Sailor."

St. Clair drops to his knee and rolls the admiral over, shielding his eyes. "Admiral, you're still wit us." He notices that the admiral's right shoulder and left side are completely iced over. "If this was not so serious it would be cool, I can see the blood, even through your ice."

Shifting his position into a squatting position, St. Clair places his right hand over the ice on the shoulder. Closing his eyes to concentrate, his hand begins to phase out, passing into and through the shoulder, taking out the bullet that was lodged in the corner of his shoulder blade.

The admiral's eyes open wide. "Okay, that felt weird."

Ignoring him, he shifts position to get to the admiral's left side.

Phasing his hand through his side, he says, "Looks like that one was a through and through."

"When this is over you are really going to have to explain your so-called condition to me."

Bose Lakeside home, Jasper, TX

July 25, 1305 hours

Removing the electronic neoprene suit, her body revels in that it can now relax and breathe. The suit was so tight she was unable to wear anything underneath it, leaving stitching impressions all over her body. Still it was good to be home. Not bothering to put anything on, she flops down in her recliner as the swamp cooler blows on high causing her entire body to goose up.

Enjoying the feeling, Dorothy closes her eyes and smiles, "That was interesting." Her mind drifts, recalling the past month and trying to imagine how she got so lucky. Her thoughts quickly float into oblivion.

The darkness creeps in, even the furthest corners of her mind become enveloped. Within the darkness, large black glass almonds form into shape. A feeling of being lifted in bliss washes over her as the almonds shimmer images of her memories off of their surfaces.

Photos of the bank flicker in fast forward. Images of the conversation with the police officer when he gave her directions pauses and slows down. The flickering speeds up at lightning speed until she is looking at a large good-looking man, the man is struggling with something then disappears. The photos flicker again as they come to a stop at the image of Admiral Julian Kay getting shot by the police officers.

The glass almonds shimmer into the darkness as the darkness retreats, letting oblivion return.

Deserted Farm,
Dry Creek, LA

July 30, 2015
0853 hours

"NO! Not happening!"

"Harvey! C'mon mon."

"Little John, it's not happening. It's taken me years to build it. I'm not just going to let some men in black reverse technology my suit."

Harvey storms out of the farmhouse, before the door can close, Agent St. Clair is right behind him. "Harv, stop. Look mon, I know, tey know it is yours and yours only. In order to get what you need, you need to work with these guys. The resources tey have is unimaginable."

"I can imagine them going nowhere near my suit!" Harvey stops just short of running into the blue SUV's crowding the dirt clearing in front of the house. He kicks the dirt out of frustration sending murders of crow cawing into the air. Causing him to duck and shield himself.

"I really hate those birds. Little John, we've already been through this. I got caught up in my comic book world as Lincoln would put it and now he's dead and the admiral was almost killed."

"I know, but I can't stop this woman by myself. With Flea gone I need your help. I need you to work with them to get your suit back up,"

"Dr. Garret, I assure you complete confidentiality."

Harvey turns to see one of the technicians standing behind St. Clair. "Look, whatever your name is again. My friend was just killed, another was shot, and now you want me to just open up my suit, my life's work, to a complete stranger. No offense, but this has been a long week." He looks around as more crows make their way into the cornfield. "I don't even have any patents on my project."

"Doctor, I know. If you did, I would already have the schematics and we would be fixing it..."

St. Clair puts his arm out stopping the technician. "I told you tey have resources. We don't have time. That quashie needs to be stopped."

"I just wanted to be the first to walk on an alien planet. I've had to keep my work hidden from these guys so that it's not exploited."

"Doctor, if I understand the concept of your suit. I would think you would have immeasurable strength when you wore the suit, with only Earth's gravity to hold you back. The inlay design is impressive."

Harvey snaps in his direction. Pursing his lips together, he rubs his chin. "Yeah."

"We can help. Under your supervision and lead, we can get you back to leaping over tall buildings in a single bound."

* * *

Lying on the couch in the living room, Admiral Julian Kay has his arm and shoulder slung and bandages wrapped around his waist.

Forcing himself to a sitting position as Director Harris comes in from the kitchen with a glass of ice water. “Admiral, you should not be sitting up.”

“I shouldn’t be doing a lot of things. Going head first into situations without a full intel or preparation would be top on the list.”

“I know, this past month has been nothing but curveballs, sending untrained and unprepared agents into the field is not a good trait for a director.” He sets the glass down in front of the admiral.

“Director, what are you the director of?”

Chuckling, he smiles, “Excellent beginning to a conversation. I am the director of aeronautical and atmospheric studies.”

“Impressive, but who do you work for?”

“I’m not sure I understand the question?”

Wincing, he reaches for the glass, “I know you don’t work for the government, the SUV’s you pulled up in don’t have government plates. Yet your agents move as if they have had extensive military training. You appear to have private money with government ties. I am asking again, who do you work for? Thank you for the water.”

Walking to the front wall, the director looks out at Harvey and St. Clair. “Now you have me in a difficult spot. You’re welcome.”

“I am getting the feeling that we are in the middle of fighting your battle, I need to know what side and who I am or rather we are fighting for.”

Taking in a deep breath, the director stretches his arms out and puts them on top of his head. "I... what makes you think we are in a battle?"

"Agent St. Clair and Agent Nomi, they appear to be straight forward, without ulterior motives. The other two, a tall red head and a shorter man, possibly eastern European descent, there's something about them. They all move like they have had the same or similar training."

"That would be under the direction of Director Rodgers. A good man."

"What is really going on here? From the beginning."

The director continues to rub his head and neck as he struggles to find the words. "We were observing an anomaly that was affecting Earth's gravitational field. I believe it is the same anomaly that the good Dr. Stevens was tracking, Agent Abergathy mentioned it to me. Anyways, she convinced me to allow her to come here and search for what was causing it. To make a long story short..." affording himself a chuckle, "...ever notice when somebody says that it is already too late?"

The admiral relaxes, "I take it this partner of Agent Abergathy, the one that was killed. She had important ties to important people?"

"Oh, that is an understatement."

He lets out a low whistle. "She was the daughter of one of our directors and she was her only child."

"Boris and Natasha must be working under this director. Kristen pulled a dash camera from one of the police cars that had our interaction with them. That must be how they got our names."

"Yes, you would be correct. She sent them to find who killed her daughter." Looking over at the admiral, "Your deduction reasoning is extremely impressive, a very good trait for a leader."

Taking another sip of water, the admiral leans his head back on the couch, stretching his neck. The room becomes quiet as the voices outside can be heard. It would seem they have come to an understanding. A thought hits him as he remembers a conversation with Dorothy DuFerot. "So those two agents are under the impression that we killed her daughter and why St. Clair first thought we did. That still does not explain Dorothy DuFerot or who supplied her with that technology?"

"That I do not know? Director Rodgers had me looking into a bank robbery under suspicious circumstances with Agent St. Clair and Nomi. Everything went South from there."

"That does not explain how she knew who we were, just like Agent St. Clair knew who we were. It felt like we walked into a trap and we had our collective asses handed to us."

"I am wondering one thing. Why did you decide to team up with Agent St. Clair and Nomi to go after this, Ms. DuFerot?"

Laying back down on the couch, the admiral puts his good arm over his eyes. "Everything seemed like a good idea at the time. Truth be told, the only two civilian names I had were Lincoln and Harvey's. Which is why, when Lincoln wanted to traipse across the country looking for a source to something, I figured why not. Then we went and fell into this hornets' nest..."

"I understand, more than you might realize. I too perhaps got caught up with the ideals of having a renewed purpose."

"Speaking of purpose. It would seem she too has a new purpose and that is to kill us."

"Now hold on a minute there, admiral. That sounds a bit extreme."

"She flat out told Agent St. Clair that she was going to kill me. She knew all three of our names. The only way she would know that would be if..." Despite the pain, he sat back up to face the director.

The director's expression pans as he takes in a slow breath as flashes of his meeting with Victoria flood his mind. "I'm not sure. Making speculations is not a good trait for a leader."

Knowing the director was hiding something, the admiral leans his head back pinching the bridge of his nose. "Look, I know you have your secrets, but make no mistake; her goal was to kill us. We walked right into a trap and had our asses handed to us. I want to know who was pulling her strings." His shoulder twinges shooting bolts of pain. "Right now, we need to rest. This will have to be your fight."

* * *

Back outside, an engine roars in the distant as a cloud forms at the end of the dirt road. "Harv, you need to get inside."

Harvey looks back at him confused, "Are you expecting some more people?"

"Harv, go now!"

"You don't have to tell me three times." Making a dash to the farmhouse, he pauses to look at the technician, "Well, are you coming?"

* * *

Director Harris is looking out one of the holes in the wall when he hears the engine and sees the cloud of dirt.

"Admiral, you need to make yourself scarce. I'm not sure who this is arriving."

"Arghh." Fighting back the pain, the admiral fights to stand up. "I remember just the other day, this was easier to do. What's going on? Who is coming?"

Just then the front door bursts open, as Harvey and the technician enter the house. "Admiral, you need a hand, we have to relocate."

"I was just telling him that." The director adds as he continues to watch Agent St. Clair watching the dirt rumble towards them, as a sense of unknown and uncertainty puts a knot in his stomach. The sound of a car plowing through cornstalks catches his attention. A grey Lexus bursts out of the cornfield as it makes its way around the SUV's. It comes to an abrupt stop, kicking up a massive cloud of dirt into the mid-day air. St. Clair phases out to avoid the dirt and rocks.

Unable to see who is getting out of the car, the director hears the car door slam shut. Everything comes to a stop, no noise, no breeze, even the dirt stops mid-air. A murder of crows flies out of the cornfields, sending everything in fast forward.

The unmistakable scream of Agent Selenia causes him to smile; however, his shoulders refuse to relax. Stepping outside to meet the arriving agents he notices Agent St. Clair phase back in.

"Chatter, welcome to the farm." St. Clair makes his way cutting them off from the house.

"Little John, fancy meeting you here. I mean after you left us at the bed and breakfast."

"Yeah well you sorta came on strong back there. I see you have your contacts in." Off the side he notices Agent Grunt finally making his way in front of the car, still waving the dirt away from his face. "Grunt, looking good."

"Little John, let's put all that in the past. Bygones be bygones and all that. I am wondering why the party here and we were not invited?" She saunters towards the large agent.

"Agent Selenia, Agent Grunt, glad you can join us?"

They both stop and look up at the porch to see Director Harris. Taking a few more steps, "Director, have you talked to Director Carol recently? It would seem you are incognito. She would be intrigued to learn that you are here consorting with the people that killed her daughter."

"Agent Selenia, I assure you that it is none of the sort. Agent St. Clair and I are regrouping to find a way to stop a woman from using a dangerous technology. A lot of innocent people have died in recent events."

St. Clair crosses his arms across his chest as he defiantly shows no fear as Selenia makes her way in front of him.

She turns to him, "Yes, and Admiral Julian Kay being one of them. Of course, was he really innocent?"

Unseen, she jabs a taser into St. Clair's abdomen causing his eyes to open in shock, as his body flickers. Director Harris yells, "Eleadora, what are you doing!"

"We're here to find answers and bring some justice. That's all." She looks down at St. Clair passed out and then examines the taser.

She then tosses it on the ground, looks back up at the Director, "I am tired of this humidity, tired of this heat, I really would like to go back home. That means we have to take a more direct approach. Kinda speed things along. Since Admiral Kay has been killed, I was hoping to find the other two and be able to question the third, the one that Agent Abergathy called, Professor."

From nowhere, a voice is coming from everywhere, "I've told you, get off my land!"

Selenia and Grunt turn in every direction to see where it is coming from. They see a man floating towards them from around the corner of the house.

Recognizing the voice, they take an aggressive stance. "After our last meeting I was not sure you would show." Selenia goads him.

"There is an old Georgian proverb, "dzaghli hk'itkha: rat'om kerki? - sheshineba mglebi. - rat'om k'etrovan tkveni k'udi? - rogor pikrobt, me ar meshinia mglebis?" He pauses to watch their dead pan expressions.

"That means, the dog was asked Why do you bark? – To scare away the wolves – Why do you wag your tail? What do you think am I not afraid of wolves?"

Scratching her head, she looks over at her partner who looks just as confused. Turning her confusion back to the man, "So, professor, does this mean you are going to bark for us?"

Immediate sounds of bending metal answers her. They step back, away from the Lexus just as the glass shatters. Shielding themselves, they watch the car being crushed as easy as they would crush a shoe box.

Concrete Bunker, Dry Creek, LA

July 30, 0930 hours

Watching the monitors, Harvey and three of the technicians are seeing the events in front of the house unfold. Harvey pushes back his chair. Running to the hidden door in the corner, he glances back to the technicians all still watching the monitors.

Making his way into the other room the vastness that he remembers is gone as the ship is taking up a majority of the space. He looks over to see Kristen still sitting by Lincoln's side.

Tring to keep his voice down, he hoarsely whispers, "Kristen, the professor needs your help..."

She looks over to him when the ship cuts him off, "You do not have to whisper, Dr. Garrett. They cannot hear in the other room."

"Ahhh, thank you? Kristen..." He notices her eyes are tired, all the spark and energy she had was gone."

"Kristen, the professor really needs your help."

"What am I supposed to do?"

Trying to find the words, he paces and massages his forehead. You understand Lincoln's equipment..."

"You're kidding right?" She cuts him off. "His body is barely cold and you already want to just give away his life's work?"

"Stop with the melodrama! He was my friend! I would like to live through this and see him laid to rest in his family plot." Taking a deep breath, "Look, I'm sorry, I..."

Walking over to his friend, he reaches out, touching his shoulder. "We may have only known each other for a brief time; but, we could have easily become life-long friends.

"It was my comic book ideals that I thought would save us. Even though, as often as he would get on to me about it, I think he liked the idea of it." Pausing to try and hold back the water forming in his eyes, "He would want you to have his project. Nobody else understands it, and his work will be lost if you do not pick up the mantle"

A monitor turns on showing the front of the house, Clarisse interrupts him again, "Dr. Garrett, I am detecting a small energy signature moving this way at a high rate of speed."

"Ummm, energy signature? Thank you?" Seeing the screens light up, he rushes over to one of them to see what is happening.

Deserted Farm, Dry Creek, LA

July 30, 0940 hours

Agent Grunt gives Selenia a pissed off look then looks back at the car as it comes to a stop, crushed to a height of his knees. Turning his attention to the levitating man, he throws his arm out towards him.

The professor shakes his head as if he is trying rid the cobwebs, with his left arm he swings it out. An intense gravitational wave sweeps across the open area, knocking Selenia end over end into the cornfields. Director Harris is hit with the wave and is sent crashing through one of the holes of the house, breaking off a piece of the wood in his lower back.

Grunt is able to withstand the wave. Bending his knees, he leans in the direction of the professor as the wave pulsates around him. Struggling, he looks up at the professor and tilts his head. The professor's shoulders drop, he grabs his head as he begins to lower down to the ground.

Agent Selenia manages to recover and comes running out of the cornfield, scratched up and bleeding from the dried leaves. She gets to her partners' side to see the professor fight off something in his mind. She notices his legs looking tired and struggling to hold him upright. With a surprise burst of energy, the professor drops to a knee and drops a fist to the dirt.

All the air begins to rush towards him as if a seal has been broken. Selenia and Grunt drop to a knee and flatten their hands on the ground to try and hold their ground.

A split second later, the area is filled with the deafening sound of a sonic boom. It sends Agent Selenia flying unconscious, landing on Agent St. Clair. Grunt grabs his ears and lets out a garbled scream.

Concrete Bunker, Dry Creek, LA

July 30, 0950 hours

Using one of the controls, Harvey pans the camera. The only person he can see is the short agent. Maneuvering the camera, he watches him struggle taking steps. The bodies of Little John and what looks like the short agent's partner come into view, both look dead.

The short agents posture drops as if defeat washed over him as he continues to rub his ears looking down at his partner.

"Holy cow...that was like...damn." Panning the camera to the right he sees the crushed car and lets out a low whistle. "That is one turkey'd car."

Continuing to pan to the right, he sees no signs of the professor. "Where did the professor go?"

"Eprem is not within radio distance."

Harvey cautiously turns, already knowing where the voice is coming from, he still looks for someone else in the room. "Ah, thanks."

"Dr. Garrett, from the sound displacement that occurred moments ago, Eprem could be, I do not know."

For the first time, Harvey looks at the ship, "What do you mean?"

Kristen gets up and walks over to him. "Clarisse, has the ability to manipulate gravitational fields. That's what got her and the professor my attention. I would imagine since they both have the same chemical and mineral make-up, that the Professor finally needed to be someplace."

"Jesus, that kind of pressure, to be able to bend gravity towards you and the just step through it and be someplace else, his molecular density has to be immense."

"Dr. Garrett, the energy signature that was moving in a high rate of speed as slowed down."

"Clarisse, What energy signal?"

Tapping his chin, Harvey ignores Kristen's question while studying the monitor. "One minute everything is happening and now nothing. Where did that short guy go?" Still panning the camera, "I have a bad feeling here. Where is the Director? Something's wrong, we need to get up there."

"Harvey, you can't just go up there."

"Sure I can, I just put on one the minion's jackets and head up there, easy day."

Deserted Farm, Dry Creek, LA

July 30, 1003 hours

Agent Grunt turns, dropping his hands, he looks around for the floating man, the one they called professor. Scratching his head, there is no movement anywhere, even the wind feels missing. Hearing a moan coming from the house, he sidesteps, waiting to see who is coming out.

Through the break in the wall, Director Harris is painfully moving, trying to get outside. Just as the director steps on the porch, he collapses to his knee, his back leg still hanging on the wall. Grunt rushes up to him. Before he can grab him, he notices a piece of plywood sticking out of lower back, blood has stained his pants and jacket.

Director Harris falls to his side, looking up at Grunt, "I always thought it would be my blood pressure or sugar levels that would have gotten me." He forces a smile then winces in pain.

Grunt fights the sadness welling up as he smiles, looking at the director.

Director Harris smiles again, the tension releases from his facial muscles as his entire body relaxes. A sense of pleasure and bliss washes over him. Closing his eyes, he fades to sleep.

Before Grunt can fully set him down, he hears a commotion of feet scuffling in the house.

With an uneasy shift in his weight, he sees four technicians hurrying towards him. Three of the technicians look like they could be clones; however, the fourth has something about him, the way he is carrying himself, has Grunt's attention.

The technician that stands out, is making the calls. "He is alight?"

Agent Grunt eyes him cautiously and shrugs his shoulder. As the technicians' step in to pick up the director. Turning to head back to his partner, he steps off of the porch and shakes his head.

The technicians are starting the bicker on who should step where and who should hold what.

"Watch where your stepping."

"Hey! that's my hand. Watch what you're grabbing."

"You're both idiots, let's get him to the admiral."

Harvey pauses, his eyes pop open as he notices the short agent come to an abrupt stop.

The technicians almost fall, nearly dropping the director, as Harvey stopped moving. One of the them give him an attempted shove. "If you had just let us fix your suit, the director may not have gotten hurt."

"What the hell, man!"

"What's wrong now?!"

Still frozen, Harvey watches the agent turn towards them. Hearing the technicians' bicker, he sets his part of the director down and backs away out of frustration.

"Jesus! What else can go wrong!"

"What's your problem?"

The three technicians lay the director down; in doing so one of the technicians get his hand incidentally stepped on. "Arhhh, asshole!" He shoves one of his friends into the other.

Harvey ignores the fight in front of him, never taking his eyes off of the agent. He watches him smile at him, as the pit of his stomach drops. All of his nerves feel agitated.

Grunt twitches his head and smiles. He goes to take a step, his head twitches again and he grabs his head as his mind clouds up. Scrunching his eyes shut, they snap open. Every blood vessel in his eyes feels like they are pulsating. A sing song voice cuts into the cloud.

"What do we have here?"

Both men watch a shapely figure step out from behind one of the SUV's. She looks over at the Lexus, "Ahhh that is a shame."

One of the technicians throws a punch at Harvey, hitting him in the jaw. Harvey falls back a step and the technician grabs his hand whelping in pain. Harvey's anger boils over and he grabs the technician, swings him around and throws him knocking his counterparts into a wall. Determined to stop everything, he steps over the director and heads outside.

The woman dances, her hands cover her mouth, "Ah oh."

Looking over to Grunt, she points to Harvey. "Isn't he one of the ones you came here to look for?"

Grunt stutters his step towards her, then turns back to Harvey. He is met with a fist that sends him back on his heels. Blood spurts out of his nose. Stabling his feet, he dabs the blood.

From the corner of his eye he catches Harvey charging him, bending his knees he thrusts himself into his gut. They both fly, slamming him into the porch.

"This is exciting." The bodies the Agent St. Clair and Selenia turn her attention. Walking over to them, she rolls agent Selenia off of him and caress his cheek, "ahhhh, you poor thing."

Harvey struggles to keep from losing his breath. He grabs Grunt's shoulders and throws his knee into his chin, sending him flailing his arms trying to keep his balance.

Grunt grabs his head, fighting the cloud, he drops to a knee.

The woman, watches this and quickly stands up. Reaching in a pocket on her neoprene suit, she pulls out a cell phone. Just as Harvey starts to charge her, she rubs her thumb across the screen. A wave of energy sweeps away from her. Both Grunt and Harvey roll across the ground grabbing their heads.

On her left she notices movement, turning to face it, she sees the admiral wearing a windbreaker, walking towards her. "You, you were shot. You were killed." Regaining her composure, "That's okay, I didn't get to say goodbye last time." Thumbing her phone again, she watches the admiral as a concern washes over her, "You're not affected?"

Wincing, he massages his shoulder, "A friend of mine said that if you could keep your mind busy, this energy may not affect you. My mind is never not busy. Dorothy, put the controls down, let's put an end to this."

Screaming, "I told you that is no longer my name! You'll show me some respect!" Thumbing the phone again, a massive wave sweeps out of her suit, knocking the admiral backwards onto the ground. The bodies of St. Clair and Selenia are thrown into the cornfields, Grunt and Harvey are sent under the porch, even the vehicles are pushed away, crashing into each other.

Looking down at the phone, she goes to thumb it again when a dark red laser shoots out of the house, cutting the phone in half. "AHHHHHH!! I can't control the suit now! Who the fuck did this!" She watches the admiral regain his footing, his hand points to her as a streak of ice hits her chest. The impact lifts her off of her feet and propels her into the cornfield.

Struggling to walk, the admiral drops his arm and buckles from the pain in his side. The stiches have ripped open, causing blood to gush down his side.

Dorothy screams out of the cornfields, "Son of a bitch! That hurt!"

Hearing the stalks snapping, he knows she is coming again, shaking his head, fighting the pain, he lifts his arms in the direction of the ruckus. Just as she tears out of the fields, the air buckles and folds stopping her in her tracks.

Between them the professor reappears, his clothes are gone, his skin is pulsating and appears fluid.

"What the fuck are you?" Dorothy yells as she absently reaches for the phone for the suit. "Shit!"

The pain in the admiral's side wins out, causing him to drop to a knee. He raises he hand again, pointing it at Dorothy. A stream of ice shoots out again. Before it can hit its mark, it takes an unnatural sharp turn into the ground, freezing it on impact. Dorothy goes to charge the professor when she finds herself having trouble moving. It is getting harder for her to see, she starts screaming.

The air begins to clear. From inside the house, Kristen walks out, her hands are holding Lincoln's visor helmet on. The energy she was projecting is trapped inside a bubble. Hearing the admiral moan, she rushes to his side. Throwing the visor off, she grabs under his good arm keeping him from falling completely over.

Screaming from inside the bubble becomes muffled. The professor levitates into the bubble. Crawling out from under the porch, Grunt and Harvey watch the bubble of energy, swirl and flex. Seconds later the energy is sent streaming upwards, leaving the professor hovering over a passed-out woman.

Her skin has a bluish-purple aura. Grunt and Harvey look at each other, without saying anything, Grunt heads into the cornfield looking for his partner and Harvey goes to help the admiral.

The professor's voice comes from everywhere, "Her suit will no longer work." He turns to see Agent Grunt helping Agent Selenia from out of the cornfield.

Grunt stops, his jaw drops in awe as he finally notices the professor.

Agent Selenia, forcefully keeping her eyes shut, "What's wrong Grunt? What is it?"

Without saying a word, he tilts his head. Harvey is the first to let a snicker escape as he watches the short agent's reaction. The admiral looks over at him, when he hears Kristen giggle as well. Shaking his head, he looks over towards the short agent and the urge to join the laughter builds.

Selenia involuntary let's out a giggle as she covers her mouth trying to keep it in. "What's so funny?"

Grunt motions his head, gesturing to Harvey and Kristen to get the admiral inside the house. He looks over at the woman on the ground and shakes his head. After a few moments of watching the professor, he gives him a slow nod of respect. Making his way over to the woman, he lifts her over his shoulder and tosses her body into one of the SUV's. Hearing the three laughing as they enter the house, he smiles as he helps his partner get in.

When he reaches the front of the SUV, Harvey yells at him.

"Hey, you are going to need these." Harvey tosses a set of keys his way. They both remain standing in place as Grunt massages his jaw and Harvey rubs his lower back.

Taking a deep breath, he smiles and starts to laugh again.

Grunt smiles back, grabbing the keys out of midair, his smiles drops as he watches Harvey go back into the house.

Arlington Cemetery, Arlington, VA

Aug 16, 1314 hours

A large, heavyset man with an intimidating build is standing next to a tall, wiry gentleman, and is watching from a short distance as the funeral unfolds someone singing a Billie Holiday tune. They take sips from their respective flasks, as they get lost in the power of the voice.

Ryan O'Connell, the larger man from Chicago, takes another sip and rubs the back of his hand across his cheekbone. "Do ya know who singin'?"

The Boston director, Richard Merrick, takes in a deep breath and says, "Na, but I've never heard such pipes in my life."

"Aye, I'll drink to that, my friend." He raises his flask before taking another sip and rubbing his cheekbones again.

"Are you cryin'?" Rich asks.

"It's the song. If you mention it to anyone, Dick, I will pound you."

Chuckling, Rich twitches his shoulders and says, "With all this tension in the ranks, I could use a good scrap."

The song ends and they see Victoria Carol smiling and taking condolences. "Well, all be damned, I never knew she could sing like that."

Watching some of the other directors gather around her, shaking her hand, Rich digs out his flask. "We've never had this kind of tension within our ranks before. We all have a job to do, a role to play in our organization. We've lost operatives before..."

Ryan looks over at him. "Yeah, we've lost operatives before, but never one so close."

"But, we have never had one of our own as an operative." Rich takes a sip; a slight shiver shoots up his spine. "Have you gotten in touch with Sydney? How's he doing"

Yeah, we talked yesterday. He's going to live; but, there are still questions the need answering. Sometimes I hate my job." Pausing to watch the crowd form a line, a jazz band initiates a procession as the crowd exits. "I've known Sydney for decades."

The procession marches towards them when a familiar voice startles them from behind.

"Did you fine men start without me?"

They both turn and look down to see Cindy. She is wearing a slimming black dress, her hair, they can tell, was brushed, but somehow still looks disheveled. Ryan gives her a subtle bow.

"Good afternoon, Director Weinheimer."

Rich's bow is a little bit more exaggerated. "Cindy, it is always a pleasure to talk with you on the same time zone."

"Director O'Connell, Director Merrick." She gives the wiry man an accepted nod. "Yeah, sorry about the other day."

Scanning the crowd in the procession, she says, "Am I the last to arrive?"

"With the exception of Sydney, I believe you are." Ryan says as he offers her his flask.

She takes it and lifts it for a mock toast. "Thank you." After taking a long sip, which gets appreciative nods from the gentlemen, she looks up at them with concerned eyes. "Does anyone know the details of what is going on in Louisiana and Texas right now?"

A familiar Texas drawl approaches from behind, "I believe the only one that can truly answer that is a little busy right now." They turn to see a well-dressed man wearing an air of cockiness in his step. "It would appear that he coordinated the apprehension of an ominous thief with suspicious circumstances. It's all very hush hush."

The four—chuckle light heartedly, which draws the attention of Director Carol and the small crowd of directors around her. Cindy notices them looking their way and gives Ryan an elbow nudge.

They stand motionless, watching Director Carol make her way over to them. A small crowd of directors stay behind within the procession.

As Director Carol approaches, she gives Rich, Ryan and Cindy a nod. "Nice of you three to make it."

Ryan offers her his hand and says, "My condolences, Victoria."

She looks him over and nods. "Thank you. Has any of you seen or heard from Sydney?" The bite in her tone is unmistakable.

Rich straightens up and with as much bravado as he can muster says, "Nah, we..."

Ryan cuts the wiry gentleman off, "I talked to him shortly after you and I had talked. We have coordinated arraignments since then."

Director Carol looks them over with suspicion, smiles and looks down at Cindy. "Well when you hear from him, let him know I need to speak to him. His phone is going straight to voicemail." She turns walks off, back into the crowd.

Rich gives the larger gentleman a quick shove. "Why'd you interrupt me?"

"Dick, you may be itchin' to scrap, but she'd kick your ass."

Cindy and Charlie grin at each other as Richard turns a few shades red; he pumps his shoulders and looks around. "I can take her."

Cindy, who was taking a sip of a flask nearly spits it up, trying not to laugh.

"Easy girl, you don't want to waste that; that would be a party foul." Charlie pats her on her back.

The three gentlemen look at Cindy as she recovers.

Ryan takes on a serious note. "Cin, what do you know? You need to be up front with us."

Wiping her mouth with the back of her hand, she looks, one at a time, at each of the men.

"You guys have heard about the robberies down there that were committed under suspicious circumstances?"

Ryan and Charlie look at each other, then subtlety nod their heads, while Rich's expression becomes bewildered.

Noticing Rich's confused look, he recalls his memories. "I heard about the big storm that rolled through there a few weeks back."

Watching everyone else smile, he can't help but feel left out of the loop.

She smiles and puts her hand on her hip. "Good, then I'm doing my job."

The wiry director from Boston points a finger. "Wait, are you talking about the random atmospheric anomalies that have been poppin' up down there, where dozens of people were killed?"

"Right, well, Sydney identified the subject and put together a team and put a stop to it and the technology she is using."

Cindy turns and looks up at Ryan. "I have been told that the subject has been nullified."

The larger man lifts his flask as a salute letting everyone know. "My team is anxious to get some answers."

They can see the excitement building in Rich's eyes as he quickly looks at Charlie, but before he could say anything, Charlie raises a hand to stop him.

"He had Little John and Yukiko Nomi, but the others I am not sure about."

"Sydney says that Little John respects them." Cindy adds.

"So, we have a man who spends most of his time looking for alternate sentient lifeforms, has now put together a team to stop people from getting killed here on Earth. That sounds like a worthy, honorable adventure," Ryan says.

The wiry gentleman raises his fists and pretends to box. "I understand now, Sydney has created his own faction. No wonder the Madam is pissed."

Ryan pushes his shoulder nearly knocking him off balance. "Rich, you're an idiot with a high IQ. Do you really think this team has a chance in the long run? Without the training from the good director here?" Motioning toward Charlie.

Charlie smiles. "I wish every team the best of luck. Since they managed to stop this subject as you call it, they may have kept Sydney out of the fire."

Rich scratches his head as he looks at the three. "An improbable team, a quixotic faction." Everyone smiles and nods. "It scores well in Scrabble."

Shaking their heads everyone starts to laugh which catches the ear of the Madam as she gives them a piercing glare; causing them straighten up.

Cindy quietly speaks up. "Would you fine gentlemen care to show a woman a good place to get a drink?"

"It would be an honor," Charlie says. "We can drink to the Quixotic Faction and hope for the best.

Deserted Farm, Dry Creek, LA

Aug 16, 1545 hours

On the remodeled porch of the rundown farmhouse, Agent St. Clair and Admiral Kay sit on some chairs drinking ice tea. They notice the arrival of a Silver Ford Taurus as a cloud of dirt envelops around it.

Director Harris slowly steps out of the car, as he closes the door a murder of crow caw and flies across the car. The director winces as he shields himself.

"Son of a...He still has not done anything about these birds?" Slowly standing himself up, he brushes off his suit. Looking up at the porch, St. Clair and the admiral are laughing. The admiral winces and grabs his side.

The director regains his composure, "I am impressed, Admiral, a good leader is a leader that knows when to take it easy."

"You are correct, sir. You should be taking that same advice." Taking a sip of his tea, "What brings you by?"

"I wish I could, there are still a lot of embers from this fire we were in that need to be put out. Besides I received a rather mysterious phone call from an up and coming agent of mine. I always try to take care of my agents."

The admiral walks over to shake the director's hand. "I want to thank you; Lincoln's funeral was appreciated and well received."

"It was the very least we could have done." He pauses for a moment to look into the admiral's eyes. "I only wish that I had the opportunity to work with him."

"He would've enjoyed that." Making his way back to the chair, the admiral looks out into the rundown cornfields. "Director, were you able to get any information on Ms. DuFerot? Like, how did she know our names? How did she know to come here to find us?"

"All very good questions, admiral, another sign of a good leader. There is a rift in our organization and some answers are not easy to come by. Still the search for Agents Selenia, Grunt and Dorothy DuFerot continues."

St. Clair smiles and whistles. "We never gonna see them again."

"Director O'Connell is spitting fire and looking to roll some heads..." Pausing to take a breath, he claps his hands together, "I bring good news. You two are no longer on the FBI's Most Wanted list and your pasts have been cleared up, no longer missing."

"Thank you, I know that Harvey will be relieved." The admiral sets his drink down. "Can I get you a glass of tea?"

Harvey bursts through the doorway with his arms raised and acting giddy. "Gentlemen. It is my honor to present to you, the ever brilliant, the ever-formidable, Kristen Abergathy."

Stepping outside, Kristen is wearing a MIT form-fitting suit, the metallic boots, gloves, and headgear of Dr. Stevens.

Everyone applauds as she takes a bow. "Gentlemen, please, call me Brittle Star," she tells them, which earns her another round of applause.

Harvey, still smiling, but takes on a more serious tone. "It took us awhile to downsize the equipment, but I think Brittle Star here will do Lincoln right with his project."

Director Harris steps up to Kristen. "Agent, it seems like only yesterday; you were tripping up the stairwell to give me information and now look at you."

"Thank you, sir."

Harvey taps the shoulder of the director and motions out to the fields. "Sir, do you have a moment?"

"Absolutely, my good man." He turns and they head down the porch, out and away from the house.

The admiral stands and looks at her. "Kristen, I am glad you are honoring Lincoln, by wearing his project. I am sure he is smiling now."

Taking off the headgear, she looks over at the admiral. "Thank you, Admiral. I hope I can serve it justice."

* * *

Out away from the house, Harvey stops the director. "Sir, what happened to Agent Yukiko?"

“She has been relocated to a medical facility.”

Tapping his fingers together, he appears apprehensive. “Last month, when we were in Texas, Lincoln made a comment that I didn’t catch until recently. He said that we need to get them into the van, not get her into the van...”

The director stops walking, puts his hand out, and looks over at Harvey. “Dr. Garret, that, I’m afraid, is Above Top Secret.”

Epilogue
2015

Medical facility, Groom Lake, NV

August 28, 0957 hours

On a television mounted on the wall of a small, sterile room, Michelle Obama is being interviewed by an attractive female reporter regarding the half billion spending project for the White House dining hall. In the room is a small twin-size bed and a young Japanese American woman sitting in a wheel chair. The girl is staring off into one of the corners, not paying any attention to the interview.

A strong female voice appears in the doorway talking in a low but audible hush tone, to an older balding gentleman. “How is she holding up?”

The young woman in the chair expresses her annoyance at the invasion of her privacy. “Igor took my legs, not my hearing.”

“Agent Nomi, you know that if you had told us that...”

Director Carol puts out a hand to stop the man from pursuing and pressing her. “Doctor, can you give us a few minutes.”

He looks up at her, nods and backs down. “She’s all yours, good luck.” Shaking his head, he turns and walks away.

The director takes a couple of steps into the room as the interview on the television catches her attention.

Watching the First Lady trying to justify the spending, she shakes her head in disgust before turning her attention to the young agent. "Yukiko, why did you not tell anyone about the parasite?"

"I didn't ask you to put that in me and I sure didn't ask you to remove it."

Keeping her voice somber as she studies the small agent, "Look, when you and Roynika came back from Kandahar, we were at our wits end trying to restore the use of your legs."

"So, you just up and went and used me as a guinea pig for your little alien symbiont." Turning her head, she catches a glimpse of surprise from the director. "Yeah, I know, Igor told me all about how you had been running tests on it since 1974." Gaining some confidence, Nomi wheels her chair around to face the director. "All those years, all those experiments, all those beings you killed, because you didn't understand."

Director Carol's expression tenses up, but before she can say anything, Nomi wheels up to her. She grips the wheels of her chair to the point that her knuckles begin to turn white.

"And then you think you can just rip it out of me and kill it!"

Anger begins to take over the director as she tries to keep her composure. Leaning over, she places her hands on the armrests of the wheelchair, backing down the young agent with slow whisper. "Look here young lady! If you weren't close to my daughter, you'd been left in that desert to become food for the hyenas and wolves. Do you have an understanding?"

For a moment they stare at each other, before Nomi wheels back a few inches, causing the director to let go and stand back up. Watching each other without saying a word, the only sounds in the room are coming from the Michelle Obama interview on the television.

"Yes, Katie, we live in trying times, where we have to put our best foot forward."

Without turning to acknowledge the television, Director Carol massages her hands. "These are trying times and she's an idiot." After a few moments of watching each other they both crack a slight smile.

"I stopped by to see how you were holding up. Yukiko, I did not come here for a fight. And please stop calling Dr. Grayson, Igor. He's a good man, he saved your life a few times now."

Nomi's facial expression goes blank. "Now you see I'm still alive and that you authorized me for experiment part two..."

Unable to keep her impatience at bay, she raises a hand stopping the young agent. "You lost control of it! You withheld information about it, despite working with Charlie at the San Antonio facility, learning to reuse your legs."

Anger taking over, Nomi blurts out, "It was sentient! You had no right!"

Turning to leave, Director Carol looks at the interview on the television, and then back over her shoulder at the young agent. "You may not have the use of your legs anymore, but you still know who's responsible for my daughter's death."

Sitting back in her chair and folding her arms. "Yeah, I figured that was why you came."

Just before the director leaves the room, she stops and her shoulders drop. "Yukiko, Roynika was my only child and I need to know who was responsible." After a moment of quiet, the director exits down the hall.

Spinning the chair around to face the corner again, she instinctively tries to push herself up and bring her feet under her. Only her legs refused to move and she falls back into the chair. Out of frustration she slams her fist onto her thigh. Not feeling anything, she pounds both of her legs; but, before she can yell out, she feels a twinge in her right leg.

Looking around she goes to call out for Dr. Grayson when flashbacks of when they found her trapped in the crunched-up van in July. Closing her eyes, a shiver shoots up her spine. Nightmare flashes of colors and Harvey and his mechanical monkey suit. Then the memory of her snapping the neck of Dr. Stevens brings her back out of her thoughts. A tear forms and makes its way down her cheekbone as she stares into the corner.

Catching it with the back of her hand, she realizes that she is absently rubbing the spot on her leg where she felt the twinge. Rubbing the location firmer with the palm of her hand she begins to feel a slight tingle in her big toe. Almost willing it, she watches her big toe begin to twitch, then realizing that she was able to move it.

Nomi looks at the doorway to see if anyone else saw, thinking out loud, “How can this be? They removed the symbiont.”

A cautious childlike voice, whispers and interrupts her thoughts. “Hello?”

About the Author

After an unknown number of years of traveling around the world, T. D. Kohler has finally found a place to call home—sitting on a secluded beach on the tropical island of Guam with his wife, one of his sons, and his two dogs. Enjoying sunsets is one of their favorite pasttimes.

T.D. served in the United States military, and has worked, shared knowledge and played games with humans from Afghanistan to Thailand, and from Australia to the United States. He has taken up writing as a means to share, for as he says: "Sharing is caring."

This, the Above Top Secret edition of *The Quixotic Faction*, is his debut work from RhetAskew Publishing, and is soon to be followed by the sequel.

Follow T.D. Kohler:

www.twitter.com/TDKohler
www.facebook.com/TD-Kohler-851197621601384/
www.goodreads.com/author/show/14795207.T_D_Kohler

WWW.RHETORICASKEW.COM

CPSIA information can be obtained
at www.ICGtesting.com
Printed in the USA
LVHW081305080719
623437LV00065B/610/P